CONQUEST

The Medieval Saga Series
Book One

David Field

SAPERE
BOOKS

CONQUEST

Published by Sapere Books.

20 Windermere Drive, Leeds, England, LS17 7UZ,
United Kingdom

saperebooks.com

ISBN: 978-1-80055-555-6

PART I

I

Autumn, 1065

Gwenyth's oldest pig had escaped again, and it would soon be dark. She tutted quietly as she persuaded herself that she would need to leave off kneading her dough and go after the beast. There would be no light left by the time she returned, but the bread could wait until tomorrow. The old sow had been her husband Alwin's favourite, but her teats had already run dry and there would be no more litters. Instead, Gwenyth would use the sow for salted pork to see her through the winter that lay ahead, and she would never again have to go wandering in the direction of Caldbec Wood to bring the wilful creature back to the wattle enclosure that it seemed able to knock over at will.

She threw her faded and well-patched cloak over her equally faded woollen gown and slipped on her sandals, because it would be rough underfoot in the copse at the edge of the wood, where escaped pigs normally went in search of the sour fallen crab-apples.

There was no sign of the pig in Crab-apple Hollow. With a sinking heart, Gwenyth looked further up the slope into the outer fringes of Caldbec Wood, which formed the boundary with Thegn Leofric's manor farm over the hill in Astenmede. The pig was probably in there somewhere, but the wood was rumoured to be the haunt of wolves.

She crept into the wood tentatively, making as little noise as possible. If her pig was here, she didn't want it to run away before she had the hempen rope around its neck.

There was the pig — in the clearing, snuffling up the first fallen acorns of the year. Gwenyth launched herself at the animal, getting the halter round its neck as it began squealing in protest. She hushed it, and miraculously it obeyed her and stopped resisting. But the hairs rose on the back of her neck as, in the ensuing silence, she heard a rustling in the foliage behind her. She turned quickly and something ducked back out of sight. Whatever it was, it was panting heavily.

Gwenyth began to tread stealthily back the way she had come, dragging the reluctant pig behind her, her eyes fixed on the foliage to one side. Something inside it moved again, but it made no move towards her. As she peered harder into the dense thicket of thorns, she spotted a pair of eyes. Not the slanting yellow eyes of a wolf, but the blue eyes of a — a *what*?

'Who's there?' she called out in a wavering voice.

Silence.

'I know you're there, so stop playing games with me. I have a heavy stick, and if you don't come out, I'll *beat* you out of there,' she lied as she scanned the immediate area for a stick with which to reinforce her threat. There was a slow movement, and a man's face appeared above the brambles. He raised his arms in surrender, and stepped out into full view.

Gwenyth let out a small squeak, but the man looked to be in fear of his life. As if a tall, albeit thin, man in his late thirties had anything to fear from an unarmed widow ten years his senior. But she had *one* advantage over him. He was naked, while she was not.

'Who are you?' she demanded. 'And what are you doing in Caldbec Wood with no clothes about you?'

The man said nothing, but simply opened up his hands to demonstrate that they contained no weapon. Emboldened by his apparent timidity, Gwenyth tried again.

'Name? Surely you have one?'

'Guillaume.'

'You don't sound as if you're from around these parts,' Gwenyth concluded. 'And where are your clothes?'

She pointed to her own cloak, and the man nodded eagerly. Gwenyth realised that the poor soul was shivering from the cold, rather than out of any fear of her. She unclipped the simple horn brooch and threw the cloak across to him, thereby preserving a safe distance between them.

'There, cover your shame with that. And you look as if a good meal wouldn't kill you. It's only a widow's humble potage, mind you, but the last batch of bread's not gone hard yet. In return for that, you can weed between my winter cabbage rows in the village strip-field. The fire in my hut won't have gone out yet, if we waste no more time. Follow me.'

Gwenyth strode off as fast as her trembling legs would allow, both the pig and the man following behind her. She looked round regularly to reassure herself that the man had not been playing some sort of beggar's trick in order to win himself a cloak. They reached the entrance to her hut, and she pulled back the thatched panel, then turned and gestured for him to go inside ahead of her. She left the flap open in case she had to run away or call a neighbour for help, but the man had lost no time in kneeling by the remains of the fire to get warm.

Gwenyth stoked it up with more foraged wood, then put the gruel pot onto the griddle plate and searched among her treasured possessions for the bone-handled spoon that had been Alwin's. She broke up the remaining bread from her bake three days ago and handed a piece to her companion. He held it up, pronounced a string of words in a strange tongue, then ripped a chunk off and chewed it with the eagerness of a starving man.

'No-one's ever appreciated my bread like that,' Gwenyth said encouragingly as she handed him another piece, then poured a ladle full of potage into her only surviving earthenware bowl. He ignored the spoon that he was handed, and simply took the bowl in both hands and swallowed its contents down with the enthusiasm of a child with strawberry curds. Three bowls later he seemed to have eaten enough, and Gwenyth rummaged in the log box for some of Alwin's old clothes.

Once the man was decently dressed, he began to nod off. Gwenyth slipped outside for fresh rushes and placed them in the far corner of the hut, gesturing for her new lodger to lie down and rest. He was snoring within minutes, and Gwenyth set about cleaning up while considering her options.

She could hardly expect the neighbours not to notice. It would probably be no later than the next sunrise before it was all over the small village that Widow Gwenyth had a new man. *Chance would be a fine thing*, she told herself. She'd been a widow for over four years now, and if she were as superstitious as some of her neighbours she might have brought herself to believe that her recent encounter had been with the naked spirit of her late husband returned from the dead. But she wasn't — and anyway Alwin had been only a little taller than her, whereas this new man was almost the height of her roof thatch.

She had told him — if he'd understood a word she'd said — that in return for his night's lodging, he would be weeding her village strip the following day. It certainly needed it, so a man would come in handy, both on her land and in her bed. The nosy neighbours would think the worst anyway, so she had nothing to lose. Despite all those years with Alwin and his healthy appetites she remained childless, so there was no risk of an unwanted birth, particularly not at her age.

By the time the man awoke and wandered discreetly outside for a piss before the sun was up, Gwenyth had washed herself and had boiled some lavender root into a potion that she smeared on the inside of her ample thighs, just in case. When the man came back in, she handed him a bowl of potage.

'What was your name again?'

The man smiled. 'Guillaume.'

'So you *do* speak our tongue? But I'll never get *my* tongue around — what you said — so I'll just call you "Gwee", if it's all the same to you. And you can call me "Gwen", to make it easier for you.'

'You are most kind to a man in need. I cannot pay.'

'You know how to weed between cabbage drills?' Gwenyth asked artlessly.

'I know "cabbage",' Guillaume replied, 'but what is "weed"?'

'I'll show you when we go outside once the sun is up.'

A look of horror spread across the man's face. 'I cannot go outside — they will find me and kill me!'

'Who will kill you?'

'Those men who took my vestment and left me with no cover for my body. The soldiers of the king.'

'You are running from the *king*?' Gwenyth demanded, her hand flying to her mouth. 'I will be killed myself, for helping you.'

The man looked wildly around the hut, then pulled a hoe from the wall and held it out in front of him in a defensive gesture. 'Please — I do not harm you — but I cannot be seen out there, where they will come for me. I am priest.'

'The shameless bitch has a man in there!' Rowena Riveracre complained as she re-entered the hut after milking her goat. She glowered at her son, Wilfrid. 'Will, put that loaf back where it belongs! It's needed for the supper, unless your father gets hungry first.'

'Tell us more about Gwenyth's man!' her daughter Elva demanded, wide-eyed with curiosity.

Rowena frowned. 'It's no business for a young girl like you.'

'I wouldn't know anyway,' Elva pouted, 'since none of the village boys shows any interest in me.'

'If they do, they'll get my sickle round their ears,' her father Eldred threatened as he raised himself from the rushes and wandered outside. There was a grateful splashing sound, and he returned with an enquiring expression on his face. 'It's quiet enough in there at present, anyway, so what makes you say Gwenyth's got someone in there?'

'I heard them talking while I was out milking the goat, so I went over and peered through the thatch. The man was fighting her off with a hoe.'

There was a guffaw from Will, which Rowena silenced instantly with one of her looks, before turning to her husband. 'If you don't want to eat, best get down to the mill. There's a good run of water since all that rain, and Thegn Leofric won't wait forever.'

Eldred Riveracre was the local miller, making use of the old water mill that belonged to the thegn's domain, in exchange for grinding as much grain as the lord delivered. The Powdermill Stream and the River Asten were both fed by Powdermill Lake, and they flowed through adjoining valleys separated by Caldbec Wood. The more westerly of the two watercourses ran faster when the lake was overflowing, and Powder Mill had been worked by Eldred's ancestors as far back as anyone could remember. They'd got their family name of 'Riveracre' from their equally long-standing allocation of the farming strip closest to the stream that powered the mill, and their superior status in the small village rankled with other churl families that were allocated less fertile strips. But Thegn Leofric, who presided over the Manor Court, was too lazy to consider change of any sort, and he relied on the goodwill of Eldred and his son to get his wheat and barley ground finely.

Eldred lost no time in collecting his mill tools from the corner of the hut, donning his cloak and heading out for the day's work, accompanied by his son Wilfrid. They had at least twenty sacks of Thegn Leofric's barley left to grind, and their lord would not be impressed if his ale supply ran out. Once milled, the freshly ground grain would go over to the thegn's brewhouse in his wagon, and his thrall labourers would load it into the oasts. It was back-breaking work.

'Why is Mother so down on Widow Gwenyth?' Wilfrid asked between breaths as he heaved the contents of yet another sack onto the bottom millstone, while his father released the brake on the creaking mill wheel and opened the sluice.

Eldred snorted, but declined to reply.

'So she's a whore, then?' Wilfrid persisted.

'Mind your language, boy,' Eldred warned him as he carefully watched the upper stone grinding down onto the barley and prepared to scoop the finely ground grain into a sack.

Since his father seemed disinclined towards conversation, Wilfrid looked out through the open door down the track that led to the main part of the village. 'Best keep going, anyway,' he told Eldred, 'since here comes Ormod with the thegn's wagon.'

'He'll have to bloody wait then, won't he?' Eldred grunted as he finished filling the latest sack and reached for a length of hemp to tie up the top.

Wilfrid's face broke into a smile as he looked down from the loading platform at the slowly approaching wagon with Ormod at the reins. His young daughter Annis was seated next to him, and Wilfrid's heart began to race as usual. He'd known Annis almost all her life, and although she was a few years younger than him — the same age as his sister Elva, who was her friend — he had set his heart on one day settling into a hut of his own with her, tilling his own strip, keeping his own beasts, bringing up their children and perhaps winning wealth and fame as a member of the earl's fyrd army. But there was a serious obstacle to all of this.

Annis was a thrall girl, part of the lowest order in the simple society dominated by the local thegn and his Manor Court over the hill. Even churls needed the thegn's permission to marry, and the lives of thralls were even more dominated by the thegns who all but owned them. It was even rumoured that some thrall girls were expected to do the thegn service with their bodies. So far as Wilfrid had been able to discover, nothing like that had befallen Annis.

Not only would Thegn Leofric be reluctant to lose the services of a girl who spent most days on the bank of the Asten, beating fine clothing and other forms of linen on the pounding stone, but Wilfrid's own parents clearly wanted better for him, and would not readily allow him to marry into a thrall family. That was why Wilfrid was planning to run away as soon as his father could spare him. He had no definite plan, but he had heard about Earl Harold's fine fortress at Winchester and the standing fyrd army that he maintained, the finest of whom served as his 'housecarls', or private bodyguards. Wilfrid was a tall youth, and had earned his sinewy strength throwing sacks of grain around his father's mill. He could throw heavy stones well past the far bank of Powdermill Stream, and he'd heard that in the fyrd men were valued by how far they could throw a spear, and how heavily they could bring an axe down on an opponent's head in battle. There was always a risk that he might be killed himself, but it would be worth it if his improved standing in the village would entitle him to choose his own bride.

Annis smiled up at him as she jumped down from the wagon and held onto the horse while her father set about loading the filled sacks that Wilfrid handed down to him from the platform. She caught his long, admiring gaze, blushed and looked down. When she looked back up again, he was still staring at her.

'How is Elva?' she asked as a polite diversion.

'Elva is very well, but bored with the household routine as usual,' Wilfrid replied.

'It's all the same in the thegn's hall,' she assured him. 'There's just more of it, that's all. But tell Elva that she must come up the hill and meet me in Caldbec Wood. The brambles have started to fruit, and there'll be blackberries soon, to make into pies.'

'I'll bring her up to meet you, if you like,' Wilfrid offered eagerly.

Her freckled face clouded slightly as she inclined her head. 'There's no need for anyone to offer her protection. There are rumoured to be wolves in there, but I've never seen one.'

'All the same,' Wilfrid insisted. 'Elva's now at an age when she could be in danger of being followed by men with lusty intentions.'

'Intentions like yours, you mean?' Annis teased him, just as the shouting began further back down the track, where armed men had begun ransacking the village huts.

It was fortunate for both Gwenyth and 'Gwee', as she had taken to calling him, that Gwenyth's hut was well to the south of Sandlake Village; the armed men had run in from the northern end, turning the folk from their huts and throwing their belongings into the mud as they conducted their search. They were armed with axes and swords, and clad in only leather jerkins, as if acknowledging that the simple peasants they had been sent to harass would be defenceless. There were six men-at-arms in all, and they split up into three teams of two.

As the shouting began Gwenyth looked briefly outside her door, saw the emblems on their tunics, and realised that Gwee had not been exaggerating when he'd claimed that the king's men were after him. Gwee himself was cowering in a corner as Gwenyth ripped off her gown and hood, throwing them at Gwee with a sharp instruction to lie down in the rushes and face the wall, wrapped in her discarded garments and with his head well hidden. Then she turned to face the hut opening dressed in only her under-shift, and adopted her most aggrieved expression as the two intruders strode over her threshold.

'Well, here's a fine thing!' she protested loudly. 'Men who are supposed to be defending us against foreigners in the name of King Edward, and all they can find to do is to burst in on a poor widow woman who's only half-dressed, and tending to the needs of her dying mother. Shame on the pair of you!'

'We don't come from the king, missus,' the soldier replied gruffly. 'We serve Earl Harold Godwinson, and he orders that we seek out a French priest who's believed to be in hiding somewhere around here. He may be without clothes. Have you seen anyone like that lately?'

'If I had, I think I'd remember. And if so, he'd be lying in the straw there, spent of all energy. Instead, there is only my dying mother.'

'What's she dying of?' the other man-at-arms demanded. Gwenyth inclined her head from side to side in a gesture of uncertainty.

'She had a bad flux, and her waste is still all over that corner. Don't tread in it if you go any closer, since they reckon it could be leprosy. It came in on a ship moored in Pevensey last month, they say.'

'We don't get paid to catch leprosy!' the first man replied, as he turned to his companion. 'Come on, Algar — we're done here.'

Checking that the two men had rejoined their companions in turning over the remaining huts to the south, Gwenyth turned to Gwee.

'They've gone, my friend. At least I know you weren't spinning me a yarn.'

'What were those brutes looking for?' Rowena asked with a sideways look at Gwenyth as they both filled their pails from the stream.

'What makes you think I might know?' Gwenyth asked as she avoided looking her neighbour in the eye.

'I thought perhaps it might be your new man,' Rowena smirked, 'since you seem to have gone to great lengths to keep him hidden.'

'*What* new man?' Gwenyth demanded.

Rowena snorted. 'Stop the pretence, Gwen. I live in the hut next to yours. I was just wondering what your new man's been up to, for the earl's men to be seeking him out. It was him they were looking for, wasn't it? An escaped priest, according to the friar from Longbottom who was here a few days ago, and nearly got mistaken for the man himself.'

Gwenyth stood up quickly and stormed back to her own hut. Her lodger backed away from her as if she had the Plague.

'You can't stay here any longer,' she told him in a low voice. 'Folk know that you're here, and that nosy old woman next door will tell half the village by dinner time. Then we'll both be dead. Is there not somewhere else you can go?'

Guillaume thought quickly, then shook his head. 'Not unless there is, somewhere by here, a *monastère* — a house of God where men live and pray.'

'A place with monks — holy brothers?'

'*Oui — les moines.* There is such a place by here? If so, I could seek *asile*.'

'Not sure what you mean,' Gwenyth admitted, 'but there's always Telham Priory, where some monks have lived for some years now. They say it's not a proper priory, but it has a man in charge who calls himself a prior. The friars who wander the countryside tell us that he's a God-fearing man with monks who tend his fields and livestock, so would that serve your need?'

'Please, you must show me the way,' Guillaume replied. 'Then you will not fear death for hiding me.'

Under the cover of darkness — which descended early that winter's afternoon — Gwenyth and Guillaume set off across the frosty ground. They rested once or twice, munching on fresh bread that Gwenyth had cooked specially earlier that day, which they washed down with water from Powdermill. As a pale dawn in the east heralded the beginning of another crisp, cold day, they heard the faint sound of some chanting, and followed it to a ruined old building in a small field surrounded by overgrown hedges.

Guillaume's face opened in a nostalgic smile as he heard the small choir of male voices intoning their way through Matins. He turned to Gwenyth. 'I must go in here, but for you it would not be good. I must thank you for being the person who saves my life, and I wish to give you God's blessing in return.'

He raised his hand high in the air above her head and pronounced a blessing in Latin. Gwenyth stood, somewhat bemused, but somehow sensing that something good had just happened. Then, to her astonishment, Guillaume began stripping off his clothes.

'Have you lost your wits?' she demanded. 'You'll freeze to death in ten minutes! What are you about?'

'These vestments, they are not mine. Soon, if God smiles upon me, I will have others. These are the vestments of your dead husband, yes? You must keep them in his memory, and perhaps for the next person you find in the trees. I must leave you now. Thank you again, Gwen, and I pray for your soul, since this is all I could give you. *Pax vobiscum.*'

Guillaume climbed through a gap in the hedge and walked towards the open door of the stone ruin from where the voices were coming. There were only six or so monks in the narrow building, and before a rudimentary altar stood a stern-faced man who appeared to be leading the service. He stopped intoning the *Te Deum laudamus*, but his mouth stayed open as he became aware of the naked man standing just inside the rear doorway, with blood running down his chest and legs from the brambles he had just climbed through. Several other monks turned and followed their leader's mesmerised stare, and for a moment they believed that they were witnessing a vision of Christ on the *Via Dolorosa* ahead of his crucifixion. Two of them crossed themselves as their wavering chant dwindled into silence.

The prior took off the heavy cloak that had been covering his simple black vestments, walked the few yards down to the rear door, pronounced a Latin blessing, and wrapped the cloak around the shivering Guillaume, before leading him to a stool behind the sparse congregation. He went back before the altar and proceeded straight to the *Benedictio* that allowed his humble following to file out through a side door. Then he came back to Guillaume.

'You are welcome in our lowly house, my son. You have obviously fallen upon hard times, but here in the house of God you will be fed and clothed, although you will find both the food and clothing to be of the most modest kind.'

'*Bien merci*,' Guillaume shivered.

The prior's face lit up, and he replied fluently in Guillaume's own tongue. 'You are French? This is good, since I learned to speak your language during my days in Cluny, and I am in danger of losing it through disuse. We are of the Order of Saint Benedict here, although we cannot yet call ourselves a priory, since we do not have the necessary twelve brothers.'

Guillaume bowed his head and sought a blessing. 'Then,' he added, 'I must make confession, since it has been many weeks since my last.'

'You are a good Christian?'

'I am an ordained priest.'

The prior's eyes opened wide, then narrowed slightly. 'You must forgive me if I ask for some confirmation of that. For all I know, you are a fugitive from the king's justice, with the death of another on your conscience.'

'The king seeks my death, I believe,' Guillaume admitted, 'but those who reduced me to this state serve Earl Harold. He has good cause to wish me dead, for the secret which I hold close in my conscience, but I have been guilty of no man's death.'

The prior looked hard into his eyes, and began the examination. 'If I were to say "*Dominus vobiscum*", what would be your response?'

'*Et cum spirito tuo*,' Guillaume replied without a moment's hesitation.

The prior smiled. 'You must forgive me for doubting you, but we live in dangerous times. I am Prior Jerome, of the Order of Saint Benedict, and you are welcome to claim sanctuary here for as long as you require it. But what leads a French priest over to our shores?'

'That I dare not disclose, even to you, since it would place you at the same risk as myself. I accept your offer of sanctuary with thanks to God in my heart. How may I best serve you, bearing in mind that it would not be safe for me to be seen outside?'

'You will serve us best by becoming our twelfth brother, so that we may seek the blessing of Cluny for this community to become a recognised house, with perhaps some financial assistance. The stonework that we occupy was, we believe, left behind by the legions of Rome when they departed some centuries ago, and it is in need of repair. But we also have need of someone to create a *Scriptorium*, and since you can speak Latin, you would be as much a gift from God to us as our sanctuary is for you. Now, let us find you suitable vestments. I will lead you to the *hospitium*, where Brother Michael will feed you and show you to our dormitory. But first you will need a name.'

'I was christened Guillaume.'

'Too difficult for our Saxon brothers to pronounce. But in English it is "William", is it not?'

'Yes.'

'Then, Brother William, welcome to Telham Priory.'

II

Will tutted loudly from his elevated position on the loading platform of the mill as he looked down the track leading through the village.

'It's Selwyn again, and Elva's sitting alongside him as usual.'

It was the fourth time in succession that the wagon from the thegn's home fields had been driven round Caldbec Hill by the thegn's younger son instead of by the thrall Ormod who used to make the trip, and it was easy to see why. Elva had no doubt jumped on board as the wagon passed their hut, and would skip back off it during its return journey in an hour or so's time, leaving Selwyn to take the sacks of ground grain back by himself. Will was not pleased with this new arrangement, for two reasons. The first was that Elva had no business playing up to the thegn's son, who would no doubt use her badly before abandoning her. The second was that with Ormod no longer at the reins, his daughter Annis was also missing.

'Leave them be, Will,' his father insisted. 'It makes your sister happy to be in his company, and it's not as if they can get up to any wrong, provided that Elva doesn't go beyond the village.'

'But Mother told her that she needed her to help change the rushes. And yet here she is, idling down the road on a wagon.'

Eldred grinned. 'You're just put out because Annis doesn't come on the wagon anymore with her father. If she *really* wanted to see you, she'd make the trip with Selwyn — doesn't that tell you something?'

It did indeed, but what it told Will was something he didn't want to contemplate. He greeted Selwyn and Elva with the curtest of nods, and began throwing down the finished grain sacks without a word, his sullen expression suggesting that the sooner this was over, the better. Elva tried to coax a conversation out of her brother and father, and the older man was experienced enough to realise that it was not in the family's interests to displease the thegn's son.

The wagon was loaded within minutes, and it was an unusually large load. An idea came to Will as he threw the last one down into Selwyn's waiting arms. 'Who helps you unload them at the other end?'

'It depends who's available when we get up there, and if we can spare someone from the field work.'

'Why don't I come with you, and that way you won't have to take a thrall from the crops?'

'I can come too,' Elva added. 'I haven't seen Annis for several weeks now, and when you've finished unloading Will can escort me back the quick way through the wood. Would that be agreeable to you, Father?'

'If it's agreeable to Master Selwyn, I'm sure there'll be no harm in it.'

Selwyn nodded, and the three of them set off, skirting Caldbec Hill and negotiating the junction at the head of the two valleys before turning down towards the manor house in Astenmede. As they hopped off the wagon at the door of the grain store, Elva called out to Aisly, Annis's mother. She was carrying a basket of washing down to the bank of the Asten, normally a daily chore for Annis.

'Aisly, where's Annis?'

Aisly looked in the direction of the manor buildings. 'She went with Master Cerdic into the hay barn, the last I saw of her.'

'And you *let* her?' Will demanded sternly. He raced towards the outhouse in question, grabbing a heavy fallen branch before he threw open the barn door.

Annis was pushed up against a hay bale with Cedric on top of her. Will saw red and raced towards them, causing Cerdic to step back with a curse and reach down for the sword he had left on the ground. Before he could rise again, Will smashed the heavy branch down viciously across his sword arm. There was a sharp cracking sound, and Cerdic doubled up in agony, clutching his arm, as the sword clattered to the ground. Will put all his anger and sinewy strength into a sideways punch to the head that sent Cerdic flying across the barn floor, landing in a crumpled heap in the far corner.

Annis had been a silent witness, her hand to her mouth, but now she called out to Will as she quickly lowered her gown. 'What have you done, you idiot? You've killed the thegn's oldest son! He'll have you hanged unless you run far away from here. Go — now! I'll swear I saw nothing.'

Without considering further, Will raced out of the barn, skidding slightly in the mud as he approached Elva and Selwyn, who were still sitting on the wagon. He ran past them, heading for the safety of the track that led north.

Will knew if he returned home, Cerdic's family would hunt him and down and kill him. He stretched his cloak across several bushes to help it dry in what was left of the afternoon sun, then set about reviving the fire on which he hoped to cook the pike he had coaxed from the lake with the aid of a long tree branch. He'd been living like this for several weeks, and he was uncomfortably aware of the rank smell from the clothing he'd been wearing when he ran from the thegn's barn after killing Cerdic. He had no regrets about that, given what the brute had been doing to poor Annis, but he had no wish to be taken up by the shire-reeve, and better to smell than to hang.

Will hadn't run far; Powdermill Lake was only a few miles from home, and he'd even managed to sneak back to the hut to collect his cloak one night while everyone was snoring. The lake also provided a ready source of fish, so he could remain here, well hidden in the beech-wood thicket, until he felt secure enough to return by night and bid his parents and sister a proper farewell before heading off for good, perhaps to London.

'Where d'yer get that fish, boy?' demanded a rough voice. A man had crept up behind him while he had been blowing on his meagre fire. Will turned quickly, and there stood a giant dressed like a man-at-arms, carrying an axe in his belt.

'In the lake, where else?' Will replied meekly.

The man glowered. 'Don't give me that rubbish, boy. We've been down there since the middle of the day, and we've not caught a thing. So how did *you* get that big one?'

The men were obviously soldiers of some sort, and Will feared they'd been sent by Thegn Leofric to find the man who had killed his son. He therefore proceeded with caution. 'Do you have a net?' he asked.

The man sneered. 'Does it look likely that we have a net, you stupid boy? We're on the march back to Winchester, in the service of Earl Harold, and he doesn't supply us with nets to go fishing in our spare time. But the muddy tracks have held us back, and we need to camp here for the night, make a fire and catch something to eat. We don't fancy rats or moles, so fish would be a good idea, if we can catch a few. You've obviously managed it, so best show us.'

The man — who introduced himself as Bearn — took Will down to the lake and announced that 'this here boy' was going to show them how to catch fish. Will had no problem doing that, and the men lit a fire and began to cook their catch. Bearn invited Will to join them, and held out a gourd containing a strong mead that made his eyes water. Several of the men laughed when Will coughed, and Bearn slapped him playfully on the back.

'You need to toughen up, boy. Where are you from, anyway?'

'Down there,' Will indicated with a vague wave.

Bearn gazed suspiciously down the valley. 'We were all down there a month or two ago, looking for an escaped priest. You didn't see one thereabouts, by any chance?'

Will shook his head as he remembered the man who Widow Gwenyth had been hiding in her hut, according to his mother. But she hadn't said anything about him being a priest, and he wouldn't want the widow to receive a return visit from these heavily armed ruffians. Instead, he changed the subject. 'How far is Winchester from here?'

'Two days at least,' Bearn replied with a frown, 'but with the state of the tracks after all this spring rain, more like three or four. Do you fancy coming along with us, boy, and helping us to catch fish?'

'Maybe Amalric will take him on as a soldier?' one of them added with a snort.

Bearn looked Will up and down before enquiring, 'Do you have work, boy, or a family that will miss you if you become one of us? Earl Harold's always looking to increase the size of the fyrd that he commands in the name of King Edward, and our commander Amalric would no doubt welcome you, while rewarding us for bringing you in as a recruit.'

Will didn't feel that he had much choice, and it made sense to hide himself away in the army of the most powerful earl in the kingdom, upon whose loyalty even the king relied.

Three days later, Will was standing in a rough field just outside the earth bank that guarded the capital of Wessex. A battle-hardened man called Amalric, with grizzled grey hair and several scars on his arms and face, was yelling at the half dozen or so youths who constituted his latest recruits.

'You look more like milkmaids or serving wenches than fighting men, but when I've finished with you, you'll either have run home to your mothers, or become men-at-arms in the service of Earl Harold. The choice is yours, but if you *do* run away, and ever get caught afterwards, there's the tree we hang cowards on.'

He pointed to an elderly oak tree in the corner of the field, from which the crow-ravaged remains of the latest escapee were still hanging, covered in flies. Will looked away in disgust, then realised his mistake. Amalric had been looking at the faces of his latest recruits for potential weaklings.

'You — pretty boy!' he yelled, glaring at Will. 'Let's see how strong you are.' He pulled his spear from the ground, walked up to Will and handed it to him. 'I'll walk away for some distance, then I want you to try to run me through with this spear when you lob it at me.' He walked for some thirty feet or so, then turned with a challenging leer. 'Go on then, boy — try and hit me from there.'

Will tested the spear's weight, then shouted back at Amalric. 'Move further back.'

Amalric guffawed. 'That will only require me to walk back further when your throw falls short. Throw it at me *now*, else it will be the worse for you.'

Will had taken a strong dislike to the man's bullying manner, and he took a few deep breaths before launching the spear at Amalric with all the anger he could summon. A look of fear crossed the commander's face before he jumped hastily sideways into the mud to avoid being run through by a spear that whistled twenty more feet past him before twanging into the muddy ground, where it remained quivering for a few more seconds. Amalric got up, red in the face, and rubbed most of the mud off his tunic and hose.

Nobody dared laugh as he walked back to Will carrying a shield and a long battle-axe.

'Very clever, boy. Now, let's see if you can dent this shield with this axe. If not, I'll have you assigned to the earl's service to clean out his midden every day. With your bare hands.'

The responding titter from the remaining recruits only served to increase Will's anger, and he whirled the axe high in the air before bringing it down hard in an attempt to split the bully's head in two. Amalric raised his shield above his head just in time, but was forced to the ground by the sheer force of the blow that left a massive split in the centre of the shield boss. He rose from the ground with a grin, and clapped Will on the shoulder.

'You seem to have what it takes, boy. Wait for me in the armoury — that's where you all assembled this morning. As for the rest of you, learn from his example.'

An hour later Will was being measured for chainmail, and the armourer was placing one sword after another into his hand, and asking him to test it for balance and flexibility. Then several different types of shield were held up against him for height assessment, and he was asked to take each one in turn, wrap the leather thong inside it around his wrist, and advise which one was the most comfortable. Halfway through this, he realised that Amalric was behind him, watching carefully.

'Where are the others?' Will asked Amalric.

'Still in the field, running up and down to get fit.'

'Shouldn't I be with them?'

'Can you ride a horse?' Amalric asked, ignoring the question.

Will shrugged. 'I don't know — I've never tried. We had horses in our village, pulling wagons, but I never climbed on the back of one.'

'I'll pick you out a quiet one, and you'll have three days to learn how to stay on its back before you depart.'

'Where for?'

'London. You just became a housecarl for King Edward. How did you get to be so strong?'

'Mainly through throwing grain sacks around my father's mill. But you made me angry, which helped,' he added truthfully, expecting a violent response.

Amalric just grinned. 'Remind me, if we ever go into battle together, to make you angry beforehand. But for the time being, save your anger for the weather and the state of the tracks to London.'

Annis looked helplessly across the field strips to where Elva was planting the family's parsnip seeds for the coming summer crop. The fifth neighbour in succession had cut Annis dead with a frown of disapproval when she tried to engage them in polite conversation. She was beginning to regret the speed with which she had accepted Cerdic's offer to speak to his father in order to have her relocated to Sandlake as a free woman, with a strip of her own in the fertile valley. It had been bought with her body and she had been cast away from the community as a result.

Annis threw down the hoe with which she had been attempting, without any great success, to clear the ground of weeds. She walked across towards Elva, but when Elva saw her coming she bent her back even lower as she made a great show of casting the parsnip seeds into the drills she had already prepared. It was only when Annis stood directly in front of her that Elva looked up.

'Why does everyone give me such foul looks?' Annis demanded. 'Come on, Elva — you were my friend, once. Have *you* turned against me as well?'

Elva stood upright and stretched her back muscles. She'd be glad of the temporary break, and it was time that Annis was told the truth by someone who genuinely cared for her happiness. 'Very well, Annis, since you ask — and since we're still friends, so far as I'm concerned. You ask why the neighbours shun you — well, perhaps you should reflect on how you came to be a churl rather than a thrall, and how you came by that strip that should have gone to the Welken family, who've been waiting for a second strip ever since the birth of their seventh child.'

'Meaning?'

'Meaning that you gave your body to the thegn's son. If we all did that, where would this village be?'

'I thought Cerdic would marry me. But now he's gone and I am on my own.'

'Well, perhaps you shouldn't have discouraged Will — you knew how much he cared for you.'

'Do you think he'll ever come back?'

'Who knows? But it's thanks to you that he ran away in the first place. Would *you* come back if you were in his place, thinking that you'd killed a thegn's son?'

With a few bland words of farewell, Annis walked back over to her strip, gave a huge sigh of resignation, and picked up the hoe again.

III

Will's thighs protested as he climbed down from his horse at their latest camp. Amalric yelled a few brief instructions, and fires were lit as others went off in search of their evening meal. It was the third such night on the open road, and Will was hoping that London was not too much further.

As they sat around the fire, taking it in turns to carve lumps with their daggers from the spitting carcass of the deer they had caught, Will was only several places away from Amalric. He voiced what many of them were thinking.

'Most of us have not yet been properly tested in battle, and yet you give us horses, appoint us as housecarls and send us into the king's service as if we were hardened soldiers. Is there some reason for this that I have not yet fathomed?'

Amalric addressed his answer to all of them. 'It is time for the planting of the summer crops, and many of you are no doubt wondering how your womenfolk will manage without you. You are not alone in that, and even the king finds it difficult to prevent his personal bodyguard from drifting back to the land, both at this time and during the autumn harvest.'

'Is the penalty for desertion not death?' another recruit asked.

Amalric replied with a hollow laugh. 'If King Edward were to put to death every man who deserted for a few months, he would have no fyrd left, let alone any housecarls. He relies on the Earl Harold to replace those men who desert, and you are those replacements.'

'Even though our valour has not been tested?' Will asked in disbelief.

Amalric nodded. 'But do not reveal that when we get to Court. Earl Harold wishes to appear loyal, but he keeps his best men back in Winchester.'

Two days later, the men wound their way slowly along the north bank of the River Thames until they came in sight of the Palace of West Minster, along with the massive cathedral that adjoined it — one of the first buildings Will had ever seen made entirely out of stone. They dismounted in the palace yard, and their horses were taken from them by grooms while Amalric led the dozen or so men on foot through the inner gate. They were halted as a white-haired man spoke briefly to Amalric.

'The king is currently at prayer in the abbey next door,' reported Amalric, 'so we may exercise our cramped limbs on the riverbank down there. We will begin with a vigorous walk, then we will attempt to run in our chainmail. It will be good practice for when we are called upon to do so in earnest. Leave your weapons with the armourer in that hut next to the stables, and follow me.'

It was several days before Will laid eyes on the king, and he was less than impressed by what he saw. The man was more elderly than he'd expected, and with white hair and a flowing beard he more closely resembled the abbot of a monastery than the King of England. His pale, watery gaze flicked without much obvious interest across the handful of men who had been sent into his Great Hall with their weapons, which included Will. Eventually he nodded in vague approval, then turned to Amalric.

'Return to Earl Harold with my thanks. But before you leave, issue orders that these men are to be properly and regularly churched, for the good of their souls.'

'Who told you that you might be of service to me?' Earl Harold demanded as he glared at the young upstart who had been admitted into the hall by his steward.

Selwyn swallowed his proud anger as he reminded himself that Earlene was relying on him. 'My mother.'

Harold laughed in his face. 'And your mother is a mighty warrior, no doubt?'

'No — she's the half-sister of King Edward.'

Harold began to laugh, then stopped himself when he caught the expression on Selwyn's face. The boy might be deluding himself, or he might have been persuaded by someone that what he was saying was true, but he obviously believed it. And if he did, there could be others of like mind, and the less claimants to the throne the better.

'And how did your mother come by this high claim?'

'Simply by being born — her mother was Emma of Normandy, who was the mother of both the current King Edward and the former King Harthacnut.'

'So this mother of yours is also related to the House of Norway?'

'So she tells me.'

'Where does she live, boy?'

'In Astenmede, two days' ride from here. It's a valley that goes down from the High Weald towards the sea at Pevensey.'

Harold's brain was working at double speed. Apart from the fact that a rival to his claim to the throne was living not a few days' ride from Winchester, the name of 'Astenmede' had been mentioned in his presence recently, and he was feverishly searching his memory when it came back to him. 'Tell me, boy, did you see some of my soldiers in your vicinity last autumn, searching for someone?'

'I didn't see them,' Selwyn replied, 'but I heard tell of them. They were in Sandlake, which is the next village across from ours, and within my father's manor estates. They would also have entered our manor lands, but my mother denied them entry. She can be very determined, and even harder to oppose when in one of her moods.'

'Your father is a thegn?'

'Yes. Thegn Leofric of Astenmede.'

'And this mother of yours is still married to him, and still alive?'

'Yes, of course. She is called Earlene.'

Harold beckoned the steward to his side, and indicated Selwyn with a nod of his head. 'See that this young man is accommodated in the soldiers' hall. I have in mind taking him into my service as a housecarl. I will speak with you again on the morrow, boy.'

Selwyn bowed out, leaving Harold deep in thought. Now it all made sense why the priest had broken out of secure custody here in Winchester. Someone — one of those hanged for what was then believed to have been his incompetence — had deliberately released him, in the pay of this Earlene of Astenmede who was no doubt planning to reveal her claim to the throne at the appropriate moment. Someone *else* who desired the death of this French priest, and had had the wretch released for long enough to ensure for herself that he was dispatched before he could destroy her claim as well as Harold's. Little wonder that she had denied entry to his men-at-arms — she did not wish to reveal that she had done away with him, thus exposing herself to trial in the King's Court. The king would not be pleased to hear of the man's fate, given that the fugitive was a priest, and Edward was so pious.

Harold resolved to keep this young man close to his side, and to learn what he could of his mother. He would discover, through her, whether the priest was still alive.

He summoned Amalric.

'You will recall the hangings of those who failed to find the runaway priest?' Harold asked quietly.

Amalric blanched. 'Very well, my lord, since I was required to supervise them.'

'Well, I wish you to take more men and resume the search, but this time in a very particular place where I have reason to believe he may once have been hidden. But that will not be the real reason why you will be journeying to this place.'

'My lord?'

'I believe that he may already have been done away with, by someone who extracted his secret from him by torture before he was killed. I need that fact confirmed, and I also require the person responsible to be brought back here as a prisoner.'

'Of course. To where will I be journeying?'

'The place is called Astenmede. It lies just above the coast at Pevensey, with an adjoining village called Sandlake. But you must go about this task using men from London, and you must not say a word regarding this mission here in Winchester. There are those here who might seek to prevent you or who may send a warning to the local thegn ahead of your departure. Are we understood?'

'Clearly, my lord. It just so happens that among those I took to London some months ago is an eager young man who comes from this place called Sandlake, or so he said.'

'But can you be sure of his loyalty, since the person I wish to seize is the wife of the local thegn?'

Amalric seemed temporarily taken aback by this revelation, and sought further details.

Earl Harold sighed, the first warning that he might be about to explode into one of his terrible tempers, but he checked himself. 'A young man arrived here, seeking to serve as a housecarl. He gave his name as Selwyn of Astenmede, and his father is Leofric, the local thegn. Leofric's father was a loyal follower of the late King Harthacnut, but Leofric himself is said to be fat and lazy. His loyalty to King Edward — or anyone else, for that matter — is suspect. I have this information from those among my advisers who make it their business — because it is also *my* business — to know who is loyal and who is not.'

'Why do you wish to seize Leofric's wife, if I might make so bold?'

'This woman — whose name I have forgotten, but who is married to the thegn — claims to be the half-sister of both King Edward and his predecessor Harthacnut. This connection comes from the royal house of Norway some years in the past, and I believe that she may be in league with Harald of Norway for him to come over here and install her on the throne. Not in her own right, clearly, since the Witan would never accept a woman ruling over them, but as his representative over here while he combines Norway with England in order to settle the long-standing dispute with Denmark. You perceive the potential threat to England?'

'And the secret that is held by this priest is in connection with this plot?'

'No, another plot entirely, but one that could cause sufficient unrest within the realm to make its conquest by the Norsemen even easier. Either that, or another invasion plan that would conflict with hers, in which case she would have sought its details from the priest who knows them.'

'I now understand why this woman must be silenced.'

'But not until we learn what the priest has told her. She must be brought back here alive at all costs, do you understand? I have men here who will be more than capable of extracting from her what information she has been given, and who will also oblige her, by very unpleasant means, to confess her treason in seeking to bring over the Norwegian king. If the priest is still alive, you must bring both him and the thegn's wife back here, unharmed. Now, when can you depart?'

'Immediately, my lord. I shall journey to London and collect the young man who is from the neighbouring village, along with some of his comrades. Then I shall employ them on the search and capture in Astenmede, thereby ensuring that no-one here in Winchester, short of yourself, is aware of what is being planned.'

'Excellent. Here, take this. There will be more when you return with prisoners.'

Harold tossed a small bag of coins onto the table, which Amalric scooped up with grateful thanks before leaving the hall in search of his chainmail and his horse.

'I think this may be your pig,' Annis said as she walked up to where Gwenyth was cutting kindling.

Gwenyth looked up and grunted. 'Where did the little bastard wander to this time? Pardon my rude language, but he's always wandering off. Just like his mother, that one.'

'I found him up on Sandlake Ridge, where I was looking for some mint to kill the taste of the last of the sheep.'

'I've got some mint you can have,' Gwenyth told her. 'It's the least I can do in return for you bringing the porker back before someone threw a line around him and added him to their collection. I've got some mead left as well, if you'd like some.'

A few minutes later, Annis was chewing on three-day-old bread and washing it down with honey mead as she looked up into Gwenyth's thatch.

'You'll have to show me how to tie up those loose bits, so that the fire doesn't catch them,' she told Gwenyth. 'The last people in my hut left it all hanging, and I'm not tall enough to get up there.'

'One of the few things that men are fit for,' Gwenyth replied. 'You should get one of your own. That thatch was fixed by my late husband — he went four years ago, so he must have done a good enough job. There are plenty of lusty men around the place.'

'Did you not find anyone for yourself after you became a widow?'

'There was a time last autumn when I thought I might have got lucky. I came across this naked man up in Caldbec Wood, but he turned out to be an escaped priest. I did my best, but I couldn't get him interested.'

'I heard you'd had a man hidden away in here,' Annis admitted.

'No doubt that gossipy old witch Rowena Riveracre was only too happy to tell you that.' Gwenyth spat into the fire.

'What happened to him?'

'Earl Harold's soldiers came looking for him, so I hustled him away to some old monastery over by Telham way. Anyway, you'd perhaps best be getting up to your own hut before it gets dark. Here's some of that mint you were looking for.'

The shadows were lengthening in the early spring evening as Annis slipped out of Gwenyth's hut and almost collided with Elva. The two girls confronted each other in shocked silence.

'Have you nothing better to do than eavesdrop on your neighbours now that Selwyn's left you?' demanded Annis.

'He hasn't left for good, he's just joined the service of Earl Harold. And when he returns, keep your eyes off him, because he's spoken for.'

'I'd wager that his mother wouldn't agree with you there.'

IV

There were several reasons why, a week later, Will was horrified to be advised that he had been selected to return to Sandlake and Astenmede with a group of his colleagues in order to resume the search for a priest in hiding. For one thing, he was uncomfortably aware that the man they were seeking may have been hidden for a short while by his neighbour Widow Gwenyth. If the brutal Amalric discovered that, God alone knew what he would do to her to discover the man's present whereabouts. The second reason was the fact that he had left the neighbourhood in a hurry after killing the thegn's son, so his own neck might be at risk. Even his position as a man-at-arms in the service of the king might not preserve his life. The third reason was more recent, and more personal.

The first time Will had laid eyes on Joan, all thoughts of Annis had been driven from his mind. He had been one of twelve men in the outer courtyard of Edward's royal palace, learning how to form up behind a wall of interlocking shields, Roman style. As they bowed their heads, with Will in the front line, and moved slowly forward with their spears held in front of them, they had heard a squeal of fear, and had received an order to halt and break the wall. As they did so, they could see a serving girl, barefoot, gazing down at an array of fruit on the ground, along with the bowl that had also been dropped as she had jumped back from the line of advancing spears.

The group had been ordered to break formation and return to their starting point, and Will had stared, transfixed by the young woman's flowing fair hair, her startled blue eyes and her open freckled face, until she saw him staring and challenged him.

'Well, are you going to just stand there and gloat over your handiwork? You might at least lend me a hand to pick up all this fruit.'

Will began to pick up the scattered fruit. As he reloaded the serving bowl that the girl held out for him with a grateful smile, he took in the deliciously overpowering perfume of rosewater that she had doused herself in.

'Thank you, young man,' she said as she took in his height, his muscular arms and his curly red-brown locks. 'My name's Joan.'

'Wilfrid,' he stammered. 'Will for short.'

'But you're not short, are you?' she teased him. 'In truth, you're one of the tallest men I've ever seen. Your woman must be very proud.'

'I don't have a woman — unless you're offering,' Will blurted out, then cursed inwardly at his own forwardness.

'I have no time for seeking a husband,' Joan replied, still smiling broadly. 'In the king's service we work all the hours, and then in our time off we're expected to attend chapel.'

'What about early morning?' Will persisted hopefully.

'Depends how early you mean. Once the sun is up, and the king's heard his second Mass, we have to be inside the Great Hall serving his breakfast. Not that he eats much, particularly since he has been so ill of late. Mainly fruit — even if it's been on the ground.'

Will was determined not to let the chance slip by. 'So if I were to be here before daybreak, you might be here also?'

'That depends whether I could rely upon a handsome housecarl to ensure that I was in no danger.'

'There *will* be a housecarl here tomorrow, to guarantee your safety, should you wish to take a turn around the outer bailey. But I fear he will not be handsome enough.'

The following morning was the first of several that they spent in each other's company. Joan was from Mercia, she told Will, and had entered the king's service as part of a gift of servants to the king from Earl Edwin. Prior to that, she had been a serving girl to a thegn on the outskirts of a large village called Tamworth, and had caught Edwin's eye during a meeting of his local Witan held in the local thegn's manor house. She was obviously well aware of her physical attractiveness, but had so far managed to avoid the usual fate of comely serving girls, and was at great pains to advise Will that this was a state of affairs that she intended to continue. Not that Will had any intention of seducing her, intoxicating though the thought might be. He was more intent on securing her agreement to become 'spoken for', and this had seemed to be growing more likely by the day when he received the order to ride back west with Amalric.

When Amalric sidled up to him on their first night's camp outside Woking, Will assumed that it was to take him to task for the sour face that he had been exhibiting. He was therefore a little surprised when, instead of chiding him for his poor attitude, Amalric put an arm across his shoulder and began walking him away from the other men.

'I haven't yet made it fully clear why we are heading where we are, but I thought that your face might be a little more cheerful at the prospect of returning to your family, assuming that you have one. Be that as it may, you were chosen especially for the task that Earl Harold has entrusted me with, because of your local knowledge.'

Will thought briefly, and decided that this might be a good time to reveal something of his recent history. At the very least, if his commander took it badly, Will would have the opportunity to escape on horseback, long before they reached their destination.

'I have a very good reason for not wishing to return to Sandlake.'

'You left a girl there with child, perhaps?' Amalric leered. 'I'll say nothing about the attention you've been giving of late to that serving girl at the palace. I can't guarantee that one of the other men won't, of course, since you and she have become the talk of the entire palace guard.'

'No, it's not that,' Will assured him. 'It's just that — well — I meant to tell you some time ago, but...'

'Out with it, boy. Did you kill your father or something? You were obviously on the run from something when you were first found by that lake.'

'Not my father — the thegn's son.'

Amalric stared back at him for a moment, scarcely able to believe his good fortune. 'You say you killed the thegn's son?'

'Yes. When we reach Sandlake, Thegn Leofric will likely have me hanged.'

'Not while you're in the king's service, let me assure you of that,' Amalric replied. 'But you should know that the thegn's son recently came to Winchester, seeking service under Earl Harold.'

'The thegn has two sons,' Will told him. 'At least, he did until I killed one of them. The one in Winchester must be the younger boy, Selwyn. I killed the older boy, Cerdic.'

'So this Thegn Leofric will be no friend of yours?' Amalric asked.

'Obviously not,' Will confirmed.

'Excellent,' Amalric murmured as he turned to look Will in the eye. 'My orders are two-fold. The first is to find a runaway priest, and you should be advised that the last search party that failed to find him were all hanged, including that fool Bearn, who first brought you to Winchester. If we find this priest, we are to take him unharmed back to Earl Harold in Winchester, where he will be *very* harmed, in order to extract some important secret from him.'

'And what is the second order?' Will asked, determined that his first task would be to warn Gwenyth to have a false story prepared.

Amalric was choosing his words carefully. 'It is Earl Harold's belief that this priest will already be dead, having been done away with by the thegn's wife.'

'Earlene?'

'Is that her name? Well, whatever, we believe that she had her own interest in having this priest silenced, and that it has to do with a planned invasion of England.'

'From where?'

'Norway, or so it is believed. This is consistent with news I obtained when back in London, collecting you and the others, to the effect that King Edward recently received a visit from King Harald of Norway. The two parted on bad terms, with Harald threatening invasion.'

'So if Earl Harold wishes to know what the priest's secret was, and Earlene has had him killed, he will need to ask Earlene?'

Amalric grimaced. 'I don't think that he intends to sit her down by the fireside and politely enquire.'

'So we are to seize Earlene, if we cannot find the priest for ourselves?'

'Precisely. You heard nothing regarding this priest before you left your home?'

'Absolutely nothing,' Will assured him — which was the strict truth, since it had only been suspected that the new man briefly in Gwenyth's life had been a priest.

It was with some trepidation that three days later Will obtained leave from Amalric to ride down to visit his family, while the rest of the armed band camped along the shoreline of Powdermill Lake.

Will hastily suppressed the cries of joy that greeted him as he lifted the door flap and walked into the family hut, dressed in his chainmail and carrying a sword and shield. Elva hugged him, then stood back and looked him up and down.

'You've obviously become a fine soldier. But you should know right away that you had no need to run away like that. Cerdic is not dead, but has been sent over the sea on a mission for his mother.'

'Let the boy warm himself by the fire, while I cut some bread and carve a portion of that cold pig,' Rowena instructed Elva.

Will joined his father on the bench and asked, 'How goes the mill?'

'Middling to good,' Eldred told him, 'but Selwyn's gone away as well, so Ormod brings the wagon down again these days. Mind you, Annis doesn't lower herself sufficiently to come across from her strip and greet him.'

'Annis is here in the village?' Will asked.

Elva nodded, with a look of distaste. 'You'll probably be distressed to hear this, but she lay with Cerdic to win herself the old strip that Oswin Shepherd used to till. She lives in their old hut since Widow Brimlad moved away, but everyone here shuns her because of her rude ways. You lost nothing by her, believe me, Will.'

'That doesn't matter anymore,' Will replied. 'I've met another girl. She's a serving wench in the King's Court in London, and her name's Joan. Which reminds me…'

'You've been to the King's Court in London?' Rowena exclaimed excitedly. 'Are you one of his soldiers now, and is that his emblem on your tunic?'

'No, it shows that I serve Earl Harold, but yes, I have been in the king's direct service, on loan from the earl. It's a long story. Before I forget, I must speak to Widow Gwenyth. She may be in danger. That man she had in her hut last autumn — was he a priest, and where did he go?'

'Only Gwenyth herself ever claimed that he was a priest, but she refuses to say what became of him. Why do you ask?'

'We've been sent here to find him,' Will replied, 'and this time we have to be more thorough than the last search party, who were hanged by Earl Harold when they couldn't find him.'

Both his mother and sister gasped, as his father asked, 'You said "we" just now. Does that mean there are more of you, and that this wasn't just a home visit by you?'

'That's right,' Will nodded. 'The rest of them are camped by Powdermill Lake, and I managed to get leave of absence to visit my family. But they'll all be down here tomorrow, and Gwenyth had better get her story right.'

'It's even worse than you think,' Elva grimaced. 'Just lately Gwenyth's got very friendly with Annis, who'd sell her own mother down the river if it meant some advancement for her. God alone knows what secrets Gwenyth's confided in her.'

'I'll get Gwenyth over here now,' Eldred offered as he lumbered towards the doorway. He peered out and advised them all that it was snowing.

When Eldred returned, Gwenyth followed him in. She looked apprehensive as she slipped off her cloak. 'What's this about more soldiers?' she asked nervously.

Will took the lead in advising her of recent developments.

Gwenyth turned pale and shivered. 'The missing man *was* in my hut, and he *did* tell me that he was a priest. But I took him to a safe place, and I haven't seen him since.'

'Don't tell us where!' Will said quickly, before lowering his voice again to continue. 'Anyone who knows where he is can be tortured for that information. We just have to make sure that you get your story right when the soldiers come tomorrow. I'll be one of them, and I'll try to help you if I can. If it helps, they think he might be dead now.'

'That's what I'll tell them, then,' Gwenyth nodded with a sigh of relief.

Eldred had a thought. 'Won't they want to see his grave?'

It fell silent, until Will remembered the second reason why armed men had been sent to Sandlake, and their possible mission on the other side of Caldbec Wood. 'Can you get someone to say that he was last seen wandering through the woods towards Astenmede? If so, then hopefully we can persuade Earl Harold that he must have died in there, particularly if he had a good reason for killing himself.'

'I can think of someone who'll do anything for the right price,' Gwenyth said. 'Just give me until tomorrow, and I'll have everything organised.'

Annis was easily bribed with a piglet, and the next morning, when Will led Amalric into the open ground between his family's hut and Gwenyth's, their neighbour was waiting demurely by her door, dressed in her cleanest gown and looking suitably widow-like.

'This is the lady I was speaking about,' Will told Amalric, who gazed appreciatively at Gwenyth as she all but curtsied.

'Come into my hut and have a mug of mead, and perhaps some of my bacon broth and fresh bread, while I tell you all about it,' she purred invitingly.

An hour later, it was all going to plan. Amalric was on his second mug of mead, into which Gwenyth had emptied a small handful of herbs she had never known to fail when her late husband had been 'off his oats'. Amalric had also been softened up somewhat by two helpings of fresh corn loaf and salted pig broth, and was in the mood to believe almost anything that this well-rounded widow lady was prepared to tell him.

'It was really all my fault,' Gwenyth assured him from under lowered eyelids. 'Being a widow and all for these past four years, I was missing the — well, you know, you being a mature and experienced man and all — so that when this lovely man came into my life completely naked, well I just couldn't help myself, could I? He was sitting just where you are now, on the floor by the fire, and I let my outer gown slip off, like this. Then when I could see he was interested in what was underneath, I dropped the under-shift to the ground as well — do you want me to show you how, so you can more easily understand how I overcame his shyness? There we go. The poor man couldn't resist, as you can perhaps imagine for yourself.'

Amalric swallowed hard as he took in her curves, and asked hoarsely, 'Then what happened?'

'Well, afterwards he burst out crying and confessed that he'd committed a great sin in God's eyes because he was a holy man of some sort. I didn't quite catch it all, since he didn't seem to speak our language all that well. Anyway, he just grabbed the few clothes I'd given him and raced off, and that's the last I saw of him. My good neighbour Annis told me she'd seen him wandering through Caldbec Wood, crying his eyes out. And that's all I can tell you.'

'Are you sure?'

'Honest. You wouldn't doubt a poor widow woman, would you? And one, what's more, who's feeling a bit flustered from showing her nakedness to a big strong man like you? Got me quite excited, it has. You couldn't by any chance oblige a poor lonely lady that hasn't known a man for a good while, could you?'

Rowena had been crouched down outside Gwenyth's hut, listening to her performance. It now got all too much for her, and she clapped her hand over her mouth and scampered down to where Will was pacing up and down the riverbank, her shoulders heaving with laughter and tears rolling down her face.

A short while later, Amalric emerged from Gwenyth's hut with a wry smile and walked down to join Will, who suppressed a grin of his own as he asked, 'How did you get on in there?'

'Fine. The lady seems innocent enough. But do you know a woman around here called "Annis", by any chance?'

'That's her, over there.' Will indicated towards where Annis could be seen prodding listlessly with a hoe in an inexperienced attempt to remove weeds from ground that still had frost in it.

'We need to speak with her,' Amalric announced as he walked over, with Will walking a few feet behind him.

Annis looked up as they approached.

'I've just come from a widow in the village who says that you saw a stranger wandering through the woods a while ago,' Amalric told her.

'That's right,' Annis replied. 'I think he was the man she had staying in her hut for a day or two, or at least that's what she said.'

'What can you tell me about this man?'

'Just that I hadn't seen him before, and he looked sort of lost. He was also crying and wandering around in circles. I asked him if he needed help, but he didn't seem to understand what I was saying, so I just pointed the way down to the thegn's manor house, in case they could help him.'

'So the last you saw of him, he was heading for the manor house, is that it?' Amalric asked. Annis nodded, and Amalric turned back to Will. 'We're done here. Follow me.'

As they picked their way between the strips back to where their horses were tied, Amalric said, 'Her story fits the information I was given before we set out. A priest, possibly French, connected in some way with the thegn's wife.'

'If he truly was,' Will argued when he could see where things were heading, 'why didn't he go straight there, instead of spending a few nights in the village?'

'Who knows?' Amalric replied as they reached their horses and climbed onto their backs. 'We don't get paid to think — just to follow orders. Show me how we get to this Astenmede.'

'We go down this track back onto the ridge, then cut down to the right at the end of Caldbec Wood. Are we going to seize the Lady Earlene?'

'Can you think of any good reason why not?' Amalric demanded. 'I left the rest of the men at the top of that ridge in case we needed to ransack the village, but now we can use them to turn over the manor house. Come with me.'

Will was desperately searching for some plausible argument to avoid arresting the innocent lady of his manor when he looked up at the sound of approaching hooves. One of his colleagues, Oswin, was pounding hard down the track towards them, and pulled hard on the horse's halter as he came to a skidding halt alongside Amalric and whispered to him with an urgent look on his face. Amalric turned back to Will.

'We need to ride hard to rejoin the main body of the earl's men, who are racing to London.'

'Why's that?'

'The king is dying, and Earl Harold wants to be there when he does.'

V

By the time they reached London, there was nowhere left for them to lay their heads. Not only had their leader Harold arrived ahead of them with a full retinue of housecarls in an overt display of strength, but they had been joined by the other two great earls, Morcar of Northumbria and Edwin of Mercia, who commanded the entire Midland region.

The outer bailey of the palace was a cacophony of competing accents, clattering weaponry and creaking chainmail as hundreds of foot soldiers from the various regional armies competed for space in which to practise their martial skills. They were under orders from their supreme commanders to appear strong enough to guarantee peace under a new King, who would be appointed by the sixty-man Witan Council.

Will sat on the hard ground of the inner bailey, sheltering from the snow. All around him was mutinous talk of walking back into the town and terrorising alehouse owners into offering sleeping spaces in lofts, stables, outhouses and barrel stores.

Then word came that the housecarls who had arrived on horseback, and had found stabling for their horses, had been granted leave to sleep in the straw beside them. Will lost no time in obeying. He dozed off wondering whether being in the earl's service was any better than heaving sacks of grain around his father's mill, and what might be happening inside the palace walls.

If he had but known it, the next few hours were to turn the tide of English history. King Edward lay covered in animal skins, but still he shivered and coughed, his rheumy eyes looking out into the chamber with its roaring fire and its attendant holy men, physicians, courtiers, earls, servants, and messengers who passed backwards and forwards with the latest news. The three major Earls were there, glowering at each other suspiciously, and mentally calculating how many of the final Witan they could rely upon for a vote in their favour.

They had few candidates to choose from inside the nation. The nearest blood relative was Edward's grand-nephew, Edgar Aetheling, an unknown fifteen-year-old who was believed to still be in hiding somewhere in Hungary. The other claimants best known to the Witan were the three great Earls, and of these Harold of Wessex was the most obvious, being not only the one with the largest standing army, but also the brother-in-law of King Edward, following the king's largely celibate marriage to Harold's sister Edith.

There were also two known foreign contenders: Harald Hardrada of Norway and Duke William of Normandy, both of whom were forever sending over envoys claiming that the throne had been promised to them — and both would attempt to take it by force if necessary. Therefore, the first task of Edward's elected successor would be to defend the realm against foreign invasion.

As he lay searching for his next breath, the king asked for Harold. It would later be claimed by the earl's supporters that Edward's final act was to beg Harold to 'take good care of the sister and nation that I leave in your most worthy hands.' It seemed that the king had nominated Harold as his heir at the most solemn moment in his God-fearing life.

Only hours after Edward's death, Harold decided on a show of strength and ordered that his immediate retinue were to be housed within the palace, whatever disruption that might cause. In the stable, Will awoke to the familiar smell of rosewater and the sensation of something soft and warm beside him. He opened his eyes and found himself staring into the face of the girl he had been dreaming of. Joan placed a restraining finger on his lips.

'Please let me lie next to you and keep warm.'

'Of course, but why?'

'We've all been turned out of our hall to make way for Earl Harold's closest attendants. It's snowing hard out there, and one of the girls remembered that the housecarls had been allowed to bed down with their horses. So, if you'll put up with me alongside you, I'd like to spend the night here.'

Will discovered that Harold was now the King of England on the morning following the Witan's vote, two days after Edward's death. Will and his colleagues had spent the first day lounging around the stables in order to avoid going out into the snowfall interspersed with drizzle, but on the second day came the command to assemble in the inner keep to be addressed by their new King.

As they stood there, heads bent against the heavy wet flakes, a horn blew a slightly hesitant fanfare, and a small procession wound its way from the Great Hall out onto the open ground. It was headed by King Harold himself, and he lost no time in making a short speech as the snow flurries skittered around his head, settling on the jewels set in the crown. It clearly going to require the services of a goldsmith to make it sit on his broad head.

'Men of Wessex,' the king shouted to the several hundred men-at-arms who stood before him, 'you came here to West Minster in the service of an Earl, and you now serve a King. Henceforth you will be required to defend not only your native

Wessex, but those parts of the entire nation that are not under the firm hand of the Earls of Northumberland and Mercia.'

Will became aware of a line of young women, including Joan, emerging from the stables in which they had spent several nights. They formed their own line behind the rear rank of the men-at-arms.

'There will be many changes as the result of these new requirements. I have divided my fyrd into two halves, one of which will return to Winchester, where it will be commanded in my name by Amalric Goodbarrow. Its duties will include the guarding of the south coast of Wessex and the Eastern Lands against any possible invasion from across the Channel, from which I anticipate that a challenge will be issued very soon by Duke William of Normandy.

'It has been reported to me that many of you from the horse-borne ranks have taken women who were formerly in the service of the late King Edward. I have ordered them to stand behind you. When the order is given, each of you may step out of your ranks and bring your chosen woman to your side. Henceforth that woman will be dismissed from the royal service, and will be free to journey with you back to Wessex, either as your wife or simply as your woman. Should you wish to marry, there are ordained priests here in the abbey who can provide that service, but, whether you marry or not, those of you who select a woman will be responsible for their welfare both here and at Winchester. You may now each identify your woman and bring her to your side.'

Will looked back gleefully towards Joan, his heart in his mouth, and let out a sigh of relief when she nodded and held out her hand. He all but ran back through the milling couples who were linking hands, hugging and kissing, and — in some cases — crying silent tears of happiness. Will took Joan's hand and looked down into her joyous face.

'Will you have me as your husband, Joan?' he asked timorously.

'Indeed I will,' she answered as she pulled him towards her.

'All I can offer you is a freeman's hut in a village by the sea.'

'That will be finer than a patch of straw in a servant's hall, and a life of running backwards and forwards for a steward who thought us all beneath him.'

At this point Amalric called his men back into line, each with his chosen woman, and addressed them himself before King Harold could command their attention again.

'By my reckoning, a dozen or so of you have taken women who will need to accompany you back to Winchester. I will arrange the necessary wagons, but be warned that the journey will be no pleasure expedition, particularly not in this weather. But married men are happier men, and I wish you every happiness in your chosen unions. You men will have good cause to be grateful for the comfort of your women before this year is out.'

Harold cleared his throat and shook the snow from his crown before placing it back on his head and continuing his address. 'I now have words for those of you who are to remain here in London. Because of the very special duties involved in guarding our nation's capital, you will be hand-picked by my most experienced warriors, and you should regard it as the highest of honours to be serving the realm in this way. It will mean that you will not return immediately to Winchester, but must be prepared to serve wherever duty takes you. We know the Midlands and North to be secure under the Earls Edwin and Morcar, but it may well be that you are required to travel north-east out of London, should any invasion threat be posed by Norse adventurers seeking to exploit the change in ruler. Or perhaps south-west, to support the men of Wessex against Norman invasion. Whichever it is, be in no doubt that in return for the honour being bestowed upon you, I will tolerate no desertions. Those who sneak away without leave will be brought back and done to death.'

'I hope we get to go away to Wessex,' Joan whispered in Will's ear, 'because I've seen quite enough of London.'

It occurred to Will that he might be one of those retained for direct armed service under the new King, and he spent the remainder of the brief address from Harold with an uneasy feeling that perhaps things had been going *too* well for him. King Harold took himself back into the palace with his small retinue, and Amalric and two other men took his place in front of the now restless ranks. It was Amalric who addressed them.

'His Majesty has graciously allowed me to retain those of my Winchester men who I select. Those of you who are seeking to return to Wessex, please step forward and form a line in front of me, but without your women on this occasion.'

Will gave Joan an apprehensive kiss and joined the line. As Amalric and the man alongside him got closer to him, the 'yes' and 'no' responses became more audible, and it seemed that a good number of worthy warriors were being rejected, either because they weren't deemed good enough for 'Wessex service', as Amalric was calling it, or because they were so good that they were being allocated to Harold's London Fyrd. Will was praying that he came into neither of these rejected categories when he found himself gazing into Amalric's quizzical eyes as he lowered his voice to speak to him.

'Wilfrid Riveracre, do you wish to return to Wessex?'

'With all my heart, sir.'

'And are you still welcomed by your family?'

'Yes indeed, sir.'

'And can you perhaps speak kindly to a neighbouring widow lady who might be prepared to let me experience the hospitality of her hearth when we have occasion to journey to Sandlake?'

'With all my heart, sir.'

'Then, Wilfrid Riveracre, it would seem that you have just been appointed to command my small company of mounted housecarls, with specific duties patrolling the coastal marshes.'

'Thank you very much, sir — I won't prove unworthy.'

'If you do, you will hang. My congratulations on your choice of woman, by the way.'

'Thank you, sir.'

'You were very fortunate to be so highly regarded by Amalric Goodbarrow, else I would have selected you myself for my London command,' came the familiar voice of the man who had been at Amalric's side as he selected his contingent. Will had not even looked at him. 'Anyone who can lay my brother out cold must have a strong arm.'

Will's mouth opened in surprise as he recognised Selwyn Astenmede. Then his face arranged itself into a self-conscious grin as he replied, 'We were both fortunate that I did not kill him, as I thought I had. It was that thought that caused me to run from the village, and I finished up a man-at-arms under the Wessex banner, as you heard.'

'Wait for me by the stable entrance when this brief parade is over,' Selwyn replied as he hurried to catch up with Amalric.

Ten minutes later, Will emerged from the stables to find Selwyn loitering outside, looking guilty.

'I cannot remain here for long,' Selwyn told him, 'since the king expects me to assemble the London Fyrd for him to address them. He is not a man to waste time in idleness, as you have no doubt already concluded. I merely wished to enquire after Elva's welfare, since I have not been home for several months now.'

'Do you and she have an understanding?' Will asked. 'But if so, how are the thegn and his lady likely to react?'

Selwyn's face clouded slightly. 'They do not yet know, but I am hoping that when they learn of the trusted position that I now occupy under the king himself they will allow me to choose where my heart directs.'

'How did you come to be so exalted anyway?' Will demanded.

'In truth, when I first presented myself at Winchester and asked to join Earl Harold's army, I expected to have to serve my time in the ranks. But when he learned who my parents were, he was sufficiently impressed to offer me a place among his housecarls, and arranged for me to receive instruction in riding a horse. It is not my favourite duty, since my behind does not take kindly to all the swaying, and my thighs get sore with the need to grip hard on a horse's flanks. But I have since proved my skill with a sword, and it is with a sword that I now command an entire wing of the fyrd, or at least the London portion of it.'

'Regarding your parents,' Will continued with a frown, 'were you aware that Harold, while still an earl, gave orders for your mother to be seized on suspicion of giving sanctuary to a runaway priest?'

'Truly?'

'Yes, truly. I can vouch for this, since I was one of those sent to carry out this duty, but I did my best to persuade Amalric, who was in command of us, to hold his hand. Then we received a counter-order to ride immediately to London when King Edward lay dying, so the order was never carried out.'

'I am grateful for that,' Selwyn replied as he placed a friendly hand on Will's shoulder, 'and I shall ensure that my mother is made well aware of the service you did her. But I fear that it will be many more months yet before I can return to Astenmede, and I would beg another favour from you — namely that you speak kindly of me to your sister, and tell her that my affections have not wandered during our separation. She still occupies a very special place in my heart, and I live for the day when we can be reunited.'

'If I can remember all that, I will of course pass it on. Do you have any message for your mother and father?'

'Tell Mother that I am still engaged in the matter that she entrusted me with, and tell Father that I shall bring further honour to the Astenmede name.'

'I shall do all of that,' Will confirmed, 'but we have not yet been told when we shall journey back west. Amalric is with the king now, receiving his instructions.'

'And I must join them as commanded,' Selwyn replied as he shook Will's hand in farewell. 'This is the meeting after which I must assemble my men to be addressed by King Harold. I am a little surprised that I was not summoned to Amalric's meeting with the king, since presumably they are arranging the division of responsibilities between the two sections of the fyrd.'

There was a very good reason why Selwyn had not been invited to attend the tersely conducted meeting between Harold and Amalric. The same reason that had prompted Harold to appoint Selwyn to a position in the fyrd well above that for which he was qualified by experience. Harold wished to keep Selwyn where he could see him, and to buy his loyalty while ensuring that no threat to his newly acquired crown could come from the meddlesome thegn's wife in Astenmede.

It was this second part of his scheme that he was disclosing to Amalric in the throne room.

'You did not bring me that woman from Astenmede, as I instructed,' he said accusingly as he twirled the wine around in its goblet.

'There was no time, Majesty, since we received your urgent summons to London before we were able to enter her demesne. I deemed it more important to be here in a show of strength when the Witan met. But it would seem from what I learned that the priest you mentioned is now dead.'

'Nevertheless, she remains free,' Harold scowled, 'and while she remains free, there is a risk to the kingdom.'

'What risk, Majesty?'

'That is for me to know, and for others to speculate upon,' Harold replied curtly. 'One day I may reveal to you what it is that this dead priest knew, but before that I must discover whether this woman knew it for herself, and if there is any danger of her passing it on to others.'

'You wish her to be taken up?'

'Make it your first task, Amalric. Do not even take the time to allocate your patrols in person, since time is precious. See to your men's return to Winchester, then take a small party and bring the lady into secure custody. But she is not to know the nature of her detention; rather, you will carry an invitation from me to attend the Court here in London as an honoured guest, given her position as the highly respected mother of a commander in the London Fyrd. See that she is securely attended at all times, and perhaps allocate a lady or two to her personal service, as if she were the Queen herself. Then escort her back here with all due pomp and reverence, and leave her fate to me.'

'It shall be as you wish, Majesty. But what of the patrols?'

'You have men who can organise those, surely? Leave it to them, but I must be reassured that the marsh approaches on the south coast are being constantly watched for invading forces.'

'Who do you fear will invade?'

'I do not *fear* anyone, you fool! But I believe that William the Bastard will bring an army from Normandy to enforce his claim to the throne. We must be ready to repel him when that day comes. Now leave me, and ensure that the London force is assembled outside.'

VI

The villagers of Sandlake were praying for the return of Earl Harold and his army. Unaware that the earl had now become the king, they were nervously questioning why he and his Wessex Fyrd had deserted them and journeyed to London, leaving them at the mercy of the foreign force that was rumoured to be getting closer by the day.

It was therefore with rousing cheers that those on the eastern boundaries of Wessex greeted the mighty force of men, horses and wagons wending its way through the Weald on its journey west. They lost no time in apprising Amalric and his men of what had been happening further south along the coast. The latest gossip was that foreigners had been seen during a brutal raid on Sandwich. Amalric sent fast riders back to London, to advise King Harold that his London Fyrd was required to journey south and send the raiders packing, then he continued west towards Winchester.

When they reached Heathfield and looked out over the downs, with the distant sea glinting in the morning sun, Will and Joan were given permission to leave the line and travel south to Sandlake. They had spent three tedious days in a long line of horses, wagons, and men-at-arms marching three abreast. Joan had been travelling in one of the wagons containing the former royal servants who had become soldier brides, along with her particular friend Quenna, who had been joined in marriage to Will's colleague Betlic.

Now Joan climbed down gratefully, took Will's offered hand and, with his assistance, jumped up on his horse. As Will was in the process of turning the horse's head to direct him down the drover track towards Penhurst and home, Amalric sidled up to them on his own horse.

'Once I have settled the men in Winchester, I shall come looking for you in Sandlake. Our work there is not completed, and we must also allocate the coastal patrols. Remember me kindly to your widowed neighbour.'

The couple had barely dismounted outside Will's parents' hut when Rowena came rushing out with a joyful cry and wrapped her arms around Will. Then she looked over his shoulder at the beautiful young woman who stood sheepishly holding the horse by its halter.

'Mother,' Will said as he regained his breath, 'you must welcome your new daughter — and my wife before God — into the family. Her name is Joan, and we believe that she may already be with child.'

His father and sister had wandered outside, attracted by the noise. Elva walked straight up to Joan, embraced her and welcomed her to Sandlake. Eldred stood uncertainly in the doorway, until firmly instructed by his wife to unstopper the mead jug and stoke up the fire for an early supper. As he disappeared back into the hut, Rowena asked of Will, 'How long are you here for this time?'

'I don't know, but the good tidings are that I have been attached to the Winchester Fyrd, so I will be closer to home than I was in London. And closer to Joan, of course, when she gives birth.'

'What of your big companion?' came an enquiring voice from the threshold next door.

Will burst out laughing as he spotted Gwenyth. 'He sends his best regards, and is as eager to renew your acquaintance as you obviously are, Gwenyth.'

'And the girl is your wife, you say?'

'That's right. We were married in London.'

'Annis will no doubt be jealous,' Gwenyth smirked, 'but that's her own fault.'

'Who's Annis?' Joan asked suspiciously.

Will leaned down to kiss her on the lips. 'You needn't worry about her. There was a time that I thought I loved her, but that was before I laid eyes on you.'

'Come in,' Rowena said, 'before the sun begins to sink. It still gets cold on these spring afternoons, and you must think of the child that may be in your belly.'

'Have you seen Selwyn on your travels?' asked Elva.

'He's still in London, and likely to remain so for a good while,' Will told her. 'Harold is now King of England, and Selwyn has been given an important position in the fyrd that guards London.' He then conveyed Selwyn's message, and Elva blushed.

'We need to get around to building you your own hut, now that you have a wife,' Eldred told Will as they stood gazing across the track at the early morning mist rising off Powdermill Stream.

'I suppose so,' Will conceded, 'but won't we need the thegn's permission, and who has the skill to build new huts these days? Where will we get the materials?'

'It's your job to get the thegn's permission to build,' said Eldred, 'and while you're at it, you'll need his permission to take the main timbers from Caldbec Wood.'

'It just so happens,' Will replied, 'that I have to visit the thegn's wife with some good news.'

'You mean the old bastard of her husband's dead?' Eldred grinned, just as they sensed movement behind them. They turned in time to see Amalric emerging from Gwenyth's doorway, fastening the straps on his chainmail and grinning at the pair of them.

'Mighty hospitable, you Sandlake people,' he said. Then he looked directly at Will. 'I heard you mention the thegn's wife just then. We must waste no time in delivering the king's invitation.'

'She's invited to Court?' Eldred asked in disbelief.

'In a manner of speaking,' Amalric replied, winking at Will. 'But King Harold requires that she have a lady or two to accompany her, and I seem to recall that your new wife is one of those who has served at Court in the past.'

'Only at the table,' Will reminded him, 'and we've only just arrived back here. We think she may be with child, and you can hardly expect her to climb into a wagon and travel back to London so soon, and in that condition.'

'Needs must, as the saying goes,' Amalric replied dismissively, 'and it's not as if she's required to attend upon the Queen herself. I'm sure a mere thegn's wife would be prepared to accept *any* suggestion that she has a lady attend upon her. For the time being, we must at least deliver the king's invitation, since she will no doubt need to make certain arrangements before departing. That will give you time to explain your wife's new duties to her.'

Will shook his head doubtfully, but untied his horse from the hut post and joined Amalric on the track out of the village, up the hill, and down its other side into Astenmede. The handful of thralls who were already labouring in the home field looked up in idle curiosity as two armed men rode up the track to the manor house. It was not long before the information was passed down to them from the house thralls that the men came from the king himself, and that one of them was the commander of the Wessex Fyrd, while the other was Eldred Riveracre's lad from Sandlake.

'I'm advised that you come from King Harold,' Earlene said haughtily as she swept into the Great Hall after being advised of their arrival by her steward. 'I trust that his Majesty is well? And is there news of my son Selwyn, who left here in his service when he was merely the Earl of Wessex?'

'I can advise you of that,' Will replied. 'I had occasion to meet with him in London before we came back here only a few days ago. He is well, and has been afforded a place of honour at the head of the king's foot soldiers, given his prowess with a sword.'

'It is to be hoped that the rumours of imminent invasion are exaggerated if he is to remain alive. I trust that you will cast a protective eye over him?' Earlene asked of Amalric as she turned to address him.

Amalric replied with a gracious smile, 'I can do better than that, my lady. The king is so impressed with your son that he would like to meet his mother. You are invited to court, where of course you can be reunited with your brave boy.'

'The king wishes me at court?' Earlene preened. 'This is indeed an honour. When do we leave?'

'Whenever you can make arrangements for travel, my lady,' Amalric told her. 'Perhaps two days' hence, when we may return with horses, a wagon for your most treasured possessions, perhaps a few more men-at-arms for an escort, and a young lady who is anxious to gain experience as a lady's maid at Court.'

'Excellent! I shall be ready at daybreak in two days' time. And perhaps you would care to sample our hospitality before you depart today?'

'Thank you, but no,' Amalric replied hastily, before Will could say anything to break the spell. 'In two days, then.' He bowed slightly and left the hall with a gesture for Will to follow him.

'That was too easy by half,' Amalric said once they were safely back on the track down to Sandlake. 'The proud woman has no idea that she is walking into a trap, and I'll thank you not to advise her otherwise.'

'What does the king intend to do with her?' Will asked, shamefully aware of what he had just been a party to.

'No idea, and none of our business,' Amalric replied. 'Just make sure that your wife is ready to travel the day after tomorrow, along with the Lady Earlene.'

'Won't the thegn raise some objection?' Will asked.

Amalric snorted. 'I would hazard a guess that his opinion will count for nought, now that she has the prospect of advancement at Court in her head. She did not strike me as the sort of woman with whom it is advisable to argue. '

Will soon discovered that he had married another such woman when he tried to explain to Joan what was being asked of her.

'We only just left there!' she protested. 'You promised me a quiet life in a comfortable hut in the countryside, where we could raise children and tend crops.'

'It will not be forever, my sweet,' Will replied, 'and you may be well rewarded, not only by the king, but also by the lady herself when she has risen in Courtly estimation and wealth.'

Joan tutted, then looked down at her gown. 'I can hardly travel to London as the maid to a fine lady without better garments than this. Would Elva loan me one of her gowns, do you think?'

'Most certainly, and then when we are in London you can obtain much finer ones. You will need larger gowns anyway, once your belly begins to swell.'

'That's another thing,' Joan reminded him. 'I'm in no condition to be travelling.'

'But once in London, there will be physicians at Court who can take care of your laying-in and delivery,' Will argued. 'Think of it in that way.'

Joan pouted. 'I will agree to what you ask of me, only because I do not wish to be parted from you again so soon. But once you return from London, so do I, is that agreed?'

'Of course, my sweet, since I would not wish to be separated from you either.'

On the return journey to London, there was only a small retinue of armed men, which included Betlic, a horseman under Will's command. He had been instructed to join the progress principally in order that his new wife, Joan's friend Quenna, could join Joan and Earlene in the wagon. Joan was much happier having her friend as a second lady-in-waiting to Earlene, who felt even more important for having two attendants, as befitted the half-sister of the former King — although she was not certain whether King Harold was yet aware of that relationship.

Only when they stopped overnight was Joan able to rejoin Will. He was riding alongside Amalric during the day, at the head of the silent group that heaved a grateful sigh when they first caught sight of the distant towers of West Minster from Richmond Hill. The night before they were to make their final entrance down the north bank of the river to the palace, Joan snuggled into Will's side on the straw pallet made available to them in the *hospitium* of their latest holy house of convenience.

'I may have been wrong in my belief that I was carrying a child,' she whispered, 'since today I saw my monthly flow of blood, which is why we cannot behave like husband and wife tonight. I'm sorry.'

'You do not need to apologise,' Will reassured her. 'There will be other opportunities, I have no doubt.'

'But will we be accommodated together once we are back inside the palace?' she asked. 'After all, my lady will require me to be in attendance on her, and you will probably be allocated to a barrack house where you can supervise your men.'

'Can you and Quenna not share your duties, so that one night you may lie with me, and the next she may lie with Betlic?'

Joan frowned. 'This I doubt, since the Lady Earlene seems to prefer me as her companion. She looks down her nose somewhat at poor Quenna, because of her shabby dress.'

'We can soon get her new dresses. As for my duties, Amalric has not confided in me yet what these may be. Perhaps I shall be drafted into the London Fyrd, to join Selwyn.'

'He's a swordsman, is he not?' Joan countered. 'You, on the other hand, are a horseman, and will surely be under a different command?'

'Who knows? Selwyn's duties may well change anyway, once his mother is at Court.'

If the mother in question was expecting to be welcomed into the inner keep of the palace by a fanfare of trumpets, with her son at the head of a noble array of men-at-arms, she would have been very disappointed. As they halted in front of the stables, it was rapidly learned that no-one had been told to expect them, and that King Harold had been meeting with the leaders of his London Fyrd since daybreak.

As a result, neither the king nor Selwyn were there to greet Earlene. It was only after Amalric had all but threatened a lowly usher with instant death that the steward was sent for. He was able to confirm that accommodation had been set aside for Lady Earlene on the second level of the River Tower, which she would be expected to occupy along with her ladies. As for the men-at-arms who had accompanied her, the steward shrugged and invited them to present themselves to the Commander of the London Fyrd.

'Leave him to me,' Amalric spat. Betlic supervised the unloading of the wagon and the transfer of Lady Earlene's possessions into the long and draughty hall allocated to her and her ladies, through which the most unhealthy of odours wafted from the river below the tower. Earlene demanded that tapestries be brought in to block off the nauseating smells, and that a fire be lit at once in the hearth. The steward told her frostily that it was not part of his duties to serve those in the River Tower, but he would leave word with an under-steward for Earlene's requests to be met. He then bowed out with the minimum of formality, and Joan looked helplessly at Will as Earlene gave vent to her displeasure.

'I feel sure that I would not be treated in this shabby manner were the king to learn of my arrival,' she sniffed, 'or for that matter my son.'

'I will advise Selwyn, my lady,' Will volunteered. 'If you would excuse me for the moment?'

He walked outside, glad to be free of the smell of the poorly appointed chamber, and apprehensive that if their living conditions did not improve, not only would Joan complain on her own behalf, but would also take him to task for the ill-humour of her mistress. He was of course aware that Earlene was about to become a prisoner in all but name, and that she would be fortunate indeed if her accommodation remained as luxurious, but this was hardly the time to make mention of that. Instead, he strode over to the main barrack house and enquired after Selwyn.

'Back so soon?' Selwyn asked breezily as he emerged from the armoury, waving and twisting a sword to test it for weight and flexibility.

Will frowned. 'We came only as an escort for your mother, who is accommodated in the River Tower. Were you not advised that she was expected?'

'By no means. But who expects her?'

'The king, no less. I thought he would have advised you of that.'

'I have been with him for most of the day, receiving orders to move my men north, since we expect an invasion from Norway shortly. This is hardly a good time for me to be entertaining my mother.'

'Do you wish me to take you over there to meet her?' Will offered.

Selwyn shook his head. 'You are not my servant. I will go and find her for myself, and in the meantime you had best see to your own lodgings, before we receive the men promised in order to swell our numbers ahead of riding north.'

Selwyn found his mother in an ill humour. No fire had yet been lit, and there was no sign of the tapestries she had ordered. But she put a smile on her face as she embraced Selwyn, then dismissed Joan and Quenna with an imperious wave of her hand.

'What have you learned of the king's plans to defend his new crown?' she asked him once they were alone.

'Only that we expect the Norsemen to come from the north, and we are to join forces with Mercia and Northumbria in order to repel them. He also seems most anxious regarding the intentions of Duke William across the Channel.'

'This is good,' Earlene told him. 'If Harold can be distracted on two battle fronts at once, it will make the prospect of a successful invasion all the greater. I believe that your brother will be in the Norwegian force, and will be well rewarded for his service. If it is William who succeeds, then he will be likely to look generously on his cousin.'

'Is there a royal house to which you are *not* related?' Selwyn frowned. 'And why do you play this dangerous game?'

Earlene snorted. 'If your fat oaf of a father could have got up off his behind occasionally, we would be much more highly placed in the governance of this land. If he cannot advance our fortunes, then I must. As you can see, I have already been sufficiently regarded by Harold that he invites me to Court, and whichever of the invaders is successful, they will make swift efforts to thank one of those who made it possible.'

'I don't suppose it occurred to you that one or both of your sons could be killed should any invasion come to pass?'

'You are both brave fighters and will be held to the rear of the company, defending your King. It is never the commanders who die in the field — that is what foot soldiers are for.'

'Regarding the reason why the king invited you to Court, do you not think that it may be in order to have you securely guarded, where he may prevent you from communicating with a foreign power?'

'Rubbish! He knows nothing of my connections with royal houses. Or does he?'

Selwyn bit his lip and braced himself for a storm of verbal abuse when he confessed. 'He may, and regrettably I may have been the cause. When you sent me to seek service with Earl Harold — who is of course now King Harold — I had some difficulty in persuading him to take me into his armed force, until I mentioned the accident of your birth that left you related both to the late King Edward and the House of Norway. It is of course now Harald of Norway that Harold of England is preparing to repel.'

'You fool!' Earlene snapped as she flung herself down on a somewhat moth-eaten couch. 'I hope you did not also tell him that your brother was in the service of Hardrada?'

'I am not *that* stupid, Mother. But since Harold knows you to be related to Hardrada, may he not have summoned you here to keep you as his prisoner, and as a potential bargaining piece should the Norsemen succeed?'

'If so, then my life will not be worth living.' Earlene shuddered. 'I must make an early excuse to leave this place — which is disgusting for a woman of my sensitivities anyway. Even my ladies turn their noses up at it.'

'Has the king not yet summoned you for an audience?' Selwyn asked. Earlene shook her head sadly, and Selwyn undertook to advise Harold that his mother was installed in the River Tower, but anxious to return home in order to see to the summer crops.

Earlene was obliged to wait another two days before she was summoned into the king's presence, by which time it had become obvious that neither she nor her two ladies were to be over-indulged in the matter of food and drink. There was meat, fruit and cheese, admittedly, but the meat was always cold, and bore every sign that someone higher up the social ladder had hacked at it before it had been passed down to those in the tower accommodation. The cheese was all but mouldy, the fruit was past its best, and there was no wine — only mead of middling quality, but at least it came in useful to force down the meat.

Earlene was therefore hardly the grateful royal guest when she was finally shown into the Great Hall in the main palace, to which she had been escorted by two men-at-arms, as if she were already a prisoner. But she swallowed her pride as she knelt dutifully before the throne dais and congratulated Harold on his elevation.

'I bring the good wishes of those people of Wessex who had occasion to benefit from your generosity and security while you were our Earl,' she murmured through gritted teeth.

'And the priest?' Harold challenged her as he swirled the wine in its goblet. 'Does *he* send his wishes for my good fortune?'

'The priest?' Earlene echoed, puzzled.

Harold's face hardened. 'Let us not waste each other's time, my lady. Some months ago, you were visited by a French priest who brought you a message from Duke William, did he not? This would have been shortly before you had him done to death.'

'I know nothing of what you speak,' Earlene replied.

Harold sighed. 'It would seem that your memory plays you false, Lady Earlene. It must be the result of such a tiring journey all the way from — what is it called again, "Astenmede"?'

'That is the name of my manor, Your Majesty, but I have fully recovered from the journey.'

'It would seem not, since you cannot remember events that occurred only recently in your humdrum life. You must rest for a few more days, then we will talk again.'

'I was rather hoping that after this audience I might return to my estates, Your Majesty, since the summer planting will soon be in full progress.'

'You may return to your estates when your memory improves. For the moment, you are dismissed.' Harold looked up to address the two men-at-arms who had escorted Earlene. 'Take her back to her chamber.'

Harold lost no time in summoning Amalric. 'I wish you to guard the room in which Earlene of Astenmede is confined. Ensure that the door is held by two of your most trusted men at all times. She is to be allowed out only for her natural needs. The same goes for any ladies who attend her. She is to receive no visitors, and especially not her son, who is in my service. I intend to send him north shortly anyway. Are we understood?'

'Yes, Your Majesty.'

'Then you are to return to Wessex with the remainder of your men to secure the south coast against any invasion. I will join you with my fleet on the Isle of Wight within the month. Now leave me and see to all this without delay.'

Amalric found Will in the stables, supervising the stable boy who was grooming his horse. Will was led outside, where Amalric broke the news.

'We are ordered back home, to meet with the king on the south coast. You, presumably, wish to remain here with your wife?'

'Of course,' Will replied eagerly.

'And the other girl who attends Lady Earlene — she is the wife of another of your men, is she not?'

'Yes. His name is Betlic.'

'Very well. Take two more men from those who accompanied us to London, and organise a guard on the door of Lady Earlene's chamber, on the king's orders. She is to be allowed out to perform her normal ablutions in the pit to the side of the tower, but no further. The same, regrettably, is true for your wives, but they may join you in your accommodation every night. The guard must be for every hour of the day and night, and you might think that the best arrangement would be for you and another man to take one turn of duty, while Betlic and another take the relief guard.'

'What is to happen when her son Selwyn discovers that she is Harold's prisoner?'

'He is not to be allowed near her, on the king's orders. You are also ordered to kill him if he makes any attempt to release her.'

'But he is likely to be promised in marriage to my sister!' Will protested.

Amalric frowned. 'That is unfortunate, I will concede. But he will shortly be sent north, to join forces with the Earls of Northumbria and Mercia. Thanks to the meddling of your lady of the manor, it seems that we are at risk of invasion from two directions at once.'

VII

Selwyn was summoned to a meeting with King Harold on the afternoon following Earlene's unnerving conversation with him.

'You will take all but my personal housecarls and march north, to meet with the Earls Morcar of Northumbria and Edwin of Mercia at York, where they await with their forces for further instructions from me,' Harold told him. 'You are to convey those instructions, which are that they must prepare to repel Hardrada of Norway wherever he may attack. You will join forces with them, and rid me of this northern threat for all time coming.'

'I will do my best, Your Majesty.'

'See that you do. And always bear in mind that your mother is now in my safe custody. But that custody may prove less than safe if you fail me. Are we understood?'

'Yes, Your Majesty,' Selwyn replied, wishing that he had for once disobeyed his mother when she sent him on this foolhardy venture.

On the day he was due to leave, Selwyn arrived outside the hall in which Earlene and her ladies were being confined, intent on making a farewell visit. Will was on duty at the door, and he explained the new restrictions.

'I can advise you in confidence that he is fearful that you will seek to arrange your mother's escape,' he said.

'How can I do that, when she is so carefully guarded?' Selwyn countered hotly. 'I just want to say farewell to her before I leave on a journey that may result in my death. Would you deny me this last meeting?'

In the end, Will relented, but first he called Joan out from Earlene's chamber. 'You and Quenna must say nothing, if asked, about this man Selwyn visiting his mother,' he said. 'And if you hear a single word exchanged between them regarding any possible escape bid, you must lose no time in coming back out here and advising me.'

Joan's face fell. 'We really *are* all imprisoned, then? Lady Earlene was fearful of such, but I chose not to believe it.'

'The king has no argument with you,' Will assured her, 'but you must remain with the Lady Earlene as your duties require, and you must also be my eyes and ears regarding whatever she may say or do. Our very lives may depend upon it.'

'Very well,' Joan nodded sadly as she led Selwyn into the chamber, where he was greeted with joyful shouts by his mother.

'I cannot understand what the king wants of me,' Earlene told him in a low voice, almost on the point of tears. 'But whatever it is, he's made it clear that until I give him the information he believes I have, I am not free to leave this disgusting hovel.'

'Did he give you no indication at all?' Selwyn asked.

'He made mention of some French priest who is supposed to have brought me a secret message from Normandy. I haven't seen any holy man since my last confession, and my only connection with Normandy is through my mother, who died thirteen years ago.'

Selwyn suddenly remembered a previous conversation with Will. 'Will Riveracre advised me that he and Amalric had been sent to Astenmede to enquire about a French priest. Will had been trying to prevent your arrest when he and Amalric were summoned to London with Earl Harold at the time of the old King's death.'

Earlene cursed quietly, then looked back up at Selwyn. 'I was clearly tricked into coming here by those two, and I trust that you will exact a just revenge when you get the opportunity.'

Selwyn shook his head. 'They were acting on the king's orders, Mother. If it were not for Will's generosity, I would not be allowed to even visit you today. He no doubt risks a terrible punishment by treating the orders he received from Amalric so lightly.'

Earlene wept when she learned where Selwyn was heading. As she said her final farewell, she hugged him tightly and whispered, 'Take care not to kill your brother. He is with the Norsemen.'

Selwyn dismounted from his horse several miles ahead of his substantial force of foot soldiers, who were trudging wearily up the remains of the old Roman road. It ran all the way from London to York, and Harold's London Fyrd had endured every mile of it as they tramped through the first warm days of September, talking, singing, cursing, laughing, thinking about the homes they had left, arguing over arrears of pay, gambling, fighting, sleeping in hedgerows and praying for safe deliverance from what was to come.

Selwyn lost no time in having himself admitted to the rooms inside the old stone tower of the Earl of Northumbria's castle. Inside he found the brothers Edwin and Morcar arguing noisily. They only broke off when they became aware of Selwyn's presence, and the emblem on his chainmail that signified that he served directly under King Harold.

'Do you bring relief forces?' Edwin demanded.

'If so, not before time,' Morcar echoed.

Selwyn nodded. 'I have two thousand men on the road behind me, but as we passed over a mighty river two days past, there were many sails in sight to the east. It may be that the Norsemen of Harald Hardrada have found a safe harbour from which to launch an attack on the north.'

'We have the same news, from men posted to the south who rode back yesterday,' Morcar told him. 'It would seem that either they will turn south for London, or come north to attack York.'

'Surely, if they have it in mind to attack London, they would have sought a landing much further south?' Selwyn reasoned. He suspected that these two men might not be seasoned military leaders with experience of battle tactics.

'You may be right,' Edwin conceded, 'but my brother here would have us remain behind his fine walls and await the invaders' approach. I, on the other hand, would urge that we venture out to meet the Norsemen on the flat land between here and the Ouse. With your reinforcements we may now count upon some five thousand, and it cannot be the case that Harald has more than that. And they will be weary if they are forced to march across the bogs of South Yorkshire to meet us.'

'My men have just marched from London,' Selwyn told them. 'How weary do you imagine *they* are?'

'So you counsel that we defend York from behind its walls?' Morcar asked eagerly, while his brother snorted and resumed drinking. Selwyn was unsure what to advise, but this was clearly not the moment to make a final decision.

'My forces require at least two days' rest, then perhaps your lookouts can further advise on the deployment of Hardrada's invaders.'

The brothers agreed, and Selwyn was invited to partake of some food and drink while his quarters were being prepared.

Two days later, Selwyn was seated on the low wall outside the stables when he was joined by Edwin.

'You must ignore my brother Morcar,' Edwin said, 'since he lacks battle experience. Had he been obliged to fight off the Danes in my Midland counties all those years ago when I was working towards my true destiny, he would have learned that invaders must not be allowed to live off your own lands. They must be harassed before they have time to grow comfortable on foreign soil.'

'So your counsel is to attack?' Selwyn asked.

'Yes. There is much fear in this town, after what Harald and his men did to Scarborough. But there is much anger also, and a thirst for revenge that must be allowed its head before it dries. The Norsemen may be skilled in fighting mountain battles in their own country, and they may be brave enough when slaughtering monks in lonely monasteries or peasants in farming villages, but they may not be so bold when faced with an entire army of angry and hardened soldiers on a flat plain.'

'For the last few days of our march, after we had sight of Hardrada's sails, we passed nothing but river marshes and bog,' Selwyn said. 'It is your belief that the Norsemen will not be comfortable fighting in such conditions?'

'Indeed not,' Edwin confirmed, 'but I need you to join me in persuading my brother of this. These northern lands are his, after all, and he is consumed by the thought that he must defend his people.'

'Sometimes the best form of defence is attack,' Selwyn observed.

'Precisely,' Edwin replied. 'So come inside with me and advise my brother of that.'

Amalric took a deep breath before ducking under the flap of the royal tent and walking in to answer the summons. He had been warned that Harold was in one of his foul moods, and Amalric knew precisely why.

'Three hundred more gone at this morning's roll-call,' Harold muttered into his goblet. 'They can't all be pleading the harvest — some of them must be genuine cowards, and we should be publicly hanging a few to deter the others.'

Harold was reaping the consequences of his obsessive belief that an invasion was pending from across the Channel in Normandy. No-one but he was aware of why he was so convinced. Amalric had been among those who had sought to dissuade him from bringing his fleet, together with the remainder of his London Fyrd, down to the Isle of Wight, which commanded the coastal approaches to much of the south coast of England. Harold had also ordered the Wessex Fyrd to be held in readiness along the coastal settlements of Sussex and Kent. The received wisdom was that if William of Normandy set sail during the summer months, when the prevailing wind was south-westerly, then his force could be intercepted by Harold's warships before it even reached the sea marshes and fishing villages. Even if a few ships made it to shore, Harold believed, they could be headed off by the land-based forces of Wessex.

But such a strategy was expensive, particularly in manpower, as Harold had begun to learn when the harvest season bore down on them with no sign of any Norman invasion fleet. The men who had been summoned to the royal banner grew restless to return home. All but the permanent housecarls were only casual fighting men, bound by their land ties to don such armour as they had and to rescue their rusting weapons from their leaky outhouses, in order to perform their annual fyrd service.

In recent weeks, the desertions had been growing. However, Amalric could not persuade Harold to break camp and send his men home until there was a more immediate need for them.

'Would that you had captured that priest alive,' Harold snarled as he launched back into a favourite excuse, 'then we could have tortured him for what he knew of William's plans.'

'What guarantee have we that he came from William himself?' Amalric asked.

Harold spat on the ground. 'Do not challenge my judgment again, Amalric, or I will have you hanged! You may rest assured that the priest carried instructions from William.'

Amalric tried another line of approach. 'May we not stand some of the men down for just a few weeks, Your Majesty? Not all of them, just a few hundred at a time, under strict instruction to return either after a month, or when summoned more urgently? This way, we will know which men are gone, and there will be an orderly coming and going, rather than the informal shambles we are enduring at present.'

Harold was about to launch into an ill-tempered retort when there was a disturbance at the tent entrance. Selwyn, covered in dried blood and limping heavily on one leg, was half carried before the king, where he hung on the arms of two attendants before managing to gasp out his urgent message. 'We have lost to Harald Hardrada, Your Majesty. His men are running amok all over the north!'

Selwyn was lowered onto a stool and given a mug of strong mead. As the colour began to return to his cheeks, and his breath came back down to its normal rhythm, King Harold was anxious for more details.

'Earl Morcar unwisely chose a narrow position between a river and a bog,' Selwyn explained. 'Somewhere near a village called Fulford, almost a day's march south of York. This was against my urgent advice, since it was obvious that there could be no escape on either side from the field he had selected. Then he allowed the lines of spearmen to spread too thinly across it, and the Norse axemen cut through them in no time. Our men fled to the side, where many were either drowned or stuck in a bog in which they were hacked to pieces; it became so bad that the invaders were able to use English corpses as a bridge across the wettest parts. We left the field as best we could, and I have not stopped riding since. I took no time to divert to London, but cut across through the Weald once I reached Barnet, so there is as yet no knowledge of our defeat in West Minster.'

'The Earls Morcar and Edwin?'

'They were alive when I left the field, Your Majesty. But where they might be now, I have no idea.'

'You were limping earlier. Are you wounded?'

'No, thankfully not, Your Majesty. But the best part of a week on horseback did nothing for my behind, not to mention my knees.'

'You fared better than most, it would seem,' Harold commented, before turning to Amalric. 'Summon the rest of the Wessex Fyrd, and any others you can press into service, and join me in London as soon as you can. Selwyn, your home is on the south coast, is it not?'

'Correct, Your Majesty.'

'Then take some time to visit those of your family who remain there, then join us in London in order to guide us back to Hardrada and his savages. We shall rid the kingdom of him before we return here and prepare to resist William of

Normandy, who hopefully will not learn that we have lifted the defences against him until we are back here.'

'My mother, Your Majesty?'

'She remains our guest in West Minster. Very well, let's waste no time, since we may not have a great deal of it left.'

Two days later, Elva threw her arms around her returning soldier hero, and through her tears she told him how relieved she was to see him back in one piece. He explained that he could not tarry long, since the king required him back in London within a week.

'Does he have no regard for the happiness of his men and their womenfolk? Or even their welfare? Look at the state of you! You smell like Gwenyth's pigsty, by the way.'

'Sorry,' he mumbled, 'but I have worn these clothes for the best part of a month now. I must go back over the hill and see how my father fares without my mother.'

'We heard rumours that she was being held captive by King Harold.'

'Sadly, that is all too true,' Selwyn confirmed, 'and it seems to be connected in some way with an escaped French priest. She knows nothing about him, or so she claims, but King Harold seems convinced that she does. He is holding her secure in a tower room in West Minster, and your brother is in charge of her guarding.'

'At least he's not out there facing a horrible death, like you are,' Elva replied as the tears began to roll down her face. 'The next time you are back here, make it for long enough for us to be married.'

'We will need my father's permission,' Selwyn reminded her, 'which is another reason why I must not delay the trip up the hill. I may not be able to get back to you before I have to leave again for London, so give me one more kiss and reassure me that I still command your heart.'

Selwyn had to tear himself from Elva's desperate hold in order to return to his horse, which he had tied to the trunk of a maple tree. He turned round, the halter in his hand, and there stood Annis.

'Hello, returning man-at-arms. I overheard what you were telling Elva just now. Is it true that your mother will only be released if she can lead the king to a French priest who was here in Sandlake?'

'What can you tell me about him?' Selwyn asked anxiously.

'What is it worth to me if I tell you where he can be found?'

'He's still alive?'

'Yes, indeed he is, and I know *where*. For the right price, of course.'

'My father would reward you richly, were you able to supply the information that would get my mother released.'

'That's not what I meant,' Annis replied. 'In return for what I know, you must renounce whatever understanding you have with Elva, and agree to marry me.'

Selwyn stared at her in amazement. Before he could think of something appropriate to say, Annis pressed home her advantage.

'Don't try to think of something different to offer me, Selwyn. Your hand in marriage in return for your mother's release.'

'But you have no reason to want me, surely?' Selwyn asked.

Annis looked away. 'I am alone and I need the protection of a man.'

'What you ask of me is impossible,' Selwyn told her with mounting anger. 'I love Elva with all my heart, and she is a true woman who can bring me a great deal of happiness. Good evening, Annis.'

He swung back on his horse and rode hard up the hill, begging his mother's forgiveness in his heart.

Joan lowered her gown before slipping out from behind the canvas surround, breathing freely again once she was clear of the nauseating smell of other peoples' waste. She was halfway back towards the tower entrance when she heard her name being called. She whipped round in surprise, but could see no-one, so she continued walking.

'Over here — behind the barrels!'

Joan stopped and stared intently over the top of the empty mead barrels that someone had stacked near the door of the grain store. She could just make out the top of a head covered in greasy reddish-brown hair, and brown eyes that looked at her imploringly as their owner spoke again.

'Don't say a word — just come over here.'

Her curiosity aroused, she walked to the rear of the barrel store, and her eyebrows shot up in amazement. 'Elva — what on earth are you doing here?'

'No time for that — just promise me that you won't tell Selwyn that I'm here.'

'The Lady Earlene's son? I haven't seen him since he left to ride north. And why should I not tell him that his woman's here?'

'I don't want him to know that I know what I have to tell you, because then he'll know that I overheard a conversation I shouldn't have done.'

'You're not making any sense, Elva,' Joan replied with concern. 'Has something overtaken your wits?'

'I need to speak to Will, urgently. Is there some way you can get him out here to meet with me?'

'He's guarding Lady Earlene, but there are two of them charged with that duty, so I suppose I could. But *why*?'

'No time to explain. Just get him out here — please!'

A few minutes later Will had joined his sister behind the barrels. He stared at her clothing and her hair in muddy disarray, and took in the faint animal smell that came from her as they embraced.

'What is it?' he asked anxiously. 'Has something happened to Mother or Father?'

'No, they're fine. At least, they're probably frantic with worry, wondering where their only daughter's been for the past few days.'

'So where *have* you been?'

'On the road here, you fool, where do you think? I came part of the way on Kenric Carter's wagon. That got me as far as Eashing, then I walked the rest. That's why I'm in this state.'

'You *walked*?' Will repeated, horror-stricken. 'You could have been set upon, ravished, murdered — *anything*!'

'Well, clearly I wasn't, and if you'd shut up for long enough, I have something to tell you. You don't have to answer yes or no, but I believe that the Lady Earlene's being held captive by the king because he thinks she knows something about a French priest.'

'How did you learn about that?'

'I overheard a conversation between two people in the village. And one of them knows where the priest can be found.'

'Still alive?'

'So she said.'

'*She*? You mean Gwenyth Longbarrow?'

'No, but she was probably the one who told Annis.'

'So Annis knows?'

'Yes. If you can get her to tell you, then Lady Earlene will be freed, and we'll all be richly rewarded, no doubt.'

Will's eyes narrowed suspiciously. 'You're not the sort to do things for reward.'

'Perhaps the reward of the man I love? If I can be the cause of Lady Earlene being released, surely she'll be grateful enough to let Selwyn marry me?'

'*Now* I understand why you walked all the way from Sandlake. And why you didn't want Selwyn to know you were here. He's still up north, anyway.'

'No, he's not. He's back in Sandlake. There was a big battle somewhere up north, and we were defeated by some Norwegian army.'

'Harald Hardrada?'

'How should I know? I only know what Selwyn told me, and he's on his way back here to gather another army and have another go. I just hope he doesn't get himself killed. So, are you going to find out what you need to know from Annis?'

'I'll need to speak with Amalric, since he and I were sent to find this priest some time ago. I'm sure he wouldn't thank me for earning all the glory.'

'Just make sure that Lady Earlene finds out where it first came from.'

'Of course,' Will replied with a light laugh. 'And now let's go inside, and you can have a much-needed wash and get your blue gown back from Joan.'

Earlene looked askance at the bedraggled creature that Will led into her presence, until Will announced that Elva had bravely walked all the way from Wessex with information that would secure Earlene's release. After that, Elva was treated like visiting royalty. She impressed Earlene so greatly with her gracious manners and deferential behaviour that when Will announced that he had to escort his sister back home to effect the next stage in the plan, Earlene threw her arms around her and begged her to visit the manor house when they were all back home. After searching his conscience, Will agreed that Joan should remain with Earlene until he returned.

Elva was still glowing with anticipation as Will flicked the reins for the horse to begin pulling the wagon on the long journey back to Sandlake. Fortunately, the weather was still fine as September drew to a close, and they made the distance in four days.

Rowena screamed with joy when she saw Elva. She hugged her tightly and gave loud thanks to God for returning her unharmed. It was Eldred who asked the obvious questions, such as, 'Where in blazes have you been all this time?'

Will did his best to explain that he would only be home for long enough to find Amalric and arrange for Annis to be seized and questioned, but his mother raised another point.

'Surely it's Gwenyth Longbarrow you should be questioning? She's the one who told Annis whatever she knows.'

Will gave her a penetrating look, but it was his father who spotted the difficulty.

'I don't think that Amalric will be all that anxious to admit that he's been lying with a woman who holds an important secret that's being kept from the king. It was Amalric, after all, who was tasked with finding the link to the missing priest here in Sandlake, and all the time the answer was under his nose.'

'Does anyone know where I'll find Amalric?' Will asked.

His mother snorted. 'Stand outside Gwenyth's hut most evenings. He's supposed to be raising the fyrd to defend us against the Normans, but he's back here most nights.'

VIII

'What the hell possessed you to leave your post?' Amalric demanded as he stormed out of Gwenyth's hut two mornings later. He strode over to where Will was waiting on the riverbank. 'I hope for your sake that Lady Earlene is still securely guarded.'

'Of course, but she may not be there much longer, and you will gain much favour with King Harold.'

'Short of putting Hardrada *and* Duke William to death with the same sword blow, it's difficult to see how I could achieve that,' Amalric grumbled. 'I seem to be his first choice of someone to blame these days.'

'Well, how would it be if you were able to deliver this French priest into his hands?'

'I thought he was dead? Have you heard different?'

'It just so happens that I've found someone we can press hard for something she knows,' said Will. 'Annis — the girl who was trying to hoe weeds from her strip on a frosty day. However, you must prepare yourself for an unpleasant surprise.'

'Meaning?'

'Meaning that it was not Annis who smuggled the priest into hiding. That was someone else in the village — someone well known to you.'

Amalric's jaw dropped as he took in the implications. 'Sweet Christ, the king will have my head if he finds out!'

'*If* he finds out,' Will reminded him. 'I certainly won't be telling him, and I doubt if the lady herself is that stupid. We simply have to pretend that the information came from Annis herself, and that she was the one who took the priest to a safe place. Once we get her to tell us where he is, King Harold will be so overjoyed to have the priest in his clutches that he won't ask any questions. We need to think of a suitable way to get Annis up to Caldbec Wood, where you can have men waiting for her.'

The next morning, Gwenyth walked over to where Annis was staring accusingly at her weed patch.

'You may not have to work that patch alone for much longer,' she announced.

'How's that?' Annis replied.

'You'll probably have thralls working it. In fact, you probably won't need to work a strip at all, since you'll be living in the manor house, no doubt.'

'Have you been at the mead jug this early in the day, Gwenyth?'

'I've been told that Cerdic's back, and he wants to meet with you.'

'Cerdic's away on a mission for his mother.'

'That's what people were told. But in fact it was a mission for the king, and that's why his mother's in London. The story about her being in prison was just a ruse. They're both about to be given great honour and reward. I got the impression that whatever the king is about to award to Cerdic, he wants to share with you. As his wife perhaps.'

'Where and when does he want us to meet?'

'Right now. In Caldbec Wood. He's in hiding up there, not wanting his father to know that he's home. I can take you up there.'

Annis threw down the hoe and wiped her hands on the smock she was wearing over her gown. Then she slipped off the smock and threw it onto the strip. 'Come on, then — let's lose no time.'

As the two women reached the darkest section of the wood, a heavily armed Amalric stepped out ahead of them, with Will at his side. Annis gave a squeal and turned round. Four huge men-at-arms stepped from the undergrowth behind her, and she was trapped.

The soldiers were on the march again. For Selwyn, it was an unpleasant reminder of his exhausting dash south only days previously, conveying the bad news of the English defeat at Fulford. But this time he was not thundering at break-neck speed both day and night, and he was riding to the left of King Harold.

Having left Amalric to gather the remainder of his Wessex Fyrd to guard the southern coast against possible Norman invasion, Harold had ordered every available man from the London Fyrd, and anyone else they could gather in the process of heading north, to rally behind his banner and expel Harold Hardrada's invaders. He rode his horse at a moderate pace up the old North Road. Scouts were then sent forward, both to warn of any southern approach by the forces of Norway and in the hope of coming across men from the previous battle, who might be persuaded to turn back north and engage the enemy again. Selwyn had been one of those sent forward, and on the fifth day of their forced march he found his path blocked by a surly group of bedraggled men-at-arms.

'You are still alive, then,' came a familiar voice. 'Do you come with reinforcements sent by Harold?'

'I come with Harold himself,' Selwyn announced as he shook Edwin warmly by the hand. 'We are some three thousand strong, by my reckoning, and they are but two days behind me. But what of your brother?'

'He is alive, and rallying what is left of his army at Tadcaster, a day's march west of York.'

'Not in York itself?' Selwyn queried.

Edwin sighed heavily. 'Hardrada's forces sacked York after defeating us at Fulford. It had formally surrendered when news came of our defeat, but that didn't stop the Norsemen raping, killing and plundering at will until Hardrada himself arrived. Then he took over a hundred children of the town as hostages and marched east. His camp has been seen by the river at Stamford, and it is believed that he is seeking to bring his fleet up the Ouse from where it first made landfall at Riccall.'

'Is this river Ouse navigable at Stamford?'

'No, it's a different river altogether, or so I'm told. But it can be reached by way of the Ouse. If we re-take York, we can prevent Hardrada's fleet getting to Stamford, it seems.'

'Surely, Hardrada would have been better advised to remain in York?'

'Clearly he does not care for sieges. And of course his army needs access to the open countryside in order to forage for food.'

'So your counsel is that we advance to York, and re-take it?'

'Indeed. Then I have no doubt that my brother will re-join us. I have several hundred men left at my command, and he has much the same. So we can harass Hardrada again with some four thousand men in all, at least a thousand of whom are thirsting for revenge.'

'Where are the rest of your men?' Selwyn asked.

'All around you, my friend. Every hedgerow, every copse of trees, every old farm building. Had you offered violence to me, you would have seen them soon enough. But they prefer to remain hidden, and some of them have hardly spoken since Fulford. They need to see King Harold for themselves, in order to lift their spirits.'

'Leave that to me.'

'We shall expect you at nightfall, and will show you where best to camp for the night. Then we may all travel together to rejoin my brother in Tadcaster.'

Selwyn lost no time in riding back and advising Harold that he had made contact with Edwin, that his forces and those of Morcar were to be found further north, and that their best tactic might be to occupy York, then sally out from there to attack Hardrada's forces before they had time to take ship, or access any supplies or reinforcements.

Three days later, Selwyn was standing on the eastern wall after they had marched back into York, reflecting on how unrealistic his mother's request had been that he keep her advised of King Harold's movements for the benefit of Harald Hardrada. The Norse King had invaded regardless of what information Selwyn might have been able to supply, and somewhere in that army of occupation was his own brother Cerdic, also sent by their mother to risk his neck in battle. A mother who was now a prisoner.

Back in York, there was a great council of war between King Harold and his two powerful Earls, who between them were confident of marching almost four thousand men east to attack the Norse invaders and scatter them all over the land between there and the coast. Selwyn was not present at that, but he was summoned by Harold a few minutes after it had ended, and told that he would be in the select group of housecarls to ride out of York with their king in the centre, intent on parleying with Hardrada and perhaps persuading him to leave England without the inevitable loss of men on both sides.

As the sun rose to its full height on a cold September morning, Harold rode out towards the western approach to the bridge over the Derwent River at Stamford, surrounded by twenty housecarls including Selwyn. A similar number of the enemy rode past the outskirts of the village and came to a halt on the eastern side, and from their centre rode a ghost from Harold's past. He grimaced as he rode out alone to meet his rebel brother Tostig in the centre of the bridge.

'Did Hardrada think it a jest to send my brother out to parley?'

'I'm the only one back there who speaks English,' Tostig replied, 'apart from a captured priest and a young Englishman who's only fit to take orders. And I'm not here to parley.'

'There's still time for you to honour your family loyalties,' Harold suggested, to a loud hollow laugh from Tostig.

'Like you honoured yours when you could have supported my cause against the twisted mind of King Edward? These lands that you trespass upon are mine by right, and when I am again Earl of Northumbria, and Harald is King of England in your stead, *then* I might honour my loyalty to a man who shared my mother's womb, but has never displayed any brotherly love towards me.'

'Brave words,' Harold sneered back, 'but from what I can see, you and the Norwegian peasants are heavily outnumbered by loyal Englishmen. Why do you and your men not cross the bridge and join what is destined to be the winning side?'

Tostig pulled angrily at his horse's head in a signal for it to return to the village, but he had one final message for Harold. '*You* may be skilled in betrayal, but it will never be said of me that I encouraged Hardrada to invade England, only to betray him in his moment of triumph. Do your worst, brother — we are ready for you.'

Harold was barely back among his housecarls before it became apparent that the Norsemen intended to hold the bridge against them. A triple line of massive axe-men moved into the centre of the narrow defile across the river, snarling and hurling oaths in their native tongue. Harold turned to his entourage.

'We need to take that bridge by force, and for that we will need horsemen armed not only with sharp swords, but also the courage to face death. Once that bridge is taken the enemy cannot withstand our superior foot force, and the day will be ours. Who wishes to place their life at peril for England?'

Selwyn was all but shamed into volunteering. There was a sickening cacophony of metal meeting metal, the shriek of wounded horses, the curses of men unhorsed, and the shouts of desperation as the enemy fell, one by one, either onto the crude planks of the bridge that rapidly turned red with their blood, or over the low parapet into the river, where they drowned in their heavy armour and clothing, too weakened by their wounds to swim to safety.

Harold's foot soldiers swarmed over the bridge and hurled themselves at the hastily erected Viking shield wall in the main street. Although many of them were impaled on the Norsemen's spears, while some were deprived of limbs by axe blows, they quickly overpowered the main enemy defences. The shield wall broke, and Norsemen began fleeing for their lives through the few narrow streets that constituted the village of Stamford.

Harold cursed as he watched his housecarls riding back to him with yells of triumph. He ordered them back over the bridge to collect the remaining English spear and axe men who had spread themselves over the village, then bring them back over to parley with him.

Selwyn was one of the first back, and was able to advise his king that both Hardrada and Harold's brother Tostig were lying dead in a pigsty up the street.

'The best place for the pair of them,' Harold replied as he spat on the ground, then looked up sharply as he heard a rider approaching.

'Your Majesty! I come from York, and from its walls we saw another army coming up from the south!'

'Get the men to form up on the far side of this bridge, in front of the village,' Harold ordered Selwyn. 'We will play the enemy at its own game!'

'The approaching army may be one of our own,' Selwyn reminded him.

Harold glared. 'If it is the men of Wessex, then they have left the south coast exposed and I will have its commander hanged. But were we not told that Hardrada had left forces with his fleet further south? Are they not more likely to be those?'

Acknowledging the logic of this suggestion, Selwyn and several of his fellow housecarls rode back into the village, rounding up the surviving English soldiers and forming them up behind a shield wall on the eastern side of the river bridge. Harold crossed the river, and turned his horse to look south and west. Then they all waited.

The oncoming soldiers were indeed what was left of Hardrada's invasion army, unaware that their main force had already been defeated and scattered. They had been summoned on Harald's command by a very nervous Cerdic.

Cerdic was in the unenviable position of riding north to his possible death, surrounded by a body of fighting men with whom he could not communicate, and who eyed his comparatively puny frame with derisive sneers. As the distant spires of York came into sight, a lone messenger, clad only in the shredded remains of his armour and covered in blood, staggered across a field to their right and into the roadway. Cerdic was unable to understand what he was saying when he was brought forward to face him, but the leader of the group that contained him cursed, and the entire army took the next lane to the right at double speed.

Cerdic let them trot past him, then sat there alone on his horse, considering his next move. From what he could deduce, things were not going well for the Norsemen, and in his heart he was glad. He could not bear to contemplate the fate of England were Harald to become its king, with his heathen followers taking their revenge for years to come. And here he was, assisting them when he wished them all dead. Time to disobey his mother.

Cerdic's most immediate problem was that he had no idea where he was, except that it was somewhere in the north of England. If he was to get back home, he would need to force this tired horse south for days, and possibly weeks, at a time. He dismounted and examined his mount more carefully. It had been captured following the brutality in Scarborough, and seemed much thinner than when he had first acquired it. He doubted whether it would last two more days, let alone two weeks.

In the centre of some strip fields to his right, he could make out a manor house. Perhaps he could steal a new horse there. While he was at it, some food and drink would be very welcome.

By nightfall, Cerdic was inside the stable, hidden in the straw. Memories returned of comfortable nights spent lying on the rushes at home, and he realised that he was dog-tired. He crawled under the warm cover of a loose bale and fell instantly asleep.

When Cerdic awoke, it was to shouts and screams. He scrambled to his feet, ran to the stable door and looked out. A man and a woman were running for their lives, and the woman was screaming at the top of her voice. Several of Cerdic's former comrades emerged from the manor, devouring lumps of meat, then stopped in their tracks when there came a shouted command. The voice was English, and sounded very familiar to Cerdic.

'Put all these Norsemen to the sword, and let's move on,' Selwyn ordered his men-at-arms.

Cerdic hastily removed his battle helm and yelled back, 'But surely not your own brother?'

Selwyn looked as if someone had hit him over the head with an axe. 'Cerdic! What in God's name are you doing here?'

'Hiding from you and your men, obviously. Are you with the English army?'

'What's left of it, certainly. But we won the day, and the king sent me to flush out the ones who are still on the run.'

'I never imagined I would be so glad to see you. Unless you intend to have me put to death, that is.'

Selwyn looked around him. Four dead Norsemen were littering the yard. 'Did you take any English lives?' he asked Cerdic.

Cerdic laughed. 'You would have been amused, had you witnessed the low esteem in which these savages held my fighting ability. I was kept close to Hardrada's side, and forbidden to take the field.'

'Then I can spare your life without disobeying Harold's order,' Selwyn replied with relief.

'You get your orders direct from the king?' Cerdic asked, impressed. 'Did Mother finally manage to persuade him that she was related to the former royal house of England?'

'Mother is being held captive in London on Harold's orders. She is only allowed out to relieve herself.'

'How did Mother get herself imprisoned?' Cerdic asked.

'It's a long story, and has something to do with a French priest. Perhaps another man who was bedded by our grandmother, who seems to have spread her favours widely. However, we have no time for that at this moment. I cannot take you back as a prisoner, nor can you continue to be clad like that. Let's see what the lord of this manor can offer by way of gratitude, shall we?'

IX

'I've been thinking a little more about our mission today,' Amalric said to Will as they approached the badly restored stonework of Telham Priory. 'It may have been that peasant girl who told us where this priest might be found, but she got that information from someone else. It might be better for that someone else if the Frenchman really *were* dead. If he is alive, and Harold has him tortured, he may reveal who led him to the priory, and an innocent woman might well suffer in consequence.'

Will had heard the Widow Gwenyth called many things, but 'innocent' was not one of them. The urge to laugh was almost overpowering. 'Are you suggesting that we kill him if we find him?'

'Kill a priest?' Amalric replied. 'I was brought up a Christian, and I'd fear the fires of Hell if I laid hands on a priest.'

'Will Harold not share that fear?' Will suggested.

Amalric shook his head as he dismounted. 'My experience of our new King leaves me with little confidence that he respects Christian values. If he finds this Frenchman, he will give him much pain, along with those who assisted him.'

'Including the holy brothers in this ruin of a monastery?'

'Those too,' Amalric confirmed. 'For that reason also, it would suit our purpose if this runaway priest is not found alive.'

'Can we not just ride away from here and pretend that we found him dead?'

'King Harold would demand to see his grave this time. If there is to be any pretence, it must be that we failed to find him alive.'

'Then why did you undertake to find him in the first place?' Will asked.

'I did not then know who had hidden him,' Amalric admitted, 'and that young girl we terrorised has a big mouth. She will tell anyone who asks — for the right price, or under fear of violence — that she pointed us to this priory. We must now at least appear to conduct a search of it, but it would be very useful if we can later swear that we found no-one alive fitting the Frenchman's description, and that we have reason to believe that he has moved on.'

Unknown to either of them, someone else had been there ahead of them. Annis had managed to slip into Gwenyth's hut under cover of darkness and warn her that they had been tricked and that her French lodger was at risk of discovery. Realising that he might lead the king's men back to her, Gwenyth had made the exhausting overnight journey to the priory. Prior Jerome had listened to her story and sent her on her way with a blessing of thanks and a pot of honey. He had then called for Brother William, and they had adopted what seemed like the best option, given that flight would achieve nothing. Without realising it, they had given Amalric and Will a way out of their dilemma.

Prior Jerome received the two armed men in the *hospitium*, with Brother Michael in attendance.

'We are seeking a Frenchman who may have sought sanctuary on pretence of being a priest,' Amalric announced.

Prior Jerome nodded. 'There was such a man, but he is with us no longer.'

'Did he move on?' Will asked.

Prior Jerome did his best to avoid another outright lie, for which he would be obliged to penance himself heavily. 'We lost several brothers recently, due to a pestilence that swept through our humble house and the surrounding countryside. You may see their graves in the next field.'

'Are the graves accompanied by crosses with the names of the dead brothers?' Amalric asked.

'Not all of them,' Jerome replied truthfully, remembering the humble plots in which they had consigned two wandering beggars whose corpses had been found in a hedge.

'We will need to search your house, and speak with each of your brothers,' Amalric insisted. Prior Jerome indicated for them to follow him.

Within an hour they had spoken with every brother they could find, all of whom spoke fluent English. They had also searched every room in the monastery, during the course of which it occurred to the prior that they were not being as thorough as they might, and his hopes rose. Then his heart sank as Amalric nodded towards a side room off the *Infirmarium*.

'What's in there?'

'Merely the most recent of those who passed with the contagion.'

Amalric looked across at Will. 'Better check, so that we can swear to have conducted a thorough search.'

With great reluctance, Will walked into the narrow room, on the floor of which were two bodies covered in shrouds. He lifted the first cautiously, then recoiled in horror from the smell of human decay.

'Get on with it!' came Amalric's stern instruction from the doorway.

Will forced himself to lift the second of the two shrouds. He found himself looking into the clear blue eyes of a monk who was very obviously still alive.

Will dropped the shroud hastily and lost no time in rejoining Amalric and Prior Jerome, the taste of decomposing flesh still in his mouth.

'Thank you for saving me the best job,' he muttered to Amalric as they took their leave, remounted their horses and rode away.

Prior Jerome beamed as the second shroud was pushed to one side, and Guillaume rose to his feet.

'That young man — he knew I was alive, but he said nothing.'

'I gained the impression that they were not all that determined to carry out the king's order,' Jerome replied. 'But is it not now time for you to be honest with me regarding why you are in hiding? I told lies and half-truths to preserve your life, for which I must spend several hours in *Pater Nosters*. Does that not entitle me to the truth?'

Guillaume nodded. 'I came to you as an ordained priest. This much is true, but you should know that I am Guillaume de Poitiers, Archdeacon of Liseaux in Normandy. In that capacity I was chaplain and confessor to Duke William, who is the rightful heir to England's throne.'

'King Harold would dispute that,' Jerome argued, stunned to learn of the man's ecclesiastical rank.

'Which is why he seeks me out,' Guillaume explained. 'It was I who was witness to Harold surrendering any claim to the throne of England, after his predecessor King Edward offered it to my master Duke William. Earl Harold, as he then was, was shipwrecked off the coast of Normandy, and Duke William gave him sanctuary after he was seized for ransom by Count

Guy of Ponthieu. Either in gratitude for this, or under threat of further imprisonment, Earl Harold swore on oath that he would not oppose Duke William's claim.'

'Men have been known to break their oaths,' Jerome reminded him.

Guillaume smiled. 'Not when they are sworn over holy relics. Under the cloth on which the oath was sworn I had placed a bone of St Anthony, one of several relics kept under the altar at Liseaux. Had your English barons known of this at the time of Edward's death, they would never have given the throne to Harold. This is why he was seeking me, because of the secret I held, but perhaps now it is too late to be of any importance.'

'But how did you come to be in England, and in hiding from Harold?' Jerome persisted.

Guillaume grimaced. 'Once he was free of Duke William, and safely back here in England, Harold sent word that he wished the English earls to be made aware of the promise he had made. He asked that I journey over here, as the witness. I foolishly came, believing that Harold was a man of his word. Harold sent men to escort me, then once we had landed I was seized and thrown into a dungeon in Winchester. Harold dared not take my life because of my holy office, but he clearly intended that I should either starve to death in there, or die of the cold. My clothes were taken from me, and I was allowed no food or water. This lasted for some weeks, until one of the men guarding me sought a blessing for his sick child, and in return he arranged for me to escape. I was still naked, and close to death by starvation, but God kept me alive until the woman who brought me here found me hiding in the trees near her home.'

'So will this Duke William seek revenge for the treatment you received?'

Guillaume gazed into the distance. 'I am as nothing, although he would regret my rough handling. But if I judge my former master correctly, he will land here to claim the throne he believes to be rightfully his, in God's eyes.'

Amalric and Will journeyed back to Sandlake, convincing themselves that they had carried out the king's orders with scrupulous integrity.

'Must we ride to Winchester so soon?' Will was enquiring. 'I wish to spend more time with my family, before we collect the whole fyrd and begin the patrols. But more than that, I would prefer to be in London with my wife.'

Amalric had been staring down the village track and out towards the ocean. 'You may see London earlier than you thought, since you may be riding like the wind to collect any men left in the local fyrd. Take a look out there — are they sails, or do my ageing eyes play me false?'

Will looked for himself, and then swore loudly. For as far as the eye could see, there were the white sails of massive ships.

Selwyn and Cerdic rode side by side, Cerdic on a horse gratefully loaned by the lord of the manor and wearing suitable clothing in which to be presented to the king. The brothers put their story together. There would almost certainly be a celebration supper back in York, at which Cerdic could be presented to Harold as a loyal subject sent by his father to offer the services of the Astenmede Fyrd. The fact that there was no such fyrd was not a matter that they need admit.

It went to plan, partly because Harold was almost sliding under the table as he received Selwyn, thanked him for his brave and loyal service at Stamford Bridge, and asked about the Norse survivors.

'They are scattered far and wide, Your Majesty,' Selwyn assured him, 'and those who make it to their ships will no doubt set sail for home, relieved to still be alive.'

'This is good,' Harold confirmed, before nodding towards Cerdic. 'And who is this?'

'My brother Cerdic, Your Majesty, come to offer the services of the Astenmede Fyrd wherever they may be required, although clearly not here in the north.'

'And how many men do you bring?' Harold asked.

'None at present, Your Majesty,' Cerdic replied, 'since there have been delays in assembling them, due to our father's distraction over the imprisonment of our mother.'

'Your mother?' Harold asked, somewhat at a loss.

Selwyn took the opportunity to remind him. 'The Lady Earlene of Astenmede, Your Majesty, detained under guard in West Minster Palace on suspicion of associating with a French priest of whom she has no knowledge.'

'Ah, yes — her. I remember now,' Harold replied as he looked more closely at Cerdic. 'If I understand what you are saying, your father will not bring out his fyrd unless your mother is released. Correct?'

'Not quite, Your Majesty. My point was that he is distracted from his main purpose by the absence of our mother, who normally arranges these matters for him, given that in his declining years...'

At that moment there was a commotion in the doorway, and an angry demand for admission.

'I must speak with him *now*! The nation is being invaded to the south!'

'Let him through!' Harold shouted as he came upright in his chair and beckoned Will forward.

Will went down on one knee, nodding to Cerdic and Selwyn, then looking back up at Harold. 'I bring an urgent message from Amalric, the commander of your Wessex Fyrd. There is a large fleet of ships bearing down on the coast at Pevensey. We believe it may be that of William of Normandy.'

'You have seen these ships for yourself?'

'Yes, Your Majesty, before I set off. I have been riding for almost two weeks, and I'm on my third horse.'

'How large is the fleet?'

'It filled the entire ocean as far as we could see. Enough for perhaps ten thousand men and their horses.'

Harold lurched to his feet and yelled at Selwyn, 'Assemble all your horses immediately, and take them to Wessex! Tell Amalric not to engage any invaders in battle until I am there to give him further orders. And collect as many local fyrds as you can on your journey south — including your father's.'

'And my mother?' Selwyn asked.

'She may be released, if it means that your father will bring out his fyrd — it may well be on the front line of our defences.'

'*What* fyrd?' Will asked as they clattered out of the castle gate.

'The one we have to assemble once you have released our mother,' Selwyn said. 'You must go by way of West Minster and see to her freedom, while we take the rest of the men to join your commander. Then we have to make good our promise.'

Back in Astenmede and Sandlake, raw panic took over. Over the course of two days, a seemingly endless line of massive warships had decanted men, horses, siege equipment and supplies onto the light shingle at high tide. Then came other vessels, carrying the materials from which the invaders began to build a fortress on the broad grass foreshore that had been evacuated by the locals at the sight of the first sail. Amalric and his fyrd had made a show of patrolling the hills that overlooked the bay, but had made no effort to engage the enemy, or even parley with them, since they seemed intent on remaining on English shores for a lengthy period.

Pevensey and its surrounding hamlets had emptied overnight, as terrified residents took all they could carry and fled on ponies and donkeys. A fortunate few had carts, and some even had horses to pull them, but in the main it was a foot-weary and apprehensive confusion of bewildered, frightened and despairing fishing folk who trudged uphill. They hoped to find shelter either in the woodland that lay at the top of the ridge of the long southern down, or in the huts of their more charitable farming neighbours and relatives.

The local fyrds slowly took shape, as Amalric and his seconds in command awaited news from the north. The Wessex Fyrd was perhaps two thousand strong at best, whereas the invaders on the waterfront appeared to consist of at least four times that number.

As the hours became days, and the days stretched into the second week, it was rumoured among the more optimistic residents of Sandlake and the surrounding district that Duke William was content to let the English come to him. The problem was that, possibly unknown to William himself, the main bulk of Harold's soldiers were two weeks' march away, and already exhausted from seeing off the Norsemen.

The first back were Selwyn and Cerdic, all but hanging from their staggering mounts as they weaved exhaustedly through lines of cheering thralls up the track to the manor house, only to discover that their father Leofric had been drunk for the past three days. Cerdic appointed himself the commander of the Astenmede Fyrd, and ordered every male thrall and churl onto the large grassy area in front of the manor house, along with whatever weapons they had. It was doubtful whether mounted French knights in full chainmail wielding swords and axes could be taken down by agricultural labourers waving scythes, billhooks and hoes, but at least it was a force of sorts. Cerdic drilled them without mercy for every hour of daylight, while envying his brother Selwyn the easier task of raising more fighting men in Sandlake.

At least Selwyn had the comfort of his woman beside him. After the long-anticipated reunion, Elva had set herself the task of raiding Caldbec Wood, along with a party of women that included her mother Rowena and their neighbour Gwenyth. They came back down five times a day on a mill wagon loaded with timber, from which some of the men began constructing shields and spears.

Before returning to Sandlake, Will had had to ride to West Minster and give orders for Earlene and her ladies to be released. Joan had cried as she'd flung her arms around him and told him of the child growing inside her. Lady Earlene gave way to undignified sobs when advised that she was now a free woman, and it was a happy company, including Betlic and Quenna, that took a wagon south-west to join the defence of Wessex.

Harold and his housecarls were in the next wave south from York, almost a week ahead of the disbelieving foot soldiers who were on one of the longest forced marches they'd ever had to endure. After five days of optimistically awaiting the return of his main army, Harold lost patience and set off again with only a handful of his elite horse warriors to ensure that he was at the head of the English army when it drove William the Bastard back into the sea.

Having arrived home, Earlene kicked her husband brutally about the body. 'You useless, pathetic lump of pig waste!' she bellowed at him. 'The nation is being invaded, your two sons are out there defending us, and all you can do is drink yourself stupid!'

'That's why I gave you sons,' Leofric lisped before doubling over and vomiting into the rushes. Earlene screamed and launched a vicious kick at Leofric's head that rendered him unconscious. She then made her way down to Sandlake to take command of her husband's fyrd.

'Is this it?' she spat as she cast a critical eye over the collection of peasants.

Will stepped forward angrily. 'If your husband had honoured his obligations to the king, and maintained a permanent fyrd, it would look more promising. As it is, we have only brave men — and women, let me point out — who have agreed to uphold the thegn's honour. They fight for their homes and families, as do I. Which is more than Thegn Leofric has proved himself capable of.'

The colour rose in Earlene's face, before she reminded herself that this was the young man who had so recently released her from her bondage in London. She looked around and asked, 'Who's that woman on Selwyn's arm?'

Elva stepped forward defiantly. 'The last time we met, my lady, I was in your chamber in West Minster, bringing you the glad tidings that the French priest sought by King Harold had been found. You were pleased enough to see me then, and you graciously invited me to visit you in Astenmede. Well, here I am in Sandlake. It is my home, and I am prepared to die defending it.'

'And why are you hanging on to my son like that?'

Selwyn gently released Elva's arm before stepping forward. 'Because we are in love, Mother, and if we survive what lies below, I intend to make her my wife.'

'And you no doubt seek my permission for that?' Earlene demanded haughtily.

'No, I do not. I will be thirty years old at my next birthday — more than old enough to make such decisions for myself. As for the tradition that all marriages within a manor must have the blessing of the thegn, you might wish to sober my father up for long enough to seek it. Whether you succeed in doing so or not, I will marry Elva Riveracre.'

An uncomfortable silence followed, broken only by several apprehensive gasps from the villagers grouped around them.

Amalric took command of the situation. 'We are wasting time. I am Amalric Goodbarrow, and on the authority of King Harold I am in charge here. Will Riveracre will now take the Sandlake men up the hill to practise with what few spears we have, while Selwyn and Cerdic Astenmede will continue instructing the Astenmede recruits in the formation of shield walls. We took the timber for those from your wood, my lady, and we took the men from your land. Should you wish to complain on either count, King Harold will be here in person soon.'

That was the signal for the gathering to break up. Earlene's mouth hung open, and Elva was left standing in front of her.

'Do you really love Selwyn?' Earlene asked shakily.

Elva nodded, and a tear rolled down her face. 'You must forgive me for that, my lady, if I am not your choice of wife for him. But he loves me also, and he may be dead before many more days have passed.' Her shoulders began to heave in anticipated grief.

Earlene was overcome with compassion. She walked the few paces that separated her from Elva and wrapped her in her arms. 'If you mean so much to my son's happiness, then you must of course marry him. I too was once in love with a fine upstanding young man. He turned into a hopeless fat pisspot, but I trust that with you beside him, Selwyn will become more than that. Now, what may I do to help?'

'When the fighting begins, we will need women to tend wounds. I can show you how to turn old garments into wound bindings.'

'Thank you,' Earlene replied. 'My first task will be to bring more cloth down from the manor house.'

The following morning, Amalric reluctantly took leave of the Astenmede Fyrd in order to return to Winchester. Everyone was sad to see him go, and everyone suspected that Gwenyth had been asked to keep a covert eye on how things were going locally. All this time there had been no sign of forward movement from Duke William's invasion force, which seemed content to forage what it could from the land immediately surrounding the foreshore. However, no-one doubted that before much longer an army of that size would either need to move further inland for additional food sources, or begin the attack that they had so carefully prepared for.

X

Early on a morning in the second week in October, Will, Selwyn and Cerdic were drilling the fyrd all together as one unit, teaching the spear throwers how to make the best advantage of the shield wall. A small group of horsemen came cantering down the track from Powdermill Lake and Will looked up, waved to Amalric, then dropped down on one knee, commanding everyone else to do the same.

King Harold climbed off his horse and walked over to the ramshackle fighting unit. 'It is heart-warming to see that Thegn' Leofric has kept such a regular and well-trained body of fighting men,' he observed. He nodded down the valley, to where the enemy camp could clearly be seen. 'The time has come to show the Normans that they are not welcome here. I'm advised by Commander Amalric that on the other side of that wood up the hill there is a convenient position from which to challenge Duke William. In less than two days, the forces that are currently resting at Winchester will be progressing through your village and taking up defensive positions on the hill. You will welcome them and give them safe passage, before joining them in a glorious defeat of the upstarts from Normandy. I now wish to speak privately with your leaders.'

He walked down the track towards the mill, accompanied by Amalric and followed by Will, Selwyn and Cerdic. Just before they reached the mill, he turned to speak to them. 'Your forces will be deployed to the left of our main army, on that hill that overlooks the coastal plain. You may be disappointed to learn that your men will not be in the front and centre of the action, where the greatest honour is to be earned. That position has been allocated to those who earned it by driving out the Norsemen two weeks ago. But you three will not be with your fyrd when the fighting begins — as senior housecarls, you will be with me, under the battle banner of England, and in the centre, at the top of the hill. Do any of you have any questions?'

Amalric coughed lightly. 'How can we be so sure that Duke William will be so stupid as to advance his army towards us uphill, while we hold the advantage at the top?'

'It won't be stupidity, Amalric, but arrogance,' Harold replied. 'We shall make a great show of force at the edge of the wood that looks down on the coastal plain, and defy the enemy to attack us. They have certainly been foolish to leave it so long as to let us gather so many warriors to oppose them, but the fact remains that their road to London is now blocked by us, unless they can blow us out of the way. We begin the deployment of men at sun-up tomorrow — see that your men are ready to be the first up there, in order to walk the length of the ridge and take up their positions on the left wing. Amalric will lead the centre and right wings up behind them, and you three will join me in the centre once your men are in position.'

As Harold rode away with Amalric by his side, Cerdic looked across at Selwyn.

'If the fight is to be in Astenmede Meadow, our home will be right in the middle of it. We must persuade Father to get out of there before that happens.'

'And Mother?' Selwyn asked.

'She seems to spend all her time here in Sandlake these days,' Cerdic observed with a wry smile, 'getting to know her future daughter-in-law, it would seem.'

They began to walk back towards their men. Cerdic recommenced their spear training, while Selwyn went in search of his mother.

He found her in the Riveracre hut with Elva, tearing her gowns into long strips, then twisting them so that they resembled rope. Selwyn stood for a moment watching them, until Earlene became aware of him looming in the entrance.

'Elva tells me that if these strips are tied tightly enough around wounds, they can stem the flow of blood,' she advised him. 'This young lady of yours clearly has great knowledge and wisdom.'

'I only hope we are not called upon to use many of them when the time comes,' Elva muttered fearfully.

Selwyn walked to her side, threw a comforting arm around her waist, and looked his mother in the eye. 'That time will be tomorrow, Mother, and the battle will be fought all over Astenmede Meadow. Our manor house on the top of the hill will almost certainly be destroyed, and we must lose no time in getting Father out of there.'

Earlene snorted. 'He has saved you the task. I was back there with Elva yesterday, collecting these cloths for bindings, and the house thralls told me that he was last seen riding away on a horse that seemed as drunk as he was. You need not concern yourself over him.'

'Is there anything we need to save from the house itself?'

'In my side chamber there is a small wooden box that contains my few treasured mementos of a former life,' Earlene replied. 'Perhaps you might wish to retrieve that for me. There are also some wall hangings left behind, which might make suitable stretchers for the wounded. Take Elva with you, and bring everything back on the estate wagon. Then tell the women and children left on the estate that they are free to remove to whatever place of safety they can find. They are no longer bound to Astenmede.'

'You are most generous, Mother,' Selwyn said.

Earlene let her gaze drop to the rushes on the floor. 'I have lately learned much from this young lady.'

Selwyn held Elva tightly. 'Come with me, and let's get over the hill.'

Early the following morning Joan slipped silently from the family hut to where Will was standing, gazing nostalgically at the mill that he had worked for so many years. She handed him a mug of mead and a chunk of bread, then leaned her head on his shoulder.

'If you need any more good reason to fight bravely today, I felt the child moving inside me as I lay in the rushes. It woke me up, and I turned to find you gone.'

'I was just remembering how I used to stand on the mill platform and watch for Annis coming on the cart with her father. I'm so glad I met you.'

'So am I,' she whispered. 'What names do you have in mind for the baby?'

Will laughed nervously. 'You're worried I won't survive the battle, aren't you? Well, how about "Wilfrid" or "Joan"?'

'No-one could ever accuse you of having a wild imagination,' Joan chuckled. 'Whatever happens, you're not allowed to die. I forbid it, and I'm your wife.'

There came the distant sound of voices in the chill morning air, and Will looked down the track to where the front rank of an army was wending its way from Powdermill Lake. The first few ranks consisted of men who were fully armed, with chainmail, battle helms, axes, swords, shields and spears. They marched in step, heads held high, and at their head rode

Amalric. There was movement from among the huts to the side, and Gwenyth slipped out carrying a mug of mead, which she held up to him.

Amalric halted the column, slipped from his horse, took the mead, placed it on the ground, then embraced Gwenyth. By the time he had remounted, the men of the Sandlake force had begun slipping from their huts, hugging their womenfolk goodbye, some with small children hanging off their tunics. Selwyn emerged from the Riveracre hut with Elva on his arm, and Cerdic came out of Annis's hut with a grim expression on his face. Both brothers joined Will on the track by the mill, and began calling their men into line.

As far as they could see up the Powdermill track there were soldiers from Amalric's Wessex Fyrd, and it was Amalric who announced that they should lose no time in wending their way up Caldbec Hill and into the woods. King Harold's troop was only just behind them, and his Majesty wished to be in position before the Normans had finished their breakfast.

The trees began to thin out at the eastern end of the ridge, and finally gave way to coarse grassland in which Amalric called a halt and instructed the men to form lines facing down into the pastures. They'd left a sizeable gap in the centre, into which, an hour later, King Harold rode with his royal housecarls, who dismounted and formed a tight group under the royal standard. They were joined a few minutes later by Will, Cerdic and Selwyn. Hundreds of heavily armed members of the English Fyrd marched in serried ranks to stand immediately in front of the royal party and turned to face down the slope. It fell eerily quiet until they heard the sound of battle horns from somewhere on the shoreline, and into the wide meadow below them processed the full might of the Norman force.

A rousing shout of challenge rose up from the English ranks, echoed a moment later by the distant responses of the invaders, who banged their axes and spears against their shields. A few moments later, the front ranks of the Norman forces below them opened to permit the exit of hundreds of archers, who walked determinedly up the slope until they were barely a hundred yards from the English front lines. Then they loaded their bows, pulled hard on their strings, and fired.

The fusillade went on for over an hour, as wave after wave of Norman shafts thunked into the heavy wooden shields held up by the English Fyrd members closest to the incoming fire. Very few Englishmen fell, and when the Normans seemed to run out of arrows, they withdrew with the catcalls of the English burning in their ears. It was now mid-morning, and some of the village women were already passing through the native ranks with supplies of bread and mead.

These were hastily lowered to the ground as the Normans moved forward in full force, waving axes and swords, or brandishing spears in a throwing position. They were obliged to bunch tightly at one point, to avoid a protruding bend in the Asten Brook, then they opened out again and kept coming towards the determined shield wall that was raised against them by terrified Englishmen.

The noise was sickening as axes smashed down on raised shields, men fell screaming with spears embedded in their guts, and here and there swords cut through chainmail and the limbs it was meant to protect. But the line held, and as the Norman progress became hindered by the mound of their own dead in front of the English shield wall, the command came for them to retreat. A mocking jeer was heard from what was left of the fyrd as the invaders hastened back to the flatter ground.

Then, to their horror, the housecarls at the top of the hill saw a section of the right wing of the fyrd break ranks and chase after the retreating invaders. Invaders who halted when they saw that they were being pursued, then turned and became the pursuers. The confused English foot soldiers had broken ranks instinctively, out of earshot by the time Amalric had bellowed at them to come back. They made for the higher ground of a small hillock on the bank of the stream, where they were quickly surrounded and hacked to pieces.

The sun had now risen to its highest, and the Normans seemed to be taking a rest from their assault on the English lines. Some of the fyrd sat down in the long grass, most of them tending flesh wounds or nursing bruises. Amalric saw the scared faces of the womenfolk peering out from the trees behind what was left of his wing of the defending army. He beckoned for them to come forward and move carefully down the slope to begin collecting the dead and assisting the wounded into the shaded groves to the side.

During this lull in the fighting, Amalric stormed over to where Will and the Astenmede brothers were grouped around the king. Red in the face, he bellowed, 'Do not under any circumstances allow the men under your command to behave like those idiots from my fyrd, and chase the Normans down the hill like that. You saw what happened to them — don't let the same fate befall your own foot soldiers. As you can see, the enemy have horses, and they know how to use them.'

He nodded down the hill, where the enemy cavalry could be seen arranging themselves into a 'charge' formation. Word was passed down the slope to re-form the shield and bring down the horses with spears. But it was not the cavalry that began to mount the slope, but another wave of archers. They leaned backwards with taut bowstrings and began firing into the air.

Shields were raised above heads in the English lines, as spent shafts embedded themselves harmlessly into oak.

Because the sun was at its highest, those who looked skywards for incoming arrows were temporarily blinded. Most of the housecarls around King Harold, including Will, Selwyn and Cerdic, had the sense to look away, lower their heads, and raise their shields. Not so Harold, and those around him heard a shriek of agony as he fell to the ground, blood pouring from a gaping hole that had once contained an eye. He fell silent almost instantly as the metal tip penetrated his brain. Horrified housecarls gathered around him as several more fell victim to the rain of enemy arrows — including Harold's two brothers Gyrth and Leofwine, who had been in command of most of the main army ranged below the housecarls on the hill.

Will was still taking in the implications when Amalric appeared at his side and grabbed him by the arm.

'I'll take over command here — you now have the Wessex Fyrd, fools that they are!' He looked across at the almost intact Astenmede Fyrd further along the ridge, and gestured to Selwyn. 'Take command of your fyrd over there!'

Cerdic was standing, white in the face and trembling, as he saw his two comrades in arms being given command positions in which they would almost certainly die. He looked fearfully up at Amalric. 'What about me?'

'You stay here and prove your courage.'

The approaching thunder of horses' hooves alerted the English to the need to brace themselves for a full-frontal assault on the central shield wall. The wall buckled, wavered, then obstinately held as shrieking horses began to fall with spears in their underbellies, and axe-wielding English soldiers raced out from the side of the wall to finish off their floundering riders. There was soon an effective barrier of dead and dying horses a few yards from the shield wall, and the remaining Norman knights pulled at the bridles of their destriers and galloped back down the slope to faint English cheers.

'When are we going to be ordered to get stuck into them, Master Selwyn?' asked an eager thrall from Astenmede Manor.

'When I order you to, and not before, understand?' Selwyn replied as he shaded his eyes against the glare that was coming from the ocean. 'But by the look of things, you won't have long to wait.'

Back in the centre, Amalric was doing his best to give orders to the seconds in command from the Northumbrian and Mercian Fyrds. They had been sent to assist by their earls, Edwin and Morcar, who considered themselves absolved from any further military service in person by their recent assistance in the north. The men regarded themselves as a rank above Amalric, and were only reluctantly coming the conclusion that, in the absence of a king or royal brother, perhaps it would be best to follow his orders.

At the foot of the hill, the mounted Norman knights who had returned from the attack on the English shield wall were climbing down from their mounts and forming up at the head of the massive horde of foot soldiers with their axes, swords and shields. It looked as if the entire Norman invasion force was about to throw itself uphill, and the English right wing was now severely depleted as the result of its earlier ill-advised charge after the retreating enemy. It clearly could not withstand any concerted attack. Amalric waved to Will in order to get his attention, then bellowed for the remains of the right wing to close up on the centre.

This left a gap between the right side of the combined force and the Asten Brook, which the Normans used to their advantage as they raced through and began attacking the defenders' shield wall from the side, where it was most vulnerable. As the marauding Normans appeared around the back of the shield wall, and began to hack at the defenders, Will gave the order for his men to come to their assistance. The severely depleted Wessex Fyrd hurled itself at the enemy, with almost inevitable consequences. Most of them were already dead, dying, or horribly dismembered as Will brought up the rear and began slashing and thrusting at Norman men-at-arms.

He had accounted for three when he looked up and realised that his own comrades were in full retreat, racing along the top of Caldbec Hill and disappearing into the dense woodland foliage to the side. He looked back up at where he had last seen Amalric, but all he could make out was a mass of flailing arms and legs, weapons flashing in the late afternoon sun, men falling dead, and battle standards being hacked to pieces and pulled from the ground. Then he looked back to his right and saw Joan, peering through the trees on the edge of the wood, one hand over her horrified mouth and the other beckoning him to safety.

Without another thought Will began to run towards her, stumbling and sliding on the shiny coarse grass of the upper slope, every step closer to her urgent outstretched arms. Then he felt an agonising pain in his left shoulder and fell down heavily. He was aware of Joan screaming and looking urgently behind her. His mother came into view, carrying what looked like a cloak. He called weakly, telling them not to risk their lives to save him, then his eyes clouded over and he lost consciousness.

Selwyn had been engaged in a similar attempt to reinforce the rear of the shield wall from the left-hand side. As he reached the rear rank of what had been the central shield, he was obliged to leap over the prostrate members of his own fyrd who had made it there ahead of him. Their crude farm implements had proved useless against Norman chainmail. He could die a hero if he chose, and perhaps account for one or two of the enemy before being felled, or he could join what appeared to be a general retreat into the trees of Caldbec Wood.

He opted for the latter, and ran with all the energy he had left towards the welcoming gaps between the oaks and elms, in which he could see womenfolk urging their men to save themselves. Fifty yards short of his goal, he felt an arrow go deep into his leg, just below where his chainmail had flipped upwards from the action of his knees. He gritted his teeth and kept limping along as best he could. Then, as he prayed for one final burst of energy, he made the tree line and collapsed on the ground. Gwenyth was nearby, and she rammed a wooden stake through the guts of a pursuing Norman foot soldier who had been raising his sword arm to extinguish Selwyn. He heard a cheer go up, and was vaguely aware of other Sandlake women putting paid to pursuing Normans, using weapons they had acquired from fallen defenders who they had carried into the trees.

In the centre of the English army, on top of the ridge and under the royal banner, Amalric and Cerdic were fighting back to back against the elite Norman knights who had skirted around the general carnage and made directly for the royal housecarls and their dead king. Then Cerdic heard a scream of anguish and a foul curse. Amalric slipped sideways under the impact of a downward swipe from a broadsword that had cut his left arm clean off. The next blow, delivered almost without a pause, removed Amalric's head, and suddenly Cerdic was exposed at his back. As he turned, a heavy blade sliced straight through his mail.

XI

Will regained consciousness as a sharp pain shot through his shoulder. The first thing he saw was Joan's tear-streaked face.

'We had to get the arrow out in case the wound became poisoned, but Gwenyth says she has something to ease the pain.'

'Some of her mead?' Will joked. 'Is she going to make me drink it, or pour it into the wound?'

Gwenyth grinned down at him as her face swam into sight. 'Once we get that mail off you and I can see the wound, it's going to get some of my best honey smeared into it. Now, shut up and rest — you've lost a lot of blood.'

'Take that, you murdering bastard!' came a woman's voice.

'Was that Lady Earlene?' Will asked in amazement.

Joan nodded. 'Not so much the lady since they told her that Cerdic's dead. That's the third Norman she's disposed of since we got you back here.'

'The enemy have entered the wood?' Will asked, aghast. 'You're all in danger! Just leave me here, and I'll pretend I'm dead.'

'The only ones in danger are the Normans!' Gwenyth assured him, wielding a captured sword. 'They took Amalric as well — the best man I've had in years.'

'What about Selwyn?' Will asked.

'I think I saw him staggering into the trees,' Joan said.

'He'll never walk straight again, probably,' Rowena told them all as she joined the group, knelt down and cradled Will's head. 'At least they didn't get you, darling one, and your sister still has a husband-to-be.'

An hour later, the news came that the Normans had gone back to their camp for a celebration, but rumour had it that Duke William would return in a day or two to exact his revenge for the loss of so many of his finest soldiers. The women collected all the heavy cloth they had available and began carrying the wounded back into Sandlake.

It was also known that King Harold was dead, and word had gone by fast horse to London that the Witan needed to choose his successor. But wiser counsels predicted that, having defeated Harold's army, there was now nothing to stand in the way of Duke William claiming the English throne. Of more immediate concern to the surviving villagers of Sandlake, most of whose households were now without a head, was whether or not William would take the traditional soldier's revenge of burning houses, putting men to the sword, and violating the women. As for Astenmede, the manor house had been ransacked and put to the torch. The handful of thralls who had survived the fighting were now landless labourers, trudging the byways with their families.

Will and Selwyn were laid down to rest in Widow Gwenyth's hut, where there was more room. Some of the cloths from the manor were laid on the rushes, and other cloths were used as insulation against the cold autumn wind. Elva insisted on sitting by Selwyn's makeshift bedding and seeing to his every need, given that he couldn't stand. Likewise, Joan stayed with Will as they whispered their way through every child's name they could think of. Gwenyth distracted herself from the loss of Amalric by cooking all day, and half into the night, in accordance with her firm belief that a full stomach helped wounds to heal.

On the morning of the second day following the battle, a dreadful silence fell over Sandlake. The children were forbidden to play in the gaps between the huts, no-one made any effort to bring in the long-neglected harvest, the mill wheel was motionless, and the only sound was nervous murmuring. William of Normandy was said to be heading their way at the head of his victorious army, and no-one knew what to expect.

'Help me up,' Will insisted, over Joan's horrified protests. 'I've still got one arm left that works, and no Norman brute is going to harm my family!'

'Best do as he says,' Eldred muttered from the corner of the hut, where he sat morosely sharpening a wooden stake. 'He inherited his mother's stubborn nature.'

'Give the bastards one from me!' Selwyn yelled as he attempted to get up, then fell back with an agonised groan.

Elva held him and kissed his cheek, before turning to glare up at her brother. 'Now see what you've done? There's no sense in playing the hero, anyway — they'll just make an example of you.'

Word had come up the valley, from a young boy who had only escaped by running for his life, that the Normans had begun the retribution. Spirals of brown smoke marked the end of the huts that had been down towards the sea. The escaped boy had also described the cold-blooded murder of his parents, and the violation of his older sister by five Norman men-at-arms. There was no reason to believe that Duke William would show any more mercy to Sandlake.

Will made his way outside, draped across Joan's shoulder, to find that most of the surviving villagers were standing silently outside their huts, their terrified eyes fixed on the track. As the Norman procession came into view up the slope, Duke William sat proudly upright on a massive warhorse decked out in fine cloth that shone gold in the morning sun. He was at the centre of the front rank of mounted knights, followed by further ranks and scores of armed foot soldiers. The procession came to a halt as William held up his hand, reined in his powerful mount, and yelled something in French.

From the third rank of mounted knights emerged a clergyman, riding a palfrey. He positioned his horse to the side of the front rank and called out in heavily accented English, 'I am Gilbert de Rouen, chaplain to Duke William. I have the unhappiness to speak your heathen language, so I will speak between you and my Lord of Normandy.'

After an ominous sounding outburst in French from William, Gilbert told them, 'Duke William tells me that you are all his prisoners.'

'Does he intend to put us all to death?' Will asked defiantly.

William sneered down at him, and spoke.

'My master asks if you took part in the battle,' Gilbert translated. Will nodded. 'How many Normans did you kill?' was the next question.

'Not enough, obviously,' Will grinned back, to the sound of hastily drawn breaths all around him, and Joan's whimper of fear.

William sat back on his horse for a moment, then his face creased in amusement and he burst out laughing.

'My master says you are a brave fool,' Gilbert announced.

'I am also still alive,' Will pointed out.

'Duke William says that this may not be for much longer,' Gilbert warned.

Joan threw her arms protectively around him.

'Your woman?' Gilbert asked.

'Yes — and she is with child, as you can probably see.'

William appeared to be absorbing this point when his gaze drifted further up the track, and his eyes opened wide. Without warning he climbed down from his horse and knelt in the dust, head down. There in the centre of the track leading from Powdermill Lake was a solitary monk with tears rolling down his face.

He walked slowly forward, then knelt in front of William. Then the two men threw their arms around each other and gave way to emotional outbursts.

The monk rose to his feet and waved in the general direction of the villagers grouped behind Will, as if for protection. Then he walked forward, placed his hand on Will's shoulder and turned back to say something to the duke, who nodded with some apparent reluctance. Then the monk passed on to Gwenyth, and he continued talking to William, who replied at length. Then Gilbert stepped forward and began to speak.

'My master says...' He got no further, as the monk interrupted him in French, then turned back to Will and Gwenyth.

'My English, it is better than his. You must know that in Normandy I was no monk, but the Archdeacon of Liseaux. My real name is Guillaume de Poitiers, and I was once chaplain to Duke William. He and I are good friends, and I have explained to him how this lady saved my life two times, from the soldiers of Earl Harold. I have also told him that this man with the bad arm could have told Earl Harold where I could be found, but did not do so. Duke William is most happy to see me alive, and will spare your lives.'

'All of us?' Will asked.

Guillaume walked back to where Duke William had remounted his horse, and knelt back on the dusty ground, his arms raised in supplication. He and William appeared to be arguing briefly, then William nodded. They clearly heard the word 'Senlac' several times, and when Guillaume walked back to the knot of apprehensive villagers, he raised his hand high in the air and pronounced a blessing in Latin, and ended with, '*Pax vobiscum.*'

'What is "Senlac"?' Will asked.

'It is how you say "Sandlake" in our language, and Duke William has promised that the lives of all who live in it will be spared, for its kindness to me.'

Duke William gave a nudge to his horse's flanks that set the massive beast walking slowly forward, followed dutifully by his entourage. As he came up to Will, he touched his battle helm in salute and spoke a few words.

Guillaume obliged with the translation. 'He invites you to join with his army. But you have a family here, *oui*?'

'Yes,' Will confirmed as he hugged Joan tighter. 'And I have seen enough of fighting. But should your master require his grain ground finer than in any other mill in the country, I'd be happy to oblige.'

Duke William received the polite rejection with a nod, then looked more closely at Joan. He said something to Guillaume.

'Duke William says that if your child is a boy, it should be called William,' he told Will and Joan. 'That is also my name in your English way, so I also would be happy if you do that.'

'My name is Wilfrid, so that's not so far away,' Will replied. 'What about a girl?'

A further brief conversation between the two Williams produced the name 'Matilde', and Joan nodded her agreement. Then the ducal party moved up the track towards Powdermill Lake, leaving the villagers to breathe more easily as they gathered around Will and Gwenyth and thanked them for saving their lives.

'We didn't really save your lives,' Will reminded them. 'It was that monk.'

'The monk who is still here,' Guillaume announced from the track. He seemed reluctant to leave.

'Will William be a kindly king?' Gwenyth asked.

Guillaume looked doubtful as he replied, 'To those who obey him he will be most pleasant. But those who displease him will die. I will do my best to save your people, and to remind him that he owes this new country to God. My first task will be to ask him to build a great abbey where I once hid as a monk, but he is not always guided by God. Those who do not learn that quickly will be put to the sword.'

'So we must take care how we behave?' Will asked. 'Will we be required to change the way we live?'

'*Oui*,' Guillaume smiled back kindly. 'England will be greatly changed in the years to come. Your child will grow into a man or a woman in a new England, which is why I wish to bless it.'

Joan was lowered gently to her knees by Rowena and Gwenyth, who each took one of her arms.

Guillaume raised his hand above her head and pronounced the blessing, then stood back and looked at Gwenyth. 'You owe all this to the lady with no husband.'

'I'm glad that old pig went wandering,' Gwenyth smiled back at him.

PART II

XII

Will Riveracre paced nervously up and down along the bank of Powdermill Stream, in front of the old mill. A few yards up the track was the hut that he had recently constructed. Despite his wounded shoulder, he'd built three huts at the same time — his own first, with help from village men who had fought alongside him, then a hut for Elva and Selwyn, and finally a hut for Earlene.

Joan was currently bringing his child into the world, with the assistance of several older village matrons. If Will moved close enough to their hut, he could hear her cries for mercy and her shrieks of pain, and his conscience drove him back to the relative peace of the gurgling stream.

Dusk was slowly descending as Will spotted movement in the doorway of their hut. Widow Gwenyth emerged, looking around. She knew nothing about childbirth, since she had never borne any of her own, but she had a comforting manner and Joan had asked her to be present.

Gwenyth finally located Will in the fading light, and she scurried over. 'You have a daughter, Will, and we need a name.'

'Matilda,' he announced proudly. 'Thank you, Gwenyth. For everything.'

Two days later, Joan was back on her feet, and the mead was flowing freely from earthenware jars, while oatcakes were being decanted from the griddle over the central fire as fast as Will's mother Rowena could produce them. The family were all there, Will's sister Elva providing the shoulder support for her husband Selwyn as he re-learned how to stand for lengthy periods, while father Eldred hid behind a grin as he consumed more mead than Rowena was able to keep track of.

There were friends gathered there too, loyal fellow villagers who had fought alongside Will and Selwyn, and had provided the muscle for the construction of the three new huts. Chief among them was Will's recently acquired close friend Deman Flesher, son of the village butcher who slaughtered and salted the local pigs, one of which was sizzling nicely on the spit outside. Deman was now installed in Annis's hut, having caught her eye with his broad shoulders and easy-going temperament.

A shadow fell across the doorway, and everyone stood back as the tall man with the white tonsure raised his hand in a communal blessing as he moved towards the fire.

'Gwee!' Gwenyth shouted gleefully as she rushed to his side and embraced him. 'What brings you back?'

Guillaume looked around until he saw the cradle, inside of which the newest Riveracre was demonstrating that she could sleep through anything.

'There is a new life to be blessed,' he said, as he extracted a cross from the side pocket of his robe. It fell quiet as he raised the cross, stepped across and dipped his finger in the water bowl to the side of the open fire, sprinkled baby Matilda's head with it and pronounced a long phrase in Latin.

As the general hum of conversation resumed, Will moved closer to Guillaume's side and thanked him for coming. 'How did you know?' Will asked.

'I was sent here on the duke's business, and I heard it from some of your men who were using Duke William's first fortress, down there near the beach, for firewood. I asked them for what the wood was required, and they told me you were having a feast to celebrate the birth of your child. But you must warn them that they risk death by such actions — that is one of them over there.' He nodded towards Deman, who was laughing heartily at what had no doubt been a filthy story from Annis.

'I will warn him, of course,' Will assured Guillaume, 'but is our new overlord so cruel as to put men to death for the theft of a few handfuls of wood?'

'It is not the wood itself,' Guillaume told him, 'but the insult. Duke William wishes to live in peace with the people of England, but he will not abide such insults to his might, and that was his castle. Which is another reason why I am here, seeking your care for your people.'

'In what way?' Will asked, troubled.

Guillaume invited him to step outside, where the sleet had begun to abate as night fell, and he nodded in the direction of Caldbec Wood. 'On the other side of that hill, have they begun to rebuild the house that was once that of your former leader?'

'It belonged to Thegn Leofric and his family, yes. Why?'

Guillaume sighed. 'My master is most pious, and wishes to establish a mighty church to mark his victory, give thanks to God, and honour the memory of his dead. He gives the task to me, and says that it is to be built at the top of that ridge where his army was victorious. When I went, with some sadness, to see it yesterday, I found labourers building a new house, led by a very rude man who called me a "meddling monk" and ordered me off "his" land. The duke will order his death if I report it, and I still owe much to your people.'

'I had heard that Thegn Leofric was back,' Will confirmed with a frown, 'and a much changed man, by all accounts. That haughty-looking lady inside the hut here — the one in the green gown that she borrowed from my mother — is the thegn's lady, Earlene. You must speak with her if you wish her husband to cease what he has begun, but I fear that she will be hard to persuade.'

'That is why I come in search of you. You are one of these people, and the warning will come better from one of their own kind, rather than a man of God who does not speak your language well.'

'You speak it *very* well,' Will assured him. 'Better than I speak French, anyway. But is it true what they are saying? That we will all have to learn your language?'

'It would be better if you did,' Guillaume said with a worried frown, 'since my master is no scholar, and will not take well to having to go back to his books.'

'Tell me more about the man,' Will urged him as they walked slowly towards the stream.

Guillaume thought for a moment. 'He is a devout man, and he believes that it is God's will that he rule this land in His name. But he is also guilty of the sin of pride regarding his image in the eyes of his fellow men, which is no doubt because he is of bastard birth. He also suffers fits of wild rage when he feels himself slighted, and I have frequent need to impose penances upon him for his outbursts, during which he orders the deaths of others, and sometimes will kill them with his own hand. But he is also a faithful and loving husband and father, and much given to prayer and devotion to the works of God. Truly a confused man.'

'And where is he now?' Will asked nervously.

'On his way to London, but he takes a wide path, showing his power to those who lie on his road to the throne. When last I was with him, it was at a place called Romney, where there is a small harbour, and some of his fleet has been moored. But now he travels to Dover, where he can rest until more of his soldiers can cross the water and join him. Not until then will he march upon London.'

'And then what?' Will asked.

Guillaume shrugged. 'That will depend upon the actions of the people of London. If they submit, it will be good for them all. But if not, then God be with them.'

Considerably unnerved by what he had just learned, Will waited until Guillaume had left before beckoning Earlene outside. He quickly relayed the monk's message.

'Duke William of Normandy — who incidentally is my cousin — is not yet King of England,' Earlene replied dismissively. 'There is still Saxon nobility left alive — such as the grandson of Edmund Ironsides, who once ruled England alongside Cnut, another of my distant relatives.'

'Leaving aside your many royal connections, who is this rightful heir to Edmund Ironsides?' Will asked.

'He is known as "Edgar the Aetheling", because he is descended from King Aethelred.'

'Who by all accounts let his throne slip to Cnut in the first place,' Will observed. 'Hardly a suitable ancestry to appeal to the Saxons who are now bowing to Duke William.'

'Not *this* Saxon. Go back inside and tell Selwyn to limp out here on the arm of your sister. We'll soon see whether or not I need the approval of a Norman bastard to rebuild my manor house!'

Selwyn came out as summoned, and hobbled to where his mother was cursing quietly. Elva released her hold on him for the last few feet. 'We leave on the morrow after next,' she instructed him.

'Leave for where?' he demanded.

'We are headed for wherever this arrogant cousin of mine may be found, to impress upon him that if he wishes to be honoured as the new king of this realm, he must work for it.'

Duke William of Normandy was bored. The serving boys kept their eyes fixed firmly on the floor as they moved tactfully around his fitful temper, trying not to spill anything or place a dish in the wrong place. They each heaved a sigh of relief as they passed back through the door that led to the kitchen of the temporary keep. This had been hastily thrown up on top of the crudely shovelled motte, which had been constructed out of soil from the surrounding ditch. From the second level it was possible to look out over the palisade towards the harbour and the ocean that lay beyond it, but today all that could be viewed was driving rain.

William glared angrily across at Eustace of Boulogne as he took another hearty swig of the wine they had brought with them. 'You seem to have brought the foul weather with you in your ships, Eustace. It always rains when I am in your territory, and it seems that you have commanded it to accompany you here.'

Eustace gritted his teeth against the ingratitude; without his fleet of ships, William would never have made it across the narrow waterway from Saint-Valery. 'I am advised that the omens are good, sire. The seagulls have not returned to their nests on the clifftops, which suggests that they anticipate good fishing, which in turn suggests good weather.'

'If you are correct,' William grunted in reply, 'see to it that the seagulls lead us to the fish, since I am tired of eating pig. If the seagulls are misleading you, then we might consider eating them instead.'

The vigorously active William hated sitting around. The pathetic Saxons would not come out to fight, however many of their villages he burned to the ground. In this filthy weather he could not even hunt. Those same sleet showers kept the rest of his invasion army in the alehouses of Calais and Boulogne, because their sea captains would not risk the crossing.

His half-brother Odo, a cleric who, despite his holy orders and status as Bishop of Bayeux, had removed many a Saxon head with his battle axe during the confrontation near Pevensey, sought to soften William's angry mood with talk of the future. 'They say that London is but four days' march of here, brother. What plans do you have for your coronation?'

'You may keep your mitre in your saddlebag, Odo,' William grimaced. 'I would be crowned by someone who still retains credit with God. After your bloodlust at Senlac, I'm surprised that you are not penancing yourself by the hour.'

'If not me, then who?' asked an outraged Odo.

William looked for guidance to the others around him. 'Is it true that this God-forsaken country has a senior archbishop who has been excommunicated?' he asked.

Robert de Beaumont nodded. 'Stigand, Archbishop of Canterbury, which is their highest clerical post. He is so dedicated to the work of God that he chose to conduct it in several bishoprics at once, for which he has been expelled from the Church of Rome.'

'Then who will crown me, and save my brother from doing so with an axe in his other hand?' William asked.

Again it was de Beaumont with the answer. 'Their second in command is known as the Archbishop of York, and the post is currently held by a man called Ealdred. He is well practised in coronations, since he conducted those of both King Edward and the usurper Harold Godwinson.'

'He will serve for the task,' William nodded as he began to peel a pear, 'although he sounds as if he would happily crown a horse if the wind blew in the right direction. I will employ him, but I will not trust him.' He looked back across at de Beaumont. 'Robert, you speak the barbaric tongue of this island of peasants, do you not?'

'I have that misfortune, yes, sire,' de Beaumont confirmed.

'Then you shall be my voice and ears while we are here,' William told him, 'which hopefully will not be for long. Once this weather lifts, and our reinforcements arrive, we shall move on London. Hugh, you have our intended route prepared?'

Hugh de Montfort was a favoured companion, given the sheer size of his contribution to the invasion fleet and those who had sailed in it. To him had been assigned the honourable duty of charting the lie of this new land with which none of them was familiar, and identifying their best route to London.

'We go first to a town called Canterbury,' Hugh told him, 'then we march through their beer fields until we reach the southern outskirts of London. I am advised that there is a hill from which one may look down upon it, and the Saxons will soil their hose when we appear in all our splendour on the ridge above them.'

'It has a river flowing through it, I am told,' William replied. 'Is it possible to sail ships up it?'

'Indeed, so it is said, my lord, but a land-borne force would look more impressive.'

'Can this river be forded?'

'In places, yes, but further upstream, according to my information. There is said to be a bridge from the southern bank into the town proper, which lies on the north side, but of course the defenders may destroy it to prevent our crossing.'

'They will pay dearly if they do,' William grunted. 'Keep your axe well sharpened, Odo.'

XIII

Edgar the Aetheling sat placidly on the old throne in the Great Hall of West Minster. Eager warriors took it in turn to bow as they pledged allegiance to him.

Edgar had spent all his life being told that he was descended from royalty. As a younger boy, he had knelt before the temporary altar in the then-uncompleted Abbey of West Minster while Edward the Confessor had placed a hand on his head and called him 'the Aetheling'. At the time, Edgar had feared that it might be some form of insult or slight, but now he was being advised by the sycophants who knelt before him that it was a reverent reference to an ancestor of his called Aethelred, who had once been king.

'Will I be expected to lead men in battle?' Edgar asked Edwin of Mercia, the bluff man kneeling nearest to him.

'No, Majesty, that will be the honour that falls to us — my brother Morcar and I — should we be deemed worthy.'

'And were you both at Pevensey when this French pretender came ashore?'

The two brothers exchanged guilty glances, and it was Morcar who offered the excuse they had agreed beforehand.

'No, Majesty, we were defending your northern regions against the Norsemen. Had we travelled south, the north might have been enslaved, thus leaving the nation exposed at both ends.'

'Then which of you fought at Pevensey?' Edgar asked of the assembled company. Of the several large men who rose from their knees, stepped forward and knelt again, Edgar chose the serious-looking one with the long silver-white beard. 'You are?'

'Thegn Leofric of Astenmede, Majesty. The battle was fought on my land, and I lost a son who fought alongside the king, directly under his battle pennant.'

'But you clearly survived?'

'Clearly, Majesty, but I have a second son badly wounded from the same battle.'

'The fighting was on your land, you say? So your forces were formally part of those of Earl Harold, before he became King?'

'Yes, Majesty — the Wessex Fyrd.'

'Who commands it now?'

'Its commander was also killed in the same battle, Majesty. His name was Amalric.'

'So we remain vulnerable on our Wessex border?'

'Not if I can prevent it, Majesty.'

'These are brave words. Does any other man here challenge this man's right to be appointed Earl of Wessex?'

No-one spoke; the wrath of Duke William was already being widely reported, and no-one wished to be directly in its path. Therefore, the next morning, Leofric humbly took his departure while he was still winning, and could travel home with the joyous tidings that for once he had not disappointed Earlene.

A week later Earlene was in borrowed clothing, but the best that she could acquire in the village. Her garments were a sort of posthumous gift from her dead son Cerdic and came, with the greatest of irony, from Annis. Annis had received several gowns from Cerdic for carnal services rendered, and when it became known that Earlene was journeying to meet with the mighty Duke of Normandy, she had handed one to Selwyn with a slightly red face, and a suggestion that if it were let out a little, it might suffice for his mother.

If Earlene regarded the recycled gown as an ill omen, it didn't show as she swept into the ducal presence in the main room of the recently erected Rochester Castle, overlooking the River Medway. The weather had improved of late, and William had been able to make considerable progress north towards London. This had lifted his mood somewhat, and there was the prospect of hunting on the morrow, so it was with curiosity — and the expectation of some mild amusement — that he had granted an audience to Earlene and Selwyn.

Earlene threw back her head regally and spoke first, against all protocol. 'Good day, cousin.'

William looked her up and down. Earlene and Selwyn recognised his interpreter as the monk Guillaume. He translated William's response: 'And who might you be?'

'I am the natural daughter of Emma of Normandy, who was your father's great aunt. That makes us cousins. And this is my son.'

'So?'

'I have estates in Wessex, close by where your victorious army overran the peasant horde of Earl Harold.'

'Why have you taken the trouble to attend upon me? Do you seek surrender terms?'

'I have no need to seek surrender, my lord, since we are not engaged in warfare.'

'But earlier you spoke of your estates being close to where our armies fought. Was that battle in fact on your land?'

'It was, my lord.'

William turned to speak in low tones to Guillaume, who nodded with a nervous expression. Then the duke turned back to glare at Earlene. 'I am advised by someone whose word I trust that you are the lady who regards herself as entitled to rebuild her peasant hut where I wish to place my magnificent church. Do you admit this?'

'My husband and I own the land of Astenmede, certainly, and we intend to rebuild our manor house, which was lost during the battle.'

'The one on the ridge — the one that I ordered burned to the ground?' William demanded, as the colour rose in his face. The interpreter's head moved back and forth almost imperceptibly in a gesture of warning, but Earlene was too busy staring defiantly back at William.

'I do not seek financial recompense for the act of destruction — merely your leave to rebuild what is mine.'

William had heard enough and banged his mailed fist on the arm of his chair before yelling an instruction. Two heavily armed attendants moved towards Earlene with a speed that prevented Selwyn from intervening, even had he been capable. She was gripped firmly by both arms as William addressed her.

'You come here uninvited, the whore of men who had the audacity to challenge my right to the English throne, and you have the cheek to demand the right to place a peasant hut where I have instructed that a great cathedral be erected. You claim to be my cousin, and in due course that claim will be further examined. If it is false, you will be hanged. Even if it is proved to be correct, you will remain my prisoner until I have decided what to do with you. As for your son, he is dismissed from my presence.'

As Earlene was led away, shouting and protesting, Selwyn remained rooted to the spot. Any attempt to rescue her would be a futile act of suicide, given that he was not armed, and was surrounded by evil-looking ruffians who were. As he stood there uncertainly, Guillaume advised him to leave while he could.

Standing outside, his head spinning with the turn of events, Selwyn became aware of Guillaume scurrying out of the hall towards him.

'Please, you must ride home to Senlac and ask Will Riveracre to come here at once,' said the monk.

'And why should I, after the way that Duke William just behaved towards my mother?' asked Selwyn.

'Because if you do not, he will behave towards her in a worse manner. Lose no time — tell Will to come alone. He is to ask for me.'

Will looked up sharply as he heard his name being called from further upstream. He heaved another bag of grain onto the grindstone, assured Eldred that he'd be back shortly, and jumped down to the ground from the platform alongside the mill wheel.

Will ran over to where Selwyn stood, red-faced, sweating and out of breath. His horse was wandering aimlessly between the huts in search of pasture.

'What is it?' Will asked nervously.

Selwyn quickly explained what had happened at Rochester Castle.

'What does Guillaume think I can achieve?' Will demanded.

'I've no idea, Will, but you may be the only hope of preserving my mother's life. William has a foul temper when annoyed, and I fear that he'll have her tortured for his own amusement.'

Will looked back at the mill, whose wheel had ceased turning. 'I can leave Deman in charge of the local fyrd. Do you think you could help Father with the mill in my absence?'

'Willingly, Will — just go, please!'

A week after Will's departure, Selwyn looked up from where he was holding open the sack into which Eldred was pouring handfuls of milled barley, and gave a shout of delight. His father was riding down the track, and he hobbled over to meet him.

'Your leg seems much improved,' Leofric observed. 'Is your mother back here yet? The men have almost finished the upper floor of the manor, and I need her instructions on where the sleeping chambers are to be located.'

It fell silent for a moment, until Selwyn broke the news. 'She was fool enough to journey to Rochester to seek the Bastard's permission to rebuild your manor house. He got more angry than befits a king, and imprisoned her. I was present, but powerless to prevent it. Will Riveracre left here last week to try and secure her release.'

To his surprise, Leofric had the suggestion of a smile on his face. 'She was asking the wrong person. England has a new King, right enough, but not William of Normandy.'

'Who?' Selwyn asked.

'Edgar, grandson of Aethelred, of pure Saxon blood. Crowned by Archbishop Ealdred, in the Palace of West Minster, in the presence of his three most powerful earls: Edwin of Mercia, Morcar of Northumbria, and Leofric of Wessex.'

'You?' he asked in disbelief.

'Yes — me. Your old pisspot of a father finally "amounted to something", as your mother would no doubt put it. Once she gets back, we must have a celebration feast. Are you and Elva married yet?'

'No, but mainly because there seem to have been no priests coming through Sandlake of late. Even the friars have stopped wandering down here in search of alms.'

'No problem there,' Leofric told him. 'I have to travel across to Winchester to claim my title, handed to me by King Edgar in person. If I can't find a priest there, I'll head to London and bring back Archbishop Ealdred.' His face lost its smile. 'I just hope that William doesn't take his revenge on Earlene when he realises that his bid for England has failed.'

'But it hasn't yet, has it?' Selwyn reminded him. 'He may not have the title, but he has the army.'

'Now that I'm the earl, I can bring my own army into the field, as can Edwin and Morcar,' Leofric explained. 'Have you kept my fyrd in readiness?'

'That was Will's responsibility, since I could barely walk a month ago,' Selwyn told him. 'But in his absence he's passed that on to Deman Flesher, and he has the men out most mornings, running and keeping fit.'

'And sword training? Shield wall drill? Spear aiming?' Leofric asked with an angry look.

'None, Father, since we were not expecting that you would require your fyrd so soon. Perhaps you'd like to take over the training? Deman has enough to do as it is, and he can still keep the men fit, while you and I teach them the combat skills. But if you plan to take on William's army, there'll need to be more of you.'

'First things first,' Leofric replied. 'I must first take a company of men into Winchester, to advise them that they have a new earl. Armed with the garrison from there, we'll go after Duke William like an arrow after a deer.'

Will slipped from the horse's back and gazed across at the crude palisade, with the double gates closed firmly against him. He heard the creaking of the gates, and there was the solitary figure of Guillaume shuffling down the bank towards him.

'Thank you for coming,' Guillaume said as he raised his hand in blessing. 'Come with me, and I will see you fed and housed, then tomorrow I will take you to my master.'

'And what do you think *I* can do?' Will asked as he took his horse's bridle and began to lead him up the slope towards the still open gates.

'It simply needs someone with a gentle tongue,' Guillaume explained. 'When you first met with my master after the battle, he seemed to respect you. You must tell him that your village lady has a pride like his, but was not aware that William is now in command of this country.'

'He has the army, clearly,' Will pointed out, 'but what claim does he have to the throne, other than physical force?'

'Since when did kings require anything else?' Guillaume asked sadly. 'As for his claim, that was the secret for which your former king sought my death. When still only an earl, he made a vow, on holy relics, to honour King Edward's offer of the throne to William long before he was on his deathbed.'

'How do I know that William will even grant me audience?'

'Leave that to me. Here are the outer buildings. You will be able to sleep here, and I will have food and wine brought to you.'

'You are William's steward?' Will asked.

'I am more to him than that,' Guillaume replied, 'which is why I am certain he will grant you an audience. But it will need to be tomorrow.'

The next morning, Guillaume was waiting for Will as he stepped uncertainly out of his overnight lodging.

'Do you have any advice on how to avoid annoying your master, and finishing up chained next to Lady Earlene?' asked Will.

'She is not chained,' Guillaume told him. 'In fact, for someone who is a prisoner she is being treated very well. William believes that she may be his cousin, and he is a man who loves family. I will speak between both of you, and if your choice of words is likely to anger him, I will use other words instead.'

'But what can I say to secure her freedom?'

'Simply that she is an old fool who speaks unwisely because of her advancing years. You must satisfy him that she no longer speaks the mind of her people, but that *you* do.'

'And why should I tell such a lie?'

'Is it so much of a lie? Why do you think I sent for you to speak for her freedom? I have seen that the people of Sandlake and Astenmede regard you as their leader. My master is anxious to secure his conquest as peacefully as possible, so saving himself the cost of keeping a large army here. He is seeking to reach out to men such as yourself, to make a lasting peace.'

'I certainly wouldn't wish my people to feel his wrath. We are still recovering from the battle.'

'Best not to mention the battle, since he also lost many friends and brave fighters. But here we are — follow me and look humble.'

Guillaume led the way into a hall that smelt of new wood, and was lined with men dressed as if for a banquet rather than battle. William himself was the most richly clad, in a dark blue floor-length robe with gold embroidery.

Will bowed slightly as he came to a halt before William, who was enjoying his third goblet of wine, even though the sun had been up barely an hour.

'You have come to plead with me for the life and liberty of the woman who claims she is my cousin?' the duke demanded, and Guillaume translated.

'I come to ask that you overlook the unthinking words of a proud lady who once ruled our small community, but now, with advanced years, has lost both her influence with our people, and — sadly — some of her wits.'

Guillaume nodded appreciatively and translated. William spoke again. 'And you now lead your people? When last we met, you were at their head, as I recall.'

'They have sent me as their representative, no more,' Will replied, uncertain of how Guillaume would translate that. He decided to play the family card. 'When we last met, you also graciously suggested a name for our child, which was then unborn. My wife gave birth to a girl, and in honour of the mercy you showed us, we have named her "Matilde", or "Matilda", as it is spoken in our tongue.'

William laughed and clapped his hands with delight. One of the serving girls mistook the hand clap for an order, and moved swiftly and silently forward to replenish his wine goblet.

'This old lady with the failing wits, you know that she claims to be my cousin?'

'She may be, for all I know,' Will replied, 'but she now resides in a hut in our village.'

'Not in the manor house she sought to rebuild on land I have chosen for a cathedral?'

'No, not at present.'

'So she has clearly handed the mantle of power to you?' William asked, which Guillaume shamelessly translated as, 'Will she approve of your coming here to explain her frailty?'

'Most certainly,' Will replied, thereby sealing his fate for the foreseeable future.

'It is my wish that the people of England accept my sovereignty without further bloodshed,' William told him. 'Do I have your pledge to assist in that?'

'Will you ensure that your people do not rise up against me?' was how Guillaume translated, at the same time selecting in his mind the penance he would impose upon himself for his lies.

'Willingly, and gladly,' Will assured him.

'Excellent,' William beamed, as he beckoned to a man who had been standing to his right, slightly behind him. The man stepped forward, and William introduced him. 'This is Robert de Beaumont, Count of Meulan, and a trusted noble from my entourage in Normandy. He speaks your language, or so he assures me, and he will be your companion and guardian as you move through the nation spreading the good word.'

Guillaume translated, and the elegantly dressed, tall man with a military bearing smiled at Will.

'I've been learning your language for some time, but it must be better. If you help me as we journey, I will teach you *le Français*.'

'You will assist in my peaceful progress through your country, in return for the lady's freedom,' William said to Will. 'But you cannot speak with the authority of Normandy while you are dressed like an English swineherd. Robert will see to it that you are adequately clothed, and after dinner you may bid farewell to the lady.'

'I had expected to travel back with her,' Will replied. 'The country tracks are dangerous for a woman travelling alone.'

'She will not travel alone,' William assured him. 'I will send men with her, to ensure her safety until she returns to your people. And now, leave us.'

An hour later, Earlene looked up from the crude stool on

which she was seated in the dank, draughty chamber on the ground level of the recently completed castle that had been her home for almost two weeks. She heard the door being unlocked, and her heart beat a little faster as she saw Duke William being admitted, along with Guillaume.

'You must forgive me for my lack of family hospitality when you first arrived, but I have only recently had it confirmed that you are almost certainly my cousin,' William said.

'Now that we have that simple matter agreed, what do you propose to do with me?' Earlene asked with her customary haughtiness. Guillaume offered a slightly more humble version of that enquiry, and William smiled unpleasantly.

'Ours is not a relationship that I would boast about to the rest of Christendom, since by all accounts your mother was the biggest whore of her age,' he gloated, which Guillaume hastily translated more diplomatically, before Earlene could retort that she was not the only bastard in the room.

'My master observes that your mother bore several children to different men,' Guillaume told her, and heaved a sigh of relief when she smiled.

'She did indeed. The royal houses of England, Denmark and Norway, in her time.'

William told her what she had been hoping to hear. 'You will be released immediately, and I should be happy if you would join me for dinner.'

'Will Riveracre has journeyed here to secure your release,' Guillaume explained.

Earlene insisted on being allowed to wash and asked for fresh clothes. She made a late appearance at the dinner table, and was somewhat slighted to find that she had been allocated a seat well down the order of importance. Will was seated only three seats down from William himself. He was now dressed in a yellow jacket and was clearly a guest of honour.

Although she had consumed nothing but stale bread and scummy water for two weeks, Earlene picked unenthusiastically at the fine dishes on the table in front of her. Robert de Beaumont, who was seated next to her, offered to cut slices for her from the roast birds that glistened on the crockery.

'These are swans,' he told her, 'and we found them in a local *monastère.*'

'I don't care where they came from,' Earlene replied ungraciously. 'I'm not hungry.'

As the last of the plundered local fruit and cheese was loaded onto the table, Duke William nodded to a pompous-looking attendant, who called out in French. It fell instantly silent. Guillaume the monk rose from his seat across from Earlene and stood behind William in order to provide an instant translation.

'Today is a day for modest rejoicing,' William announced, 'since it is the day that I am able to send my long-lost cousin Earlene back to her people, the people she once led. But even more cause for toasting comes with the appointment of Wilfrid Riveracre as my special envoy among the people of England. He now commands the people formerly ruled over by my cousin. This excellent warrior has wisely accepted that England now belongs to Normandy, and he will be journeying far and wide to advise the people of England accordingly. Let us drink a toast to his success.'

Everyone except Earlene rose to their feet, wine goblet in hand, and William beamed down the row at Will.

'I give you our new ambassador to the English people — "Wilfrid of Pevensey".'

Earlene shot from her seat like a scalded cat and screamed down the table at Will. 'You turncoat! Traitor! Pig! A man fit only to grind our family's corn, now sold out to the invader! A thousand curses on your head, Will Riveracre! Rot in Hell, you spawn of scum!'

Guillaume and William stood open-mouthed at this outburst, but a crimson-faced William, who recognised her tone, if not all her words, was the first to regain his voice as he beckoned to several guards.

'Take this woman and hand her over to the company that stands in readiness to return her safely to her pigsty. Get her out of here before I change my mind. And see to it, Wilfrid of Pevensey, that you reward me adequately for my forbearance.'

XIV

Leofric rode proudly at the head of what was, by any standard, a token force. He and Selwyn were the only two on horseback. Those following behind on foot, led by Deman Flesher, were already tired and a little apprehensive as they approached the closed gateway cut through the earthen mound that guarded Winchester from incursion. They had been on the road for two days, and although their weapons were the best that Sandlake could produce, they were past their best, and some of them still bore traces of Norman blood.

An armed guard on the top of the mound yelled down at them. 'The Earl of Wessex is not in residence.'

'Indeed he is not,' Leofric replied. 'He is here, seeking admission.'

'I see only an old man with a few peasants in his train,' came the reply.

Leofric's face reddened. 'You will hang for that insult! Open up immediately, to your new earl.'

'When he is sent by the invader, we will.'

'You should know that I am Earl of Wessex by the hand of King Edgar himself.'

'Never heard of him.'

'By God you will, when I return with both him and his army. I'll use your guts for bowstrings when that day comes!' Leofric turned to address his humble band. 'We'll return with our full fyrd. In the meantime, I'll get King Edgar to send a messenger to the commander of this fly-plagued midden, confirming my appointment.'

As they turned back and retraced their steps, Selwyn was concerned, and deeply embarrassed, to see the smirks on the faces of their small contingent, including Deman. Leofric had never been a popular thegn among the folk of Sandlake, and once they returned it would be all over the manor that 'the old pisspot' had been refused entry to what he claimed was his own capital.

Leofric's mood was in no way lightened by the sight of Earlene waiting for them at the side of the road near where the track led off to their partly reconstructed manor house. He'd been forced to abandon work on it because he could no longer afford to pay the labourers and journeymen their daily hire fee. She stood with her hands on her hips and she was red in the face.

Selwyn jumped down from his horse, then winced as his leg reminded him that it had seen better days. He limped heavily over to his mother and threw his arms around her. 'Thank God you're safe!' he enthused, but Earlene kept her stare firmly on Leofric as she yelled past Selwyn's ear.

'Get off that damned horse, and explain how a jumped-up miller's son can claim to preside over our manor!'

'I'm now Earl of Wessex,' Leofric announced as he slid from his horse's back.

'But no longer Thegn of Astenmede, according to Duke William. He seems to have bestowed that honour upon the son of the man who once worked your mill.'

'Will Riveracre?'

'Will Riveracre no more. "Wilfrid of Pevensey", now.'

'How did that lanky churl get to have a grand title like that?'

'He was given it by William the Bastard himself. But wait until you hear *why*! Help me up onto your horse, and take me back into the village. I have news that everyone should hear about their beloved hero!'

Eighty miles to the east, Will was asking himself what would be expected of him in his new role. Duke William had secured his agreement to some sort of position from which Will could ensure that English lives were not lost needlessly, or mercilessly, but Lady Earlene's reaction had worried him. Her insults suggested she considered that he had thrown in his lot with the invader — could she have so swiftly forgotten that he had been at the head of the Sandlake Fyrd?

If he could, Will would gladly give up what appeared to be a position of some trust within the invader's force if it meant that William would go quietly back to Normandy, and take his heavily armed savages with him. As it was, Will would have to use his new position to stand between English families and this unpredictable man.

'Where are we heading?' he asked Guillaume listlessly as they stood watching the baggage being loaded.

'London,' Guillaume replied. 'This will be the first — and biggest — test of your value. If the people of London hand over the town, Duke William will be in better spirits, and will not take revenge against the people of that town, and any towns that lie beyond it. If not, then he will leave a pile of dead bodies to show others that they should not dispute his right to rule.'

Hours later, as the winter sun was sinking, they came to the brow of a hill and looked down on a glittering river, which Will was almost certain was the Thames. In the far distance he could just make out the struggling figure of some poor peasant who had been pulled from his hut, and was being gripped by the throat and shaken by Duke William. Then the grip was released and the man fell to the ground, clutching his throat. A message was shouted up the slope by relay, summoning Will de Pevensey to the front.

Will reached the muddy riverbank and reined in his horse. This was obviously reclaimed marshland, but there was a bridge spanning the swift-flowing water. Or at least, there had been once. So far as Will could make out, a central span of the rickety old wooden structure had been removed. Duke William was stamping his feet in rage, and finally hurled his mailed glove down onto the soggy ground and screamed.

Hugh de Montfort and Guillaume walked over to where Will was sitting on his horse.

'What does the name "Sudweca" mean in your language?' Guillaume asked.

'It is Saxon for "south work", and probably refers to these raised riverbanks, which are intended to hold back the river at high tide. They are not very effective, to judge by the marshes you can see all around us.'

Guillaume provided the translation, and William, still red in the face, yelled across at them.

'The duke wishes to know whether the bridge was broken recently, or if it has been like this for a long time,' Guillaume told him.

'I cannot lie; I would guess that it was done recently, to prevent his crossing into the main town on the north side,' Will replied gloomily.

The information was shouted across to William, whose face changed from red to crimson as he bellowed out orders. Will looked on, horrified, as men-at-arms kicked down the doors of the nearest huts, dragged out around a dozen people, and cut off their heads with swords and axes. Other men stomped onto the southern side of the broken bridge armed with spears, which they rammed into the gaps between the crude planks, with a head impaled on each tip. A smile of satisfaction flitted across William's face as he shouted across to Will and Guillaume. Then he kicked his destrier into life and galloped back up the slope.

'He says,' Guillaume told Will sadly, 'that this will show the people of London that resistance is not good for them.'

'Where is Duke William going?' Will asked.

Guillaume shrugged. 'Who can tell? Perhaps to kill more of those who resist. It would be good if you could warn them not to show defiance — that is why you are here, is it not?'

'Yes, for all the use it seems to be,' Will replied sourly. 'Duke William did not even consult me before cutting off heads.'

'I will penance him heavily,' Guillaume assured him, 'if he will once again accept my services as chaplain. He seems to prefer his brother these days — that fat old bishop Odo, who enjoys cutting off heads himself. Who will remind William that human life is sacred?'

Will caught up with the royal party long after night had fallen, encamped a few miles back from the river. He was guided by the light of a hundred fires — some of them having once been peasant huts — and eventually he found Robert de Beaumont sitting outside a hastily erected tent, staring into a fire on which a servant was attempting to roast a bird.

Robert nodded towards the flame and grimaced up at Will. 'If you can give a name for that *oiseau* in the fire, I will give some of it to you.'

'It is called a "goose",' Will told him. 'It must have been stolen from near a hut.'

'*Oui, vraiment*,' Robert replied. 'William burns the houses of the people, I eat their "goose" — *oui*?'

'*Oui*,' Will replied sadly as he sat next to Robert. 'Where is William going next?'

'He will play "round the ring" with these London fools. We go to the west side, then we cross this river, then we go back east.'

Will's heart sank even further. There was little doubt in his mind that William would make an example of every settlement he came to on his way west until he found a safe crossing point across the Thames. Then it would be the turn of the people on the north side to suffer the same fate. 'Robert, William has put me under your supervision, has he not?' he asked as diplomatically as he could. 'Well, I wish to return home and visit my wife and child.'

Robert nodded in the direction of the main camp, where William's grand marquee was clearly visible with its ring of fires and the shadows of armed guards patrolling up and down in front of its entrance. 'You do not wish to stay and save the lives of your *compatriotes* — your English comrades?'

'How many have I saved so far?' Will asked bitterly.

'Not one have you saved. You will lose nothing if you visit *ta famille*.'

'Will Duke William be angry if I go?'

'He may not know, since he pleases himself with killing. But if he is angry, it will only be with me, and many of these soldiers are mine. But you will return?'

'Of course,' Will assured him. 'I would not wish William to put you to death.'

'He would not dare,' Robert replied. 'Have some of this goose with me, then go when everyone sleeps.'

Five days later, mid-morning, Will smiled when his horse quickened its pace without being instructed, as it recognised the last half mile down the Powdermill Track to Sandlake. On the broad grass strand to the north of the village, before the start of the arable strips, a large group of men — some of them little more than boys — were practising the all-too familiar 'thrust and parry' exercise under the shouted guidance of Selwyn as he eased the pressure on his wounded leg by leaning on a stout stick. Next to him, his father Leofric stood watching.

Will called out a cheery greeting, and it fell silent. All the men stopped what they were doing, and several of them looked across at him with frowns of disapproval. One of them twisted his mouth in a grimace and spat on the ground, before being rebuked by Selwyn, who hobbled quickly over to Will.

'What foolishness brings you back here?'

Will's jaw dropped. 'My own home village? Where I have a wife and daughter? What do *you* think?'

Leofric called out to Selwyn. 'Leave the traitor and get back here, Selwyn.' There were cries of agreement, and at least one obscenity from the men on sword training.

'Traitor?' Will echoed, as he slipped down from his horse's back.

Selwyn took him by the arm and led him further down the track, out of earshot of the men. 'Is it true that in return for aiding the Norman invader, you have been given a title and command over the manor that belongs to my family?'

'Of *course* not!' Will insisted, horror-stricken. 'I ride with Duke William's force in order to prevent unnecessary bloodshed among our people, that's all. And now I have returned to visit my family.'

'That is not what Mother is telling the village. It is believed that you have sold out to the Norman, and there is much anger. You will find Joan and Matilda in our hut, for their own safety. They are part of my family now, of course.'

'But surely you cannot believe such nonsense, even from your own mother?'

'She was there, Will, and we were not. When she returned to the village, she told everyone that you had been appointed Lord of Pevensey, in return for guiding the Bastard through England.'

'I agreed only to accompany Duke William as he rode north, since I speak the language, and he wished me to persuade the people that resistance would result in death.'

'Is that not precisely what Mother is saying?' Selwyn challenged him.

'No, it is not!' Will argued back fiercely. 'You were there when we stood against William on the ridge. There were several thousand of us that day, many of them hardened soldiers, and we still lost. William has a vicious temper when thwarted, but he has promised peace and goodwill if the people recognise that he is now our king. If not, he has enough soldiers to wipe out the entire Saxon people. I am merely trying to prevent that — does that make me a traitor to those people?'

'*They* believe so,' Selwyn replied with a sad nod. 'You saw the reaction of the men just now — the men you once led into battle. Even they believe that you have sold out.'

'And who do *you* believe, Selwyn? Me, or your mother?'

'Much though it grieves me to say so, I fear that my mother grows feeble in the head. As for my father, he still does whatever my mother decrees. For myself, I have never known you to be anything but true to your own people, and I was there when you stood to defend them against the Bastard's first attack. But I'm afraid that some of the men burned down your hut, Will.'

'Your mother has much to answer for,' Will spat back as he turned and strode swiftly up to Selwyn and Elva's hut. As he strode in, he heard a scream and saw Joan cowering in a corner, clutching their daughter to her.

'Have you come to kill us, on the Bastard's orders?' she asked as she looked pleadingly up at him with quivering lips.

Devastated, Will shook his head and tears flooded down his face.

Elva got up and put her arm tentatively over his shoulder. 'Welcome home, brother,' she said gently. 'It's not true what Lady Earlene told the whole village, is it?'

'How could *any* of you think that of me?' Will demanded. 'I've spent three weeks watching my fellow Saxons being slaughtered by that animal who claims to have conquered them, and for all that I was able to stop him I might as well have pissed in his boots. And now I come home to — to *this*! I may as well be dead, for all the use I am to anyone!'

Elva beckoned to Joan, who got up from the corner in which she'd been cowering, placed Matilda in the cot, and walked up to Will. She reached out a tentative hand to touch him. He clung onto her and began howling like a child with a broken limb. Elva tactfully slipped outside.

Will seemed unable to break his grip around Joan, who whispered in his ear.

'I *tried* not to believe what Earlene was saying, but none of us was there. Where have you been all this time? It was meant to be only for a few days.'

'I went back to London with Duke William, but he seems intent only on putting people to the sword, and huts to the flame. I thought I could stop him, and to begin with I thought he wanted me to, but the man's a monster when he feels challenged or frustrated. And while I was away, trying to save Saxons from the sword, my own people were turned against me. And had it not been for Selwyn and Elva, they'd even have taken the most important people in my life. Thank God I came back when I did!'

'Take us well away from here, Will,' Joan pleaded. 'Even though we are physically safe, because Selwyn has threatened the life of anyone who harms us, the village women still treat me like dirt. They call Matilda "the spawn of the Devil", and me "the whore of a traitor", and recently they've taken to throwing pig dung at me whenever I try to leave the hut.'

Will's face reddened in anger, and he released his hold on Joan, turned, and stormed out of the hut, striding angrily down to where the men were still in training. It fell silent as they saw him rage towards them, grab the sword from Selwyn's hand, and wave it in the air.

'Those of you who wish to call me traitor, step forward and prove your courage! Those of you who take pleasure in insulting my wife and daughter, take a pace forward, and let me cut your heads off! One at a time or all at once, I don't care. Say these things to my face, or shut your ignorant mouths!'

No-one could look him in the eye, and Leofric looked genuinely frightened. After several minutes of excruciating silence, Selwyn stepped forward to stand alongside Will, and shouted to the men.

'None of us — not even me — dare take up his challenge, because we've seen him in battle. A battle he fought alongside most of us, to defend this village against the Norman bastard.

He's still fighting that battle, while the rest of us are in our huts, with our families to comfort us. And how do we repay him? We burn down his hut, threaten and insult his loved ones, and spit at him on his return. Is that the way to welcome home one of the greatest warriors Sandlake has ever known? Has the time not come for us all to offer a heartfelt apology to Will Riveracre?'

'Wilfrid of Pevensey,' Leofric muttered.

Selwyn's face grew crimson. 'Do *you* wish to take up his challenge, Father? And where were you when I was obliged to lead the fyrd that by rights should have been led by you? You claim now to be the Earl of Wessex, but God preserve Wessex if you are all we can rely upon. You would be best employed seeking out Mother, and prevailing upon her to apologise to our comrade here.'

'Selwyn, please…' Will began, having calmed down considerably.

'No, Will, let me finish. My family has done you a great disservice, and the least we can do is to correct our error as publicly as it was committed. I make you a gift of my sword, and any man here with a shred of honour will pledge you his. Should you wish to lead us back into battle against the Norman Bastard, Will, we are all yours to command — and *this* time I'll make sure that my father is in the front line.'

There was a faint cheer from the men, partly in approval of the insult to Leofric, who slunk away towards the huts, while Will thanked Selwyn for his offer, then turned to speak to the men.

'You have no doubt heard tales of my treachery — that I've sold out to William of Normandy for my own ends. You should know — because she probably didn't bother to mention it — that I first journeyed to William's camp at the request of Selwyn here. He begged me to secure the release of Earlene, and I did, by promising to travel with William to tell the people that if they acknowledged his right to the throne of England, they would not be harmed.

'That offer is also open to you, and before you reject it out of stubborn pride, ask yourselves what alternative you have. We have proved that we cannot defeat him in battle, so all we have left is stubborn defiance. I've witnessed for myself how that is rewarded — I stood and watched while a dozen severed heads of my own people were impaled on spikes. Is *that* what you wish for yourselves and your families?

'I see the looks on your faces. You believe that I've been sent here to secure your surrender. Well, consider this — you already surrendered when you failed to defeat the invader on the ridge behind us. There are still the bones of some of our former villagers being bleached white by the weather where they lie in Caldbec Wood. If you wish to add to that number, go ahead and try again. As for myself, I'm leaving here for good, with a very bad taste in my mouth. I'm taking my wife and child with me, God alone knows where. But I will not remain where my very name is reviled, my birthright challenged, and my family threatened. I'll do my best to persuade Duke William to show the hand of mercy, while you must ask yourselves whether it makes any real difference to any of you who is King of England. What did Harold of Wessex do to defend you when you were invaded? Before that, when he was merely your earl, did he put food in your mouths? Till your fields? Clothe your children? Life in Sandlake will continue as it ever was, and please God you will never set eyes on William of Normandy again.

'So farewell for the final time. May God be with you, and may you never again be stupid enough to fight a battle you cannot win.'

With that Will strode back towards his hut, praying for the courage to act in accordance with his own words.

XV

'You *will* come back for us, won't you?' Joan asked nervously as she clung to Will in the hut entrance. A small group of people had gathered to say farewell.

'Just try and stop me,' he smiled back reassuringly. 'I don't know how long it'll take me, but once I know where we can settle, I'll be back.'

'Don't let Duke William distract you, or command you into more titles and responsibilities,' Selwyn counselled him. Elva choked back a sob and buried her head in Rowena's shoulder as they both let their tears flow.

'No risk of that,' Eldred asserted. 'The boy has the patience and determination of a hawk hovering above its prey. I'm just glad that the loudmouths in this village have finally recognised that he's working for common people like us, and are not listening to any more lies from that woman a few huts away.'

After four days of travelling, Will came across some burned-out huts. William and his retinue could not be far away. Will pressed on, trying not to gaze too long at the shattered expressions of those who sat on the hard frosty ground, surrounded by their few remaining possessions, or the hopeful looks on the innocent faces of the children who called out to him for bread and water.

As Will approached a river in a village called Wallingford, he could see the lengthy procession splashing through a shallow ford to the other side, and he could hear the faint cheers from those who had successfully crossed to the other side. A camp was being erected on the far bank, and even from the near bank Will could clearly make out the banners and pennants of the invader embedded in the earth around the familiar marquee in which William would no doubt shortly be having dinner.

Will tagged on to the rear rank of a group of *chevaliers*, as he had been taught to call them, and together they clattered over the stony riverbed and up the mud of the far bank, worn smooth by the passage of those who had gone ahead of them. Safely back on dry land, he looked carefully around him until he spotted the familiar red and yellow chequers of the coat of arms of Robert de Beaumont on a pennant stuck into the ground in front of a smaller marquee. Small it might be, when compared with William's, but de Beaumont's canvas would stretch across at least three Saxon huts.

Will dismounted a hundred yards short of de Beaumont's temporary residence, and walked the rest of the way holding his horse by its bridle. He was challenged by two men-at-arms with crossed spears, and Robert looked up from where he was seated on a rock, sharpening his sword. He shouted a greeting, while ordering his men to let Will through.

'You have kept your promise,' he said. 'William never asked for you, so he doesn't know you left. But where are the woman and child?'

'In the village,' Will replied.

Robert nodded grimly in the direction of the duke's tent. 'One of those that the Duke has not yet burned?'

'How many has he burned on the march south of London?' Will asked.

'All of them,' Robert replied, 'since you were not here to stop him.'

'But they offered no resistance?'

'None of them. It is not enough that they do not stand and fight. William wishes to see the tops of their heads as they kneel before him.'

'But without understanding what he commands of them, how do they know his wish?'

'That is perhaps why it is best that you are returned.'

Two days later they were on the move again, and Duke William called for Will to ride alongside him. Guillaume did his best to keep up.

'Stigand, your Archbishop of Canterbury, rides with the baggage train,' Guillaume told Will, with a backwards jerk of his head. 'He surrendered yesterday. He says that there are others waiting to surrender, including some of your earls.'

'The Earl of Wessex?' Will asked.

Guillaume shook his head. 'I have no knowledge of him, but Duke William wishes to know how important this Stigand is to your Saxon people.'

Will thought for a moment. 'Not very, except that he is the head of the Christian faith in this country, or so we have been taught by the friars who come through our communities from time to time. The larger villages have a priest, and some are close to monasteries in which monks may be found, as you know for yourself. But in the more backward-looking villages the old Saxon gods are still worshipped by many, so that the Church of the Christ is little regarded.'

'William is very pious, as I have told you before, and the worship of old gods will be stamped upon by people like me, on his orders.'

As the days passed, it was obvious that William intended to follow the north bank of the Thames all the way into London. If they came to a village of any size, Will would be called forward, and he would explain to the terrified villagers that William came in peace as their new king, and that he would pass by peacefully if they would kneel. They all did so — some of them muttering quietly to themselves — when Will described what had befallen those who had failed to show obeisance. Duke William seemed pleased by the sight of so many bent knees, to judge by his benign smiles as he rode past.

William's other obsession seemed to be the building of castles. At a place called Reading, and another called Windsor, he selected suitable plots, and left men behind to dig a ditch, throw the earth into a giant mound in the centre, then raid the local woods for timber to construct a keep. He never stopped to see one completed, but the size of his retinue grew noticeably smaller as men were left behind to complete each construction. Will was wondering how long this could go on for when there came a shout from a forward scout, who was standing in his stirrups to get a better view. When Will did the same, the familiar towers of West Minster were just visible in the far distance.

Then, for reasons best known to him, Duke William ordered the entire procession towards a range of hills that ran for several miles to the north of the Thames. As they pitched camp, and Will led his horse down to a stream to let it drink, he heard English voices and saw several coarsely dressed men drawing water in pails on the opposite bank. Encouraged, he called out to them.

'Are you from around here?'

'Are you with the Norman army?' one of them asked in a heavy accent.

'In a kind of way,' Will told him. 'Duke William requires my services to advise the English throughout the land that they have been conquered.'

'You'll have a long bloody walk, then,' another man replied. 'We've been almost a month on the road south, and we still don't know why.'

'Where are you from?' Will asked.

'York,' he was told. 'A long way north of here, as my blistered feet could tell you.'

'I think I've heard of that place,' Will told the man, 'because my sister's man fought the Norsemen somewhere near there.'

'Is he dead?'

'No, back home in Wessex. Several days south-west of here by horse.'

'Not near London?'

'No, why?'

'That's where we think we might be going when all this is over. Our lord is here to surrender to William, before he burns us out.'

'And who's your lord?'

'Morcar of Northumberland. Edwin's lot are here from Mercia as well. There are almost enough of us altogether to send the bastards back where they came from, but the earls seem keen to negotiate terms.'

'I'll probably see you sometime in the next few days,' Will said as he pulled his horse back from the stream.

'Not us,' one of them said. 'We'll be cooking or serving, as usual.'

Back in his own camp, Will sought out Robert de Beaumont and told him what he'd just learned.

'This is a good thing to hear,' Robert replied, 'since it tells me why we have been ordered to be with the duke when the sun rises tomorrow. We must speak to these English who have come to bow the knee. Stay with me and eat goose — it was caught only yesterday. Then you may bring your blanket into

176

my cloth house, because it looks as if the rain it will start coming again.'

The following morning Will was served bread and wine, and assisted into a tunic that had once belonged to Robert de Beaumont. He followed closely behind Robert as they pushed their way through the throng that filled William's marquee. Eventually, they found themselves standing in front and slightly to the right of William's chair, and they turned to look back at the assembly.

In the front row were several well-dressed middle-aged men clad in the simple Saxon fashion, with plain tunics and dark hose. They carried no weapons, and Will had caught sight of them handing over swords and shields, so he assumed that these were the men who were surrendering. A herald called for order, and gradually the noise subsided.

'I am Robert de Beaumont, Count of Meulan, and I am speaking for my sovereign lord and master, Duke William of Normandy,' called Robert. 'He is happy to receive your submission to him being your new king, but my English is not good. This man in red is Wilfrid de Pevensey, and his English, it is better. So I will let him speak.'

Will was horrified at being placed in such a sensitive role without prior warning, but perhaps this was deliberate. He cleared his throat, prayed for inspiration, and began. 'You heard me introduced as "Wilfrid of Pevensey", which is the name that Duke William has graciously required me to adopt. But I was born Wilfrid Riveracre in a village called Sandlake, in the manor of Astenmede, near Pevensey. It was there that the forces of Duke William overran the fyrd of King Harold, of which I was a member. I faced the full might of his army, and I hope never to have to endure another such ordeal. We were soundly thrashed by superior arms, even though there were thousands of us, and I have since seen two sides to the man who conquered us. To those who accept his sovereignty he is merciful, even gallant and chivalrous, but to those who do not accept his military superiority he is the most ruthless and unforgiving man I have ever encountered. If you have come here to recognise what I have already accepted, there is only one way you can demonstrate that you pledge yourselves to his service, since the duke does not speak our language. That is by bowing the knee, which is what I urge you all to do now, if we are to avoid the most grievous shedding of noble Saxon blood.'

Two of the men in the front row exchanged glances and got down on one knee.

'As the more senior of us,' the older one announced as he looked Duke William in the eye, 'I, Edwin of Mercia, pledge my loyalty to my new liege Duke William of Normandy, in return for the title and continued possessions that I held under the former pretender to the English Crown, Harold Godwinson, Earl of Wessex.'

Robert said something to the duke, who beamed back at Edwin and waved his hand to indicate that he might rise. Morcar of Northumberland then mumbled precisely the same words, albeit with slightly less enthusiasm. Duke William beamed again, waved his hand for Morcar to rise, then raised an eyebrow as he called a single name in a loud and commanding voice.

'Edgar?'

A youth not yet in his twenties was led forward by a clergyman dressed in such finery that he must be at least a bishop, Will surmised. He was then startled to hear the youth admit to having been crowned King of England by mistake.

Edgar begged William's pardon for his insolence, borne only out of youthful ignorance, and with no offence intended.

The clergyman who had led the boy forward, who introduced himself as Ealdred, Archbishop of York, pleaded with William that if anyone was to suffer as the result of the recent presumptuous coronation, it must be himself, since he had been the one responsible for placing the crown on the boy's head. He offered to foreswear his holy office and retire to a monastery for the rest of his days, should William so desire, otherwise he was ready and willing to provide any holy office that might be required.

Robert translated. William replied briefly, and Robert smiled at Ealdred.

'Since you do coronations, you will do another in London soon, yes? My master, he would be crowned.'

Ealdred rose to his feet, raised his hand in the air, and pronounced a long stream of Latin that presumably meant more to William than it did to Will.

'The duke, he is pleased with you,' Robert told Will after the gathering, as they dined on cold goose and freshly baked bread. 'The English earls have been asked to remain in his company on the way to London, but you and I must go early tomorrow morning. William wishes to be crowned at the former king's palace.'

The next morning they set off shortly after daybreak, a body of men forty strong and armed to the teeth. As they moved slowly eastward, they came across increasingly larger villages, and in every one they halted for Will to impart the same message — that Duke William was on his way into London, that he intended to claim the crown of England, and that they should simply kneel at his passing, unless they wished to be put to the sword with their huts burned over their heads.

In the main the villagers took the news philosophically, confirming what Will had said to the men in Sandlake; it made no difference to the ordinary man and woman who was King of England, provided that he treated his people mercifully. But occasionally they would hear murmurs, sometimes oaths, and more than one mouthful of spittle hit the dusty ground when they heard what Will had to tell them.

By mid-afternoon they had been granted entry to West Minster Palace. It was as if a biblical plague had recently passed through. Former men-at-arms lounged listlessly against walls, their weapons hanging from disinterested hands. Serving girls sat shamelessly in the sun, their gowns hitched to their knees, calling out in seductive tones to the few armed men who displayed interest in them. Inside the Great Hall, the rushes on the floor reeked of neglect; the hangings on the walls dropped cobwebs; there was stale food on the tables, over which rats were scurrying; and the elderly steward who enquired about their business gave the distinct impression that he could not care less about their answer.

All this changed dramatically when Robert announced in his broken English that he had been sent by Duke William, and that if the palace was not suitably organised in readiness for his arrival in less than two days, the outer palisade would be festooned with hanged corpses. The steward ran out, calling for assistance. By the time the sun went down, the Great Hall been transformed into something approaching its former glory, and tapers were brought in to provide light. Fresh bread had been baked, and an entire roasted deer appeared from the kitchens, which they washed down with the finest Rhenish from the royal wine store.

Duke William arrived as predicted, and if he was aware of the considerable effort that had been made to render the palace habitable he said nothing, merely nodding and demanding to know where his chamber could be found. His priority seemed to be his forthcoming coronation, and the steward was ordered to ensure that a grand dinner would be prepared following the ceremony.

Robert and Will deemed it wise to check that the steward did what he was told, and that none of the food or wine for the banquet was being poisoned. They therefore missed the start of the coronation, which was conducted in the abbey on Christmas Day by a very relieved and obsequious Archbishop Ealdred.

The coronation had been proceeding smoothly, and Robert and Will's orders were to remain outside the abbey, guarding its entrance against any possible uprising by the Londoners. Then it occurred to Will that an expression of delight might be appropriate, and he passed among the throng gathered in the inner bailey, encouraging them to wave their hands in the air and proclaim loyalty to their new sovereign. Unfortunately they did so in Saxon, and the guards on duty at the palace doors misconstrued their shouts as those of rebellion, and ran amongst them with their swords. Robert and Will tried desperately to restrain them, but once the first few local corpses hit the ground, their relatives and friends began to fight back with crude weapons they had hidden in their roof thatches.

This was all the excuse the Norman men-at-arms required to set fire to the huts that were ranged inside the palisade and were occupied by those who laboured in the palace. But they had failed to account for a strong westerly breeze, and embers began drifting towards the wooden abbey. In panic, the man commanding the Norman troops ran into the abbey, interrupting the coronation and calling out that the abbey would shortly be engulfed in flame. An irate William ordered Archbishop Ealdred to get on with it, but to go a little more quickly, and fortunately the terrified clergyman had enough French to know what '*plus rapidement*' meant.

A few minutes later William stormed out of the abbey, quivering with rage, and his eyes lit upon Will, standing to the side of the entrance and covered in soot after his success in supervising the dousing of the flames. William strode up to him, grabbed him by the collar and began screaming at him in French, some of which Will was able to comprehend. He thought it best to bow his head and look suitably chastened, even though he burned with indignation at the injustice.

XVI

For the next few weeks, Will kept as far away from the newly crowned King William as possible. He stayed in the hut that had once belonged to the royal armourer, which he shared with several middle-ranking warriors in the service of Robert de Beaumont. Robert himself left him in peace; he was always the one chosen to stand by William's side during various ceremonies that took place in the Great Hall as the new year of 1067 progressed into early spring.

Will's thoughts dwelled on the loving wife and beautiful daughter he had left behind in Sandlake. He was all but convinced that the time had come to discreetly leave West Minster when he was approached by a familiar face early one morning, as he was supervising his horse's feed in the stables.

'You're the young man from Sandlake, aren't you?' his visitor asked. 'You were there when my brother and I paid homage to our new king.'

Suddenly, Will remembered: this was Earl Edwin of Mercia. 'Yes, and it is high time that I returned,' he replied.

'And Sandlake lies within the manor estate of Astenmede, does it not?'

'It does indeed,' Will confirmed.

'My reason for asking,' Earl Edwin went on, 'was to enquire after the fortunes of a young man from Astenmede who fought bravely with us at Stamford Bridge, when we took the field against Harald Hardrada. His name was Selwyn. Did he survive the fighting at Pevensey?'

'He did indeed,' Will replied, 'and he is now married to my sister.'

Edwin's face broke into a wide smile. 'He was a brave man — and no doubt still is. I would have him in my service, since our new king has confirmed me in my Mercia estates, while also confirming my brother Morcar in his.' He lowered his voice. 'Despite what we see around us, I do not believe that the nation will remain at peace. Morcar confides in me that the people of Northumbria are warlike and argumentative at the best of times, and even he has trouble preserving the peace. When they learn that their new king speaks no English, and has so far done nothing but burn Saxon villages, they will be eager to take up arms against him — particularly since he has announced his intention of returning to Normandy once the spring gales have subsided.'

'And the people of Mercia?' Will asked.

'They are likely to react in the same way, which is why I would be reunited with your sister's husband. You would be welcome yourself, of course — you have family?'

'A wife and daughter,' Will told him.

'You would all be very welcome in my earldom. Give Selwyn my regards, and tell him that I would value his sword arm at my side in these uncertain times.'

'I will, and gladly,' Will confirmed, 'but he may well be required back home. When young Edgar was falsely crowned, he raised Selwyn's father to the Earldom of Wessex, and I don't recall hearing King William saying anything about changing that.'

Edwin frowned. 'You should have attended more frequently at William's side than you have of late. He plans to return to Normandy, as I mentioned, taking some of us with him, and in his absence he has left the governance of England in the hands of two men. The first is his half-brother, the murderous priest Odo of Bayeux, who has been made Earl of Essex. The other is one of his most trusted followers, William FitzOsbern, who has become Earl of Hereford and Wessex.'

'So Earl Leofric is not confirmed in his estates?'

'Indeed not, but it bodes even worse for him, should he not concede immediately. William is aware that much of the west remains outside his control, and there are rumours that the Welsh are preparing to take this opportunity to settle old scores. I have been ordered by William to strengthen my own borders in anticipation of this, and FitzOsbern has been given the task of holding down any sign of rebellion to the west of Wallingford. If Selwyn's father does not bend the knee and bow the head at the first signs of FitzOsbern's approach, his head will be spiked for public display. Is he likely to surrender meekly?'

'*He* may well be prepared to do so, since he is past his best years and too fond of his pleasures. But his wife is another prospect altogether, and she has a mouth that would scald metal and strip it of rust. She will be bound to bring about her own death, unless I can persuade her otherwise.'

'Then you must do so without delay,' Edwin told him, 'since William heads for Dover by the end of the week.'

It was a sweet homecoming for Will. Climbing wearily from his horse's back, he caught sight of Joan, standing at the entrance to Selwyn and Elva's hut, Matilda in her arms and tears rolling down her face. She held their daughter up to him, then laughed as he reached out and pulled her face gently towards him for a long-anticipated kiss.

Next to welcome him was Elva and her new son, Elston, and then he was almost bowled over by Rowena, who hugged him and cried. Finally, Eldred stepped forward and shook his hand.

'We heard that William has returned to Normandy,' he said gruffly. 'Does this mean that he has given up with England?'

'Far from it, Father,' Will told him. 'He will return, and has taken the Earls Edwin and Morcar with him as hostages to England's good behaviour. Also poor young Edgar, who was briefly king, and Stigand, Archbishop of Canterbury, along with the Earl of Huntingdon and Northampton, a man called Waltheof. All the earls have surrendered to William, and been confirmed in their lands and titles.'

'And the Earl of Wessex?' asked a friendly voice behind him.

Will turned to shake Selwyn's hand. 'I am glad you are here, Selwyn, since you may now advise your father that he is no longer Earl of Wessex. That honour has been bestowed on a man named FitzOsbern, who is one of two who will govern the nation in William's name in his absence.'

'My father will no doubt be relieved,' Selwyn replied, then winked as he added, 'although my mother will not be so content with that news.'

'How are they both?' Will asked.

'My father grows fatter, despite insisting on exercising with what passes for the fyrd, which Deman is keeping in good shape. As for Mother, she continues to insist that Father do more to assert his authority in Winchester — hopefully she will now desist, although I doubt it.'

'And the village?' Will asked.

'The summer planting's completed,' Eldred told him, 'and we have enough grain left from the last harvest to ensure bread until the next. The animals are fattening nicely on the new spring shoots, and there's still a plentiful supply of salted pig, so come in and get some food and drink.'

An hour later, Will sat back from the crude table and gave a sigh of satisfaction. 'For all the rich food that I tasted at West

Minster, Mother's bread and pickled meat, washed down with Gwenyth's mead, is still the best meal. But now, if Elva would have Matilda for a short while, I want to take Joan for a walk down the mill track. We have much to decide.'

'They probably think you're taking me for a quick embrace in the mill,' Joan grinned up at him as they neared the building in question.

'Now *there's* a good idea,' Will replied as he held out his hand to assist her onto the platform.

As Joan breathlessly lay on her back ten minutes later, her eyes glowing with satisfaction, she looked up at him. 'I really missed that while you were away,' she said. 'I hope you weren't rolling in the stables with serving girls at the palace.'

'I only ever did that with one,' Will teased, 'and look where that got me. A married man with a child.'

'*Two*, if I have my way,' Joan giggled, then her face grew more serious. 'You *did* have something to talk about with me, didn't you?'

Will told her of Earl Edwin's proposition, and they agreed to leave Sandlake together when the time came.

A few weeks later, an ominous silence fell as a heavily armed knight dismounted from his courser and haughtily surveyed the Sandlake villagers who had risen early to till their crops before the sun rose too high.

With his hand on his sword hilt, he asked in broken English, 'Who speaks French?'

One of the men at the rear of the group slipped away to fetch Will, who hurried down the track to confront the French man-at-arms. Selwyn joined him.

'I speak some French,' Will addressed the man in his own language.

'I'm pleased that someone does, although soon everyone will,' the man replied. 'I am Gilles de Feauville, emissary of Earl FitzOsbern of Hereford and Wessex, Regent for King William while he is in Normandy. I wish to find the man who has been unwise enough to persist with the building of that straw house on the ridge behind the hill.'

'Tell your father to stay well hidden,' Will whispered hoarsely to Selwyn, who began to slowly back away. Will tried to occupy de Feauville's full attention. 'The man you seek is not here, but I can give him a message.'

'An invitation, rather,' the man replied sourly. 'He is invited to come and watch his pathetic attempt at house-building being burned to the ground. Then he is invited to lose his head if he attempts to rebuild it.'

'I will pass on both messages,' Will assured the knight.

'Your face is familiar, I think. You were in the train of Robert de Beaumont?'

'I was,' Will confirmed, 'but I was mainly in the train of King William, to advise the conquered people of England that resistance is useless. Since the king is no longer in England, he does not require my services, and I have returned home.'

'You live in this pigsty of a place? God help you.' And with that, the knight turned to leave.

'Well, what are you going to do about it?' Earlene demanded of Leofric an hour later, as Selwyn and Will broke the news.

'What do you suggest?' Leofric asked sarcastically. 'I can go and watch it burn, or I can rebuild it and lose my head. Which would you prefer?'

'This would not be happening if you had more influence with the new king,' Earlene insisted.

Selwyn voiced his thoughts. 'This may not be the last indignity inflicted on the family, or for that matter the village. Without Will being present to speak to the man in his own language, things might have got a whole lot uglier.'

'Are you telling me I can't leave?' Will demanded.

Selwyn shrugged. 'I'm just suggesting that the village will be more exposed if you leave us.'

'Joan and I will not be more than a week's ride away,' Will argued, 'and when King William returns, I can intercede on your behalf should he make any threat towards Sandlake.'

'Or Astenmede?' Earlene asked.

'He's already done the worst he can to Astenmede, and you should regard yourselves as villagers of Sandlake from now on. It's a big climb down from where you once were, but times are changing rapidly.'

Selwyn was not the only villager to express concern about Will's intention to leave the village with his family and head for Tamworth, the capital of Edwin's earldom. However, they reluctantly came to accept it, and were determined to make amends for the way they had once treated him. One morning, as Will was outside the hut collecting kindling for the fire, he looked up at the sound of half a dozen men manhandling a large cart through the summer ruts in the hard baked earth. They stopped at his hut entrance, and looked embarrassed until one of them broke the silence.

'We thought you might need this, Will. We built it ourselves from timber taken from Caldbec Wood, and the wheels are from a wagon abandoned by the Normans on the beach.'

Deman Flesher appeared from around the back of Will's hut with a fully saddled warhorse. 'That wasn't all that the Normans left, Will. I found this wandering up by Powdermill Lake while I was fishing, and it seemed content to let me ride it home. As you can see, it's still fitted with one of those fancy seats that the Normans use.'

Will was overcome with emotion, wondering how he could possibly thank his fellow villagers for their generosity. Then he heard Joan's voice from the entrance to their hut, where she stood holding Matilda.

'You are all very kind, but if I may speak for my husband, does this mean that you do not resent us leaving?'

'Resentment doesn't come into it,' Deman replied on behalf of the rest. 'We shall sorely miss Will Riveracre — and his wife and child, of course — but he has promised to return should we need him. In the meantime I'll do what I can to replace him at the head of the fyrd, along with Selwyn. But we once treated him very poorly, and this is our way of apologising. God speed you all, and don't forget where your home is.'

XVII

Since she had been born in Tamworth, Joan was doing her best to guide Will on their journey there. However, this was proving difficult. They were into their third week on the road and had eaten everything they'd brought with them. They had no money, and for the past three days they had been relying on Will's ability to trap food.

'There's a church of some sort coming up,' Will observed as he stood in the stirrups and squinted into the sunset. 'To judge by the sun, it's a mile or so to the north and west. Perhaps we can at least find out where we are.'

The 'church' turned out to be a monastery, whose kindly abbot took pity on the weary-looking family of three, offered them accommodation in the *hospitium*, found some goat's milk for Matilda, and arranged for the hospitaller Brother Simon to feed them a bowl of soup and some bread. Refreshed, they fell asleep gratefully in the rushes, and were awakened by the Lauds bell just as the sun was rising.

Abbott Benedict asked where they were headed.

'Tamworth,' Will told him. 'Do you by any chance know the track to follow?'

The elderly monk thought for a moment. 'If you continue on this same track for three or four more days, you will come to a large village called "Lichfield". Beyond that, I cannot tell you.'

'I've heard of Lichfield!' Joan blurted excitedly. 'I've even been there! My Aunt Wilda came from there, and we often went there for family visits. I haven't been back there since I was about eleven years old, but I remember that the journey to there from Tamworth only took two days or so. I seem to recall that the road was a straight one.'

Relying on that simple childhood memory they headed north, and in the late evening of the third day they were being welcomed into a large hut in Lichfield that belonged to one of Joan's older cousins, Boden, who remembered her. His original trade as a woodworker had been passed down to two of his sons, Camden and Morton, who were never without work in the rapidly expanding community.

Boden had kept in touch with other branches of the family, and from him Joan learned that her mother had died while living with Joan's older sister Kendra and her husband, who had four children. Fortunately, Morton Merriweather had ambitions to work as a house builder in Tamworth, and when he learned that Will had actually met with Earl Edwin, he offered to build him and Joan a house there for nothing. Will would just need to find the land and materials, and contribute his own manual labour.

They were given detailed directions to the brewhouse in Tamworth run by Kendra and her husband Lucan. Two days later, the sisters were reunited, and they clung to each other with tears in their eyes. While they talked, Will and Lucan sat in the shade of the overhanging brewhouse roof, drinking some of Lucan's ale.

'Is it true that you once met Earl Edwin?' Lucan asked, highly impressed. 'My reason for asking is that I now have enough barrelage to be able to supply his garrison with ale. If I could get the regular business, I could increase the size of my enterprise. Would you be able to speak with the earl for me?'

Will laughed lightly and shook his head. 'I have met the man but once, and I was helping King William to speak with English people, mainly in an effort to prevent them being slaughtered. Other than that, I could provide you with no introduction.'

'It's still better than nothing,' Lucan replied, as Kendra called them in for the evening meal.

For the next few months, as the summer of 1067 merged into autumn, Will was happily engaged in restoring himself to the level of fitness he had previously enjoyed as a soldier in the Wessex Fyrd, while helping Joan's cousin Morton to build them a spacious hut on the southern outskirts of Tamworth. It was almost complete when Will turned up for work one morning and found Morton talking with an unfamiliar man. Morton looked down uncomfortably before opening the conversation.

'Will, this is Delbert Thatcher, and he can continue the work if you would agree to hand him up the yelms. He has already been paid for his services, so you need not concern yourself over that. But I have a very important new client, and the finest opportunity I will ever have of becoming known in this town for my woodworking skills.'

'Don't worry, Morton — I have more than enough cause to be grateful for your generosity so far, and I am happy to complete the work alongside Delbert. But tell me, what is this new venture that has got you so excited?'

Morton puffed out his chest with pride. 'Earl Edwin will be returning within the month, and has sent word ahead that he requires a new fortress to replace his old manor house. Men have already been sent to supervise the digging of a huge ditch to surround a massive earth pile in the centre. A two-level keep will be built on top of that, which will act as his hall as well as his main defensive position. I am told that the system is Norman, and the man who sought me out to do the work is one of the earl's retainers. He has chosen me because I am already being spoken of as the best woodworker in Tamworth! And that's all because of you!'

'No it's not,' Will chuckled modestly. 'It's because you have a well-deserved reputation. But are you saying that Earl Edwin is back in England?'

'He must be, I suppose. If that's so, then we may expect to see him once his new "castle" is ready for his occupation.'

They in fact saw him much sooner than that. Lucan and Will were enjoying the cool of an early October evening when a cloud of dust and an increasingly loud noise announced the appearance of a large body of horsemen from the south. First into view was a line of four heavily armoured mounted knights, two of them holding pennants aloft. The first depicted two gold lions on a field of crimson, declaring the presence — or at least the authority — of William of Normandy, while the second was less familiar. It was a simple yellow diagonal cross on a field of blue, and Will would soon come to know it as the traditional battle standard of the Earl of Mercia.

There were several more lines of horsemen, and in their centre rode Edwin himself, much thinner in the face than when Will had first met him. In the rank immediately behind him, armed to the teeth and all but hidden under a Norman helm, was a face that Will had last seen outside his hut in Sandlake, and he gave a loud shout of recognition.

Selwyn looked in his direction, and their eyes met. Then he gave a cry of his own, said something to the man next to him, and nudged his horse out of the procession as it wound its way on into the town centre. When still a few yards short of where Will had risen to welcome him, Selwyn slid from his horse and closed the gap, throwing his arms around Will and yelling in sheer delight.

'Come inside and enjoy a mug of ale,' said Will. 'Then tell me how on earth you finished up here.'

After Selwyn had been introduced to Joan's family, he reported back for duty at Edwin's grand manor house in the centre of Tamworth, only to be told, along with the vast majority of the earl's other seconds in command, that they would need to find temporary lodgings among the townsfolk, for which Edwin would pay while his new castle was constructed. Will and Joan were happy to accommodate Selwyn in their newly completed hut on the south road, and after a hearty supper, the two men sat down outside, warmly wrapped against the chill.

'The time has finally arrived for some explanations, Selwyn,' Will said. 'How do you come to be in Tamworth, serving Earl Edwin? The last I recall, you were about to be recruited at the head of the Sandlake Fyrd to fight for Earl FitzOsbern.'

'Indeed I was, and indeed we did,' Selwyn nodded. 'Myself and Deman, plus a score or so of our men. We were set to defend the walls of Winchester, while FitzOsbern planned to march north to defend his new castle at Hereford. Then came the news that the castle was safe, but that the town itself had been looted, and the Welsh were moving south behind their own lines along the border. Rumour was that they were heading for a place called Exeter, and FitzOsbern decided to head them off, rather than return to Hereford.'

'And where was Edwin while all this was going on?' Will asked.

'Still in Normandy, it would seem. But he was getting restless, and increasingly annoyed as William continued to delay the promised marriage of Edwin to one of William's daughters. When news came that FitzOsbern did not intend to march to the defence of Hereford, Edwin demanded to be allowed to return in order to do so, making his point that the town lies within the old boundaries of Mercia, and that if William had not given Hereford to FitzOsbern, it would never have suffered at the hands of the Welsh.'

Will chuckled. 'Edwin must be either wrong in the head or so angry that he no longer cares.'

'William is much preoccupied with uprisings in his native Normandy. According to Edwin, William didn't enjoy his first stay in England — particularly the food and the weather — and he would prefer that others govern it for him, merely passing on the plunder. For this reason he was prepared to let Edwin return, along with his brother Morcar, who is headed north to command it in William's name, along with a man called Gospatric, who has purchased everything north of York from William. He is now Earl of Bernicia, which lies between York and the border with the Scots.'

'So what happened to bring you back into Edwin's service?' Will persisted.

'When Edwin returned, he decided to visit FitzOsbern, in an effort to agree between them which of them was to march on Hereford. They do not like each other, and seemingly never did, and in the garrison we heard tales of one screaming argument after another. In the end Edwin announced his intention of marching north whether FitzOsbern approved or not, and by then he had discovered me, in charge of the east gate defences of Winchester. Since I was by his side when we fought the Norsemen, he insisted that I be drafted into his retinue, and FitzOsbern agreed.'

'I had already been asked by Edwin to send you to him at West Minster, but I remained silent because I deemed it more important that you organise the defence of Sandlake in my absence. But FitzOsbern surely undervalued you as a warrior, to let you leave like that?'

'He undervalued the entire Sandlake Fyrd by that stage.'

'So you journeyed north in Edwin's retinue? Were you able to return home before coming here?'

'Edwin proved very generous,' Selwyn said. 'He allowed me a week to return home, let Elva know where I was bound, and make arrangements for her to come and join me once we had reached the safety of Tamworth.'

'What news of your parents?'

Selwyn's face clouded. 'An ague swept through the village, not long after you left. It was still summer, so no-one was expecting it, but it took Mother — and Widow Gwenyth, God bless both their souls. My father took it badly, and stopped eating or drinking, which was almost unheard of for him. I knew nothing until my brief visit home, obviously, so I wasn't able to bury Mother or look after Father. But Elva took care of everything. Father lives with her and Elston now, and your parents have kindly offered to look after him when Elva comes to Mercia to be with me. Your father caught the ague, but survived it, tough old bird that he is. He's still working the mill, with a couple of local boys to help with the heavy work. Your mother's fine, by the way, and told me to give you all her love if I ever caught up with you.'

'At least your father will keep out of trouble, now that your mother's not there to urge him into defying King William, so that's one consolation,' Will observed.

Selwyn smiled. 'But I may be destined to keep up the family tradition, it seems. Once or twice on our way up here, Edwin was asking me questions intended to test my loyalty to the new Norman rulers. Given his annoyance with William, and his near hatred of FitzOsbern, I wonder if he's planning some sort of uprising. If so, I'll be at the forefront of it, and what will become of my life then? The sooner I get Elva and Elston up here, the better.'

'You can borrow my cart,' Will offered. 'And the horse, too, if you need it. Don't waste any more time — head back to Sandlake and get them both, before Edwin has you on the march again.'

'And what about you, Will? What do you intend to do for your livelihood?'

'I hadn't really given it much thought — perhaps labouring for Morton in his busy house-building business. Or for Lucan, shovelling barley into the tuns.'

'Given any thought to becoming a soldier again?' Selwyn asked. 'I have no doubt that Edwin would afford you a position of some authority within his army.'

Will shook his head. 'I've seen enough of soldiering. And I certainly want nothing to do with the new Norman way of governing the nation's affairs, which seems to consist of little more than cutting off heads. If anything, I'd be inclined to take up arms again in order to prevent it.'

'I have a horrible feeling that the day is not far away when you'll be called upon to do just that,' Selwyn replied glumly.

XVIII

Elva and Elston finally arrived in Tamworth the following spring. She brought all the news from Sandlake: Deman and Annis were expecting their third child; the last harvest had proved adequate for the winter, and they had experienced no further harassment from Winchester, mainly because FitzOsbern had been laying siege to Exeter, where the wild Welshmen had been holding out.

But the main news was that as Elva and Selwyn had travelled north over the Thames at Wallingford, the locals they had encountered were recounting recent memories of a massive army that had ridden westwards, headed by King William himself. Selwyn had therefore lost no time in taking Elva and Elston north, in the belief that the return of William to England would be valuable news for Earl Edwin.

A week after his return, Selwyn took Will by the arm and led him outside with a worried expression. 'Did you mean what you said about standing against King William if he continued his policy of slaughter?' he asked in an urgent voice.

'Of course,' Will confirmed, 'but why do you ask?'

'A messenger arrived for Earl Edwin today, and he summoned his seconds to hear the news repeated. William's first act upon his return was to attack Exeter, which FitzOsbern had been trying to take with minimum loss of life. It seems that William blasted through the place like a March gale, slaughtering every person he could find. There is said to be barely a soul left alive, yet those who were really responsible for the defiant stand against FitzOsbern were able to escape to the west as soon as William's force was seen approaching from the east. Apparently William's anger was terrifying to behold, particularly when he was told that one of those who had escaped was the former King Harold's mother, an old lady called Gytha. Apparently he had intended to have her burned alive as a witch.'

Will shuddered. 'Where is William now?'

'According to the messenger, who is a deserter from William's English force who couldn't bear to witness any more, William has sworn to ride north and make an example of any town in Mercia that shows the slightest sign of resistance. He is ordering the building of castles wherever he goes, and Exeter already has one nearly completed. He remained there long enough to see it started, then fell back on Winchester, where his woman Matilda was crowned Queen of England. The next place he was heading to was Warwick, which he intends to place under the command of Henry de Beaumont. Did you not have dealings with him when you first left Sandlake?'

'No, that was *Robert* de Beaumont. But he had a son called Henry — a youth barely out of his teenage years. But is Warwick not within Mercia anyway? Why is he giving command of that town to a de Beaumont, and not Earl Edwin?'

'It is said that he no longer trusts Englishmen to govern in his absence, and that Normans are to be installed wherever he builds these new castles.'

'And what does Edwin say to that?' Will asked.

'He is not pleased, and is determined to prove that north of London he can govern the nation far more effectively than any Norman incomer.'

'And more mercifully, no doubt,' Will replied ruefully. 'So how long will you be with us this time?'

'We've been told to prepare to leave within the week. I think we go to Hereford first, then Edwin plans to travel to York, to meet with his brother Morcar. From little bits of conversation I've heard, it seems that the people up there are threatening trouble.'

'That will be all the excuse William needs,' Will muttered. 'At least I'll still be here to provide protection for our families if William comes north, determined to prove his point.'

It fell silent for a moment, then Selwyn looked Will firmly in the eye. 'Edwin is seeking more men to enter his service, to guard Tamworth while he's away. If you have no better plan, may I take you to him as a volunteer?'

'I haven't wielded a sword since we took to the ridge against William,' Will pointed out, 'and I'm not sure how good my shoulder will prove to be. That said, I've had no problem labouring for Morton and Lucan. If it comes to that, how is your leg these days?'

'As long as I'm on horseback, it's not a handicap. However, if I'm ever unhorsed it might be a different tale. But don't avoid my question — will you volunteer to remain here as part of the town defences?'

Will nodded, but with some hesitation. 'If I'm defending the town, then I'm defending both our families as well. But our hut on the south road is too vulnerable to any approaching force, so I may have to seek leave to withdraw them within this new castle that Edwin is building.'

'I'm sure he'd agree to that,' Selwyn assured him.

The next morning, Selwyn took Will to see Edwin, offering his services as a soldier. Edwin accepted immediately. 'Consider yourself appointed. Selwyn here will see to your weapons and armour, and he'll arrange for you to be given a horse, which will then be your responsibility. You will be given duties at the south gate, where we expect the main threat will come from.'

'Surely, the Welsh lie to our west?' Will queried.

Edwin grimaced. 'Who said aught about the Welsh? If he keeps true to form, our greatest threat will come from the Norman who has set himself up as our new king. We ride north within the week, to join my brother Morcar at York. William will no doubt come through here, on his passage through the nation building castles, and will not be pleased to discover that I have built one of my own without his leave. You will need to pacify him, as you have shown yourself capable of doing in the past. Will he remember you, do you think?'

'It is to be hoped that he will,' Will replied, 'if we are to keep Tamworth safe.'

Selwyn was reminded of the magnificence of York. Less than two years previously he had stood on its walls with the brothers Edwin and Morcar as they made plans to resist the invasion of Harald Hardrada. Later, he had ridden out at the side of King Harold Godwinson to drive the Norsemen away. Now he was back, and little seemed to have changed.

He was once again in the presence of the two brothers, as part of a select bodyguard that Edwin had brought with him to this meeting in Morcar's large manor house. But this time there was a third man present, who had been introduced by Morcar as Gospatric, Earl of Bernicia to the north. He had been appointed by William to govern the remaining land between York and the border with Scotland, and he was bringing them up to date with the information he had recently received.

'The Norman was unwise to leave Edgar Aetheling so imperfectly guarded when he returned here from Normandy,'

Gospatric was explaining. 'Rumour is that Edgar escaped, and travelled to Scotland, where he is currently at the court of King Malcolm. Malcolm has ever coveted the land to his south, and we are reinforcing our defences at Bamburgh against a possible incursion on the flimsy pretext that Edgar is the rightful King of England.'

'So he is, to many in this town,' Morcar muttered, 'and who is to say that we would not be better offering our forces to Malcolm, in order to show William that while he may strut around in London and Winchester, he would not be well advised to push his luck anywhere north of Lincoln?'

Edwin looked nervously round at his bodyguards, some of whom — including Selwyn — appeared shocked by what they had just heard.

'You heard nothing of that, understand?' Edwin demanded, and his men shook their heads in unison as Edwin turned back to address his fellow earls. 'It would be too early to show our hands. Rather let the arrogant Norman butcher display his true nature, then the people will rise up even without our leadership. What is the popular feeling further north, Gospatric?'

The burly Northumbrian shrugged. 'The men of villages such as Alnwick and Berwick regard themselves as Scots anyway, and would need little persuasion to send *any* English king away, let alone one who speaks a foreign language and by all accounts treats ordinary folk with less kindness than his horse.'

'So they would rise against William if commanded?' Morcar asked.

Gospatric gave a savage leer. 'Even *without* command, if pushed too far.'

Will was thankful that he had brought Joan, Matilda and Elva within the keep of Tamworth Castle when advised by a breathless and slightly apprehensive Joan that she was with child again. His first euphoric reaction was almost immediately tempered by the fact that the child would be born during the most uncertain times he had ever experienced.

'When is it likely to be born, do you think?' he asked as he held her in his arms in the cramped quarters they had all been allocated, just inside the wall of the inner bailey.

'Probably around Christmas,' she replied. 'You *will* still be here, won't you, and not marching around the country behind Earl Edwin?'

'That's Selwyn's job,' Will reminded her as he kissed the tip of her nose. 'I deliberately chose to remain here to guard the town, since then I can also guard you and the rest of the family.'

'Is it true that King William is marching on Tamworth?' she asked fearfully. 'And that he slaughtered everyone in Exeter?'

'I'm not sure where he is now. But by all accounts Exeter suffered because it resisted his advance. Here in Tamworth I have strict orders to welcome him into the town, and to afford him all respect and obedience.'

Will awoke from a restless sleep to hear horsemen cantering into the keep past the south gate. He dressed hastily and walked outside to where King William was yelling in French to a bewildered Brodic Wilbond, temporary Captain of the Guard. William was interspersing his yells with furious hand gestures towards a serene-looking lady in her mid-thirties. She sat sideways on a white palfrey, accompanied by Ealdred, Archbishop of York. William was red in the face by the time that Will walked over and addressed him in French.

'May I be of assistance, sire?'

William glared down at him briefly, then his face softened. 'I remember you. Since you're here, although God knows why, would you advise this peasant how to properly treat the Queen of England? Matilda of Flanders is accustomed to being assisted from her horse even in ordinary circumstances, but she is currently expecting our child.'

'If you would allow me, sire?'

William nodded, and Will walked to the side of the horse from which the Queen's legs were protruding and held out both his hands. She slid daintily to the ground as Will steadied her descent. She thanked him quietly in her native language, and looked back expectantly towards William, who gave orders for the best suite of rooms in the castle to be made available. Will translated for Brodic's benefit. Brodic yelled instructions back to the main door of the inner keep, and a handful of servants ran forward, bowing and scraping as they indicated the way.

William had dismounted, and he turned back towards Will before following Matilda into the keep. 'Since you have once again proved your value to me, remain by my side while I organise these peasants.'

Will, Joan, Matilda, Elva and Elston were obliged to give up their accommodation inside the keep, and they returned to the house on the south road. Joan's first months of her second pregnancy were proving to be uncomfortable ones, with much vomiting and backache. King William required Will constantly by his side. As well as continually criticising the living conditions that he and his queen were expected to tolerate, he demanded more than once to know by whose authority Edwin had set about the construction of the keep, and why the earl had not been there to welcome him on the royal progress following Matilda's coronation.

Will did his best to stem the royal wrath by pretending that Edwin had ordered the construction of the moat, earthworks and keep in the Norman style in order to keep the new king's Mercian capital safe against the marauding Welsh, and that Edwin had marched north in order to assess the mood in the more isolated parts of the kingdom. Whether William was convinced by these explanations or not, he clearly intended to do things his own way. Will's heart fell to his boots when he was ordered by the king to make arrangements for an early departure from Tamworth with all his retinue, including Will himself.

'My wife is expecting another child,' Will offered by way of excuse, which William waved away with an impatient hand gesture.

'So is mine, but she is required to travel on horseback, whereas yours will enjoy the comfort of your home, wherever that may be. We march north in two days' time, and I expect you to show your loyalty.'

Will bowed his head and said a silent prayer, wondering what lay ahead.

XIX

A week later, the royal procession approached the market town of Snottingham from the south.

'That's a fine defensive rock on which to build a castle,' William observed over his shoulder to the second horse-borne rank behind him, which contained Will and several of his closest entourage. Five rows behind, and in the centre of a tight group of armed men, rode Queen Matilda in a litter, accompanied by two of her ladies. Archbishop Ealdred, as usual, trotted alongside on a pony.

'It also has a fine broad river in front of it,' the king continued, 'and would therefore only be vulnerable from the north and east. There seems to be some sort of township to the east — if we burn that down, we could erect walls, and that would leave just the north.'

'It might be more advantageous to employ the local people as labourers for the construction of the castle,' Will observed as casually as he could, hoping not to have to witness mass bloodshed.

'Wilfrid, you are right,' William conceded. 'Seek labourers from among the peasants, then recruit the best of them for a castle guard. Those who refuse can be put to the sword, and their hovels burned to the ground.'

They were a week in Snottingham, mainly because Queen Matilda seemed to take a liking to the place, with its wooded valleys and clean water. Then it was back onto the track that led through hillier country, where colder winds blew from the east as the autumn bore down on them.

Next, they passed through Lincoln. There they were joined by the Earl of Huntingdon, a man named Waltheof Siwardson, who seemed to be highly favoured by William. The earl ate at the table reserved for the king's closest advisers, and chatted happily in French. Waltheof had taken the trouble to learn the language while he had been exiled in France, along with the other leading English earls. Will overheard snippets of loud conversation, and learned that Waltheof was to become betrothed to William's niece, Judith of Lens.

Will's language skills were, however, sorely tested the further north they rode, as they encountered more local dialects among the country people of Yorkshire. Will had resumed his former cautionary habit of riding ahead whenever they approached a settlement of any size, urging the inhabitants to their knees. It took Will some time to decipher what they said to him in reply, and it was not always polite, but they seemed capable of understanding him.

Selwyn's terror grew as news of the royal progress travelled north. In York, for the last two weeks Edwin, Morcar and Gospatric had been playing host to Edgar Aetheling, who was now into his manhood and had repaid William's clemency poorly.

Edgar had travelled to Scotland via Denmark, and had been brought south in secret by Earl Gospatric of Bernicia with plans to invade England from the north, taking advantage of York's distance from London and the fact that everything north of Lincoln had once been firmly under Danish rule. As the most important town in the old 'Danelaw', York had a long tradition of resistance to even Saxon rule, and could hardly be expected to welcome an invader from Normandy. King Malcolm of Scotland could also be relied upon to take this unique opportunity to strike south against his old enemy, whoever their king might be, and a large resistance group was rapidly forming against the Norman usurper.

Selwyn had inevitably become aware of the plotting as he stood guard at the conspirators' meetings, and he feared for the entire region if William got wind of it. He was also concerned for his own life, given his position as a leading warrior in the retinue of one of those heading the planned rebellion. He was therefore relieved when Gospatric and Edgar slid silently back north, once the advance scouts of King William's approaching army rode through the south gate and began commandeering houses for the accommodation of the several hundred Normans.

As part of Edwin's immediate entourage, Selwyn was standing smartly in line behind his leader as King William swept into the central marketplace on his mud-spattered courser, and remained aloofly in the saddle as Edwin and Morcar stepped forward and knelt. William's first command was for the best house in the town to be made ready to receive his queen, and while he was preoccupied in inspecting those that were suggested, Selwyn smiled across at Will as he accompanied the king. Will grinned back in acknowledgement.

It was several hours later before the two men could sidle casually up to each other in the great hall that their respective commanders had selected for the reunion banquet.

'I am meant to be dining at that table to the side,' Will explained to Selwyn in a hoarse whisper, 'in case the king requires me to translate into English for him. But our family is safe — or at least, they were when I left Tamworth, bringing the main danger with me.'

Selwyn laughed. 'You had best not let the king hear those words. But in truth, you may have walked into the greatest danger you could have imagined.'

'Your meaning?'

'Not now,' Selwyn insisted. 'Meet me by the royal stables at daybreak. They are the ones to the side of the old cathedral, and one of Edwin's grooms will have taken your mount there. Mine is there also, and we can pretend that we are merely catching up on family matters while seeing to the grooming of our mounts.'

Just then, Will heard William calling for him to take his seat at the banquet. He was surprised to find himself seated next to Waltheof of Huntingdon.

'It is good to be eating under a proper roof, and to be fed real meat for a change,' Waltheof remarked. 'Who was that you were speaking with? He seemed to be wearing the emblem of Mercia on his tunic.'

'He's my sister's man,' Will explained, surprised that Waltheof should be interested in his choice of companion. 'I was in Tamworth when King William came north, and since I have in the past been of service to him in the matter of English, he insisted that I join his progress north.'

'And do you approve of William's methods?' Waltheof asked quietly. Will looked at him sideways, and Waltheof hastened to reassure him. 'You may speak your mind, without fear that your words will be reported.'

Will still felt it safer to be circumspect. 'It is a source of some concern to me that William seems to feel that the only way into the hearts of his new subjects is on the point of a sword. I would assist him in becoming a ruler who enjoys the loyalty of all his new subjects, but perhaps a little more in the way of kindness and generosity might achieve that more swiftly. Or so

I sometimes try to advise him, but I am no statesman. I fear for my own head, should I be too outspoken.'

'You need have no fear of confiding your advice to me first,' Waltheof said, 'and perhaps I can prevail upon William to listen. Although since I have this evening been consigned to a lower table, perhaps my influence over him is on the wane.'

'His current interest is here in the north,' Will reminded him, 'so perhaps it is appropriate that seated closest to him is the Earl of Northumbria, with his brother on the other side. Between them they govern most of England.'

'But not the lands to the east,' Waltheof insisted with a grimace. 'If William wishes to build castles wherever his foot leaves the stirrup, then he will no doubt consent to my constructing a few in East Anglia. That's everywhere east of Lincoln. You have perhaps heard of Peterborough and Cambridge? Or perhaps Huntingdon?'

'Huntingdon certainly,' Will confirmed, 'since it is the place of which you are earl. What are your lands like?'

'Very flat and windswept, with marshes and bogs. Also, as you move towards the ocean, of which there is much bordering my realm, the land becomes salty, and will not yield any grain crop. Even such grain that will grow is often flattened by the winds that howl in from the east.'

'It is as well for me that I was born on the south coast,' Will said.

'Where William first invaded?' Waltheof asked.

'*Exactly* where William first landed. My home village was right in his path, and our two armies met on the ridge above us. I commanded the local fyrd, with my friend over there. We were both in King Harold's main force. We were both wounded, but not before we had accounted for several Normans each.'

'Then how do you come to be one of William's most trusted companions?'

'That is a long story, but it was my willingness to speak English on his behalf that led me into his service. I have, of course, taken the trouble to learn French as well.'

'Were many of your people put to the sword afterwards?'

'No, due to the fact that we had a friend who spoke for us. A former chaplain of William's who we had been hiding from King Harold.'

'So you are a man who does not scruple to betray your leader at any given time?' Waltheof asked quietly.

'I remain loyal to King William,' Will insisted, suddenly fearful of the way the conversation had drifted.

'That will, of course, remain to be seen,' Waltheof replied enigmatically, 'but when we journey south once again, you must visit me and see more of these lands of mine.' Then he turned to speak to the man on his other side, and Will heaved a sigh of confused relief.

The next morning, Will rose at the first glimmer of red in the sky. As he approached the stables, Selwyn slipped out from the shadow of the main doorway, and signalled for Will to join him down the side of the old timber wall that leaned ominously sideways.

'Once again,' Will asked, 'why the secrecy, and what did you mean about danger?'

'There's an uprising being planned by the earls — Edwin, Morcar and Gospatric,' Selwyn told him, his eyes wide. 'They're against the king. Gospatric is the Earl of Bernicia — everywhere north of here until you reach Scotland. And the Scottish king is also involved.'

'But Edwin and Morcar surrendered and swore allegiance,' Will objected. 'I was there when they did so.'

'You were also there when Edgar gave up his claim to the throne of England?'

'Yes — why?'

'Because he's behind it all. He was here with Gospatric until just before William arrived from the south, and they brought with them the promise from King Malcolm of Scotland.'

'How do you know about this?' Will demanded.

'Because everywhere Edwin goes, I go, as part of his personal guard. I've been there while they've been hatching their plans — as soon as William goes south again, it will begin.'

The previous evening's conversation flashed back into Will's memory, and he frowned. 'It may well be that Earl Waltheof is also part of it,' he told Selwyn. 'When we spoke during the banquet, he was clearly seeking to test my loyalty to the king. What are we to do? Did you wish me to warn William?'

Selwyn laughed hollowly. 'Do you think he would believe you? Your word against three earls and a former king? As well as imparting information that will require him to wage war on Scotland?'

'A good point. And where does that leave you, should the uprising fail?'

'On the wrong side, clearly. But if it succeeds, it will be *you* on the wrong side. Whichever way it goes, one of our wives will be a widow, dependent on the generosity of the survivor.'

Will let that sink in before replying. 'We must clearly both make plans to desert before the storm breaks.'

Another hollow laugh from Selwyn. 'And how would the king react to your desertion? You would be hanged from the nearest tree, as an example to all others who might be considering the same thing. Me likewise, if I judge Earl Edwin correctly. Or, if it became known that I had revealed their plans to King William, I would have my throat slit in some quiet place, and my body thrown into the river.'

'You have clearly had longer to think about this than I have,' Will replied, 'so have you come up with any plan of your own?'

'Only that you must do your utmost to ensure that William leaves here with no suspicion of what might be afoot. Accompany him back to London, or wherever, then travel home to Tamworth and take our family to some safe place where no-one would think to look for you, and somehow get a message to me as to where that is. Or perhaps come and collect me, although by then the whole of the north will be in uproar, no doubt. William will be bound to send his army against us, and my best hope would be to escape from any battle that ensues, and let them think I am dead. Then I can rejoin you all wherever you have made our new home.'

'That all sounds very risky,' Will observed.

'If you think of something better, get word to me. Now, we must go our separate ways, because we cannot risk even being seen together.'

Deeply disturbed by what he had learned, Will reported for duty leading his horse by the bridle. He was required to report to William Malet, who King William had appointed to the position of High Sheriff of Yorkshire the previous day. Malet was to supervise the construction, and ongoing defence, of a castle on a strategic strip of land between the two rivers called the Ouse and the Foss. Malet spoke no English, and Will's services were required in order to explain to several hundred local peasants why their huts were to be put to the flame, because they were in the way.

Will could barely endure the sight of devastated elderly folk, shattered once-proud men, wailing mothers and shrieking children, standing in a pathetic cluster while burly men-at-arms set about destroying their shelters and their memories with torches. He silently cursed the man who claimed to be their king for his indifference to their welfare, and shuddered at the cruelty with which his bullies carried out their work. The sooner they went back south again, the happier Will would be. Perhaps one day he might be able to square his conscience for what he had been a silent participant in.

King William remained in York for long enough to ensure that his castle was being constructed to his liking, then announced his intention of progressing south to build new ones. For Will it was the same depressing round of warnings to villages that they passed through — bend the knee or lose the head.

There was an angry argument between William and Waltheof once they reached Lincoln. The king insisted that since the castle he had ordered was a royal one, it would be constructed to his now well-established specifications, and would be manned by men of his choosing, rather than men in the service of the Earl of East Anglia, whose domain it was. Will was outside the temporary stables on the morning after the dispute when Waltheof appeared silently by his side.

'Presumably you heard our argument, even though it was conducted in French?' Waltheof asked.

Will nodded. 'I imagine that everyone heard it, my lord, as I would imagine that most of us could see your point of view.'

'Really?' Waltheof asked, obviously pleased. 'Do you really hold the view that an earl should be given leave to construct his own defences?'

'Most certainly,' Will replied cautiously, 'but of course King William is slowly ensuring that the entire country is properly defended, in his name, and with his castles.'

'Such as the one in York?' Waltheof asked. 'You will be aware that Earl Morcar resented that? And the one at Warwick, handed over to the son of one of William's flatterers, when it should have been left to Edwin of Mercia to construct? Presumably your brother, who serves Edwin, told you of his wrath when that decision was taken out of Edwin's hands?'

'I was myself in the service of Edwin when that happened,' Will told him, 'but I don't recall any outburst of anger. Mind you, I was only guarding the south gate at that time.'

'Indeed, and of course your brother would be closer to him, as part of his inner retinue.'

'He is my brother only by law,' Will told him, 'since he is married to my sister.'

'And, like you, he lives in Tamworth with his wife, and is no doubt anxious to be reunited with her, as are you with yours?'

'Indeed yes,' Will confirmed. 'It is to be hoped that such a day is not long away, and that presumably we may both return there when King William returns to Normandy.'

'And what makes you so confident that he will?' Waltheof countered. 'There could be matters in the north that require his more immediate attention.'

'But we have just left there, surely?' Will asked as his heartbeat became swifter. 'The king left York well-guarded by the Earls Edwin and Morcar.'

'Yes, but against *whom* do they guard it?' Waltheof asked, before turning on his heel and walking away, leaving Will with more questions than answers.

The atmosphere between King William and Earl Waltheof became even frostier after they paused briefly, first at

Huntingdon and then at Cambridge. William ordered the construction of castles at both locations, and insisted that Waltheof travel with him to the second of those places, even though this meant only a brief stay in his own manor of Huntingdon, where messengers awaited him from various other places. It was late in the evening of their fourth day in Cambridge when Will found himself at the supper table with Waltheof once again. His companion looked round cautiously at where William was laughing heartily at some jest or other from one of his travelling sycophants, then whispered, 'Meet with me tomorrow at sunrise at the base of the new castle, and we may always claim that we are admiring William's new work.'

'And why would we need to make any such false claim?' Will asked.

'Tomorrow at sunrise,' Waltheof repeated, then turned and looked the other way at the minstrel who had entered the hall.

The next morning Will was waiting apprehensively where requested. The sun had just begun to creep up the spire of a church to the east when Will was aware of a furtive footfall behind him. He turned and looked at Waltheof, who broke the uneasy silence.

'If I judge you aright, you are a sturdy warrior who would rather be with his family, out of the immediate line of battle. Am I correct?'

'Yes,' Will answered truthfully, 'although it's some time since I had the opportunity to test my battle fitness.'

'That time is rapidly approaching,' Waltheof told him as he lowered his voice, 'but before then, you would wish to be in a safe place with your family?'

'Of course.'

'And in exchange for that, you would wield a sword by my side?'

'Of course. We are all soldiers of King William.'

'Not all of us,' Waltheof replied softly. 'Your brother confided in you, did he not, that the north will shortly rise against William?'

'Yes, he did,' Will replied hesitantly, 'but I did not so advise the king because…'

Waltheof raised his hand for silence. 'You did not advise William because you feared for your brother's life?'

'My brother-in-*law*, yes. Where is this leading?'

'If I were to offer you a safe place to which to take your family when the storm breaks, would you pledge yourself to my service?'

'Of course, but I cannot speak for him.'

'He already pledged himself, when we were at York. Did he not ask that you contact him when you found a safe place?'

'Yes, he did, but…'

'That place is four days' ride to the north-east of here, and the lady who occupies it has been told to await your arrival. Selwyn will follow when he is able, since he already has the directions. They are here on this scroll, which you must keep close about you before you leave.'

'But King William may not grant me leave,' Will objected.

Waltheof burst out laughing. 'You are slower than I thought — or perhaps more loyal, in which case I will be obliged to end your life here and now, after what I have imparted. Did you not realise that the price of this safe haven for your family is that you desert the service of the king?'

'But that would be treason!'

Waltheof sighed. 'Not half as much treason as that which Selwyn will be committing within days, once the north rises up, to be joined by the Scots under Malcolm and Edgar. To add to William's problems, there will also be another Danish incursion from the east. My family name is Siwardson, and my father was one of King Cnut's leading jarls when he conquered this land. Emma of Normandy exchanged bedchambers in order to give England two half-brothers, both of whom became kings of England. One of these became Edward of England, but before him came Harthacnut. It is time that Denmark claimed back what is rightfully its own. Not without just cause was this land upon which we stand once called "The Danelaw", and it shall be so again.'

XX

'Thomas needs to be fed,' Joan told Will testily, 'and if I hang my breast out in this cold wind it'll probably turn into an ice block, so the next monastery we come to will be the last for today. I'm sure Elston needs feeding as well.'

It had been like this for the past two weeks, and the euphoria of the initial reunion had long ago worn off. Will had slipped away from Cambridge under the cover of nightfall, with his horse tied to a wagon stolen from King William's train. These were both offences that could lose him his head, he'd reminded himself almost hourly during the uncertain journey across England from east to west, when the only established tracks ran north to south.

When he'd finally reached Tamworth, he'd been smothered in wifely kisses, and breathlessly advised that he had a son, only to be reminded barely an hour later that he hadn't been there for the birth. And that had proved to be the first of a seemingly inexhaustible list of complaints, which had increased in both volume and frequency when he'd announced that they were all leaving Tamworth for some unnamed place at least two weeks' journey away.

Elva had remained diplomatically quiet in her enforced loneliness. All that Will had been able to advise her was that Selwyn was in a place weeks to the north of where they were heading, as part of what was shortly to become a rebel army. She could soon become a young widow. Her muted sobs as they lay each night in the *hospitium* of yet another monastery were enough to remind Will and Joan that the immediate future was bleak with uncertainty.

It became drier after Cambridge, but much colder and windier. They spent what they hoped was their final night on the road in the ancient abbey of Hempton, where they cleaned themselves up as best they could before presenting themselves to the lady of the manor at Walsingham.

The lady who came out of the substantial house when summoned by her steward was willowy and above average height. She had a regal bearing and a countenance reddened by the wind. Her radiant smile bathed them in a warm glow as she bid them welcome, indicated a building to the side of the main manor house, and invited them to make themselves comfortable after their long journey while she ordered food and drink.

The taste of meat and freshly caught fish made Joan cry tears of relief and gratitude. After they had eaten, the steward reappeared and informed Will that the lady would like to speak to him in the privacy of the manor house. Will walked into the spacious main hall and thanked her for her charity.

'It is not I you must thank, but my very good friend here.' The lady nodded towards a man who slipped out from the corner in which he had been concealed, and Will instinctively dropped to one knee.

Earl Waltheof chuckled as he indicated that Will should rise. 'There's no need for any of that Norman nonsense in *this* company, Will,' he assured him.

Will rose. 'Nevertheless, it's the least that you deserve, given the favour you have shown to me and my family.'

King William listened in mounting anger to the messenger who knelt at his feet, then he dismissed him and sent for Robert de Comines.

It took a while for the middle-aged Norman count to appear, green-faced and bleary eyed from his seven hours in the royal presence the previous evening, celebrating the birth of the latest addition to the royal brood. The boy had been christened Henry almost as soon as he'd been cleaned up and loaded into a baptismal shawl. William himself had drunk more the previous night than anyone, and if his head was clear, he was paying the price with a rebelling stomach.

'Robert,' William announced, 'you have long sought a title in this country, have you not?'

'Indeed, sire.'

'And you have seen York?'

'Regrettably yes, sire.'

'But you have not travelled beyond it, I assume?'

'No, sire — York was quite enough.'

'Well, the opportunity has come for you to assume a title.'

'Sire?'

'It seems that Earl Morcar is not to be trusted, despite the mercy I showed to him, and the foolish generosity that led to my unwise decision to allow him to retain his title. You are to ride north and replace him. I will arm you with the necessary seal of authority. You speak English, do you not?'

'After a fashion, sire, but the noise that comes from the mouths of those northern clods could hardly be described as English.'

'Then you may take with you that Saxon peasant who I raised for the purpose — the tall one with the red hair — Wilfrid de Pevensey.'

'I haven't seen him since Cambridge,' Robert said. 'I sought him out for some task or other when you commissioned the new castle by the river here in London, but no-one had seen him. Rumour is that he has deserted.'

'No matter,' William replied dismissively. 'If he has indeed deserted, then even if he is recaptured he will be of no use to you, since I shall have him hanged from London Bridge, in full view of the peasants from whom he is descended. You must therefore go north without him.'

'Of course, sire, but may I perhaps enquire why this honour is being bestowed upon me?'

William snorted. 'I am reliably advised that Morcar has encouraged that idiot Gospatric to wander north and parley with the Scots, who have given sanctuary to the pretended boy king Edgar. When you take up your new office, you may also advise Gospatric that his claim to the title of Earl of Bernicia has proved as brief as his loyalty to me. He should be keeping the Scots out, not entertaining them at Bamburgh. Your new earldom of Northumbria will extend all the way from Derby and Lincoln in the south to the Scots border.'

'Derby is surely within the earldom of Mercia?' Robert pointed out, to another snort from William.

'It was — until today. Edwin is still in York, I am told, and no doubt encouraging his brother. Edwin's loyalty is suspect. Either he distances himself from what his brother is plotting, or he too will be living on memories — if I allow him to live, that is. Now go!'

Two weeks later, Selwyn was an unwilling audience to the urgent conversation between brothers Edwin and Morcar and their clandestine visitor. Selwyn was one of two men guarding the entrance door to the great hall of Morcar's manor house, the other being a trusted man-at-arms in the service of Morcar. This was a conversation that might only be overheard by those whose loyalty was above suspicion. But loyalty to *whom* was a very vague matter.

'How can you be sure of this?' Gospatric asked with alarm.

Edwin smiled knowingly. 'You have no doubt heard the expression that a dog that can fetch may also be trained to carry? Or, in this case, bribed. My messengers all court death while earning a double payment for their services, and as swiftly as information travels to William, it comes back to me.'

'But why did you make the king privy to our plans?' Gospatric asked.

'To test the water,' Edwin replied, as usual talking for both himself and his brother. 'We wish to stir up the people against William, do we not, while keeping our own hands clean? We wait to see who William sends north, then we have him done to death by the people, in an open gesture of defiance that will bring William back north. This way we test not only the depth of hatred for Normans this far north, but also William's strength in responding to it.'

'He will put the entire town to the sword, no doubt,' Morcar responded gloomily.

Edwin smiled. 'And why would he do that, when the uprising will be further north?'

'*Now* I understand the reason for my being summoned south,' Gospatric muttered as he turned pale. 'Where do you propose that the deed be done, and which of my towns do you deem to be dispensable?'

'Durham,' Edwin replied, as if consigning hundreds of locals to Norman swords were a simple matter. 'But William will not reach that far north, trust me.'

'And how can you be so sure?' Gospatric asked, wishing that he had declined the invitation to leave the sanctuary of Bamburgh.

'Because on his way north, he will be assailed from the east,' Edwin explained. It fell silent, and Gospatric's eyes widened in disbelief.

'King Sweyn of Denmark,' said Morcar. 'He will set sail in a week, and by the time that William reaches Huntingdon he will find that there is an entire Danish army moored in the Humber, and about to pillage from his baggage train.'

'But…' Gospatric began, almost lost for words, 'I mean … Earl Waltheof…'

Edwin regarded him with a look bordering upon pity. 'Do you think we could have planned this *without* him? The offer to invade came through your honoured guest, the former King Edgar. While in Denmark he pledged his crown to King Sweyn, in return for ridding England of Normans. Saxon rules, or Dane rules — either way, it is better for this realm that the ruler is not Norman, as we have learned to our cost. And Waltheof is of Danish lineage.'

'So Earl Waltheof will not ride to William's assistance?'

'No, he will in fact attack him from behind as he approaches York, while Sweyn sweeps in from the east. We hold firm here in York, King Malcolm crosses the border with his forces, and William is history.'

The meeting broke up an hour later, and Edwin and Selwyn strolled side by side back to Edwin's temporary manor house, each deep in thought. It was Edwin who broke the silence.

'I hope that you are committed to all that you heard, Selwyn. I would be sad at heart to have to organise your murder. You have heard too much for your loyalty to be suspect, and I have a special task by which you may demonstrate it beyond all doubt.'

Selwyn swallowed hard as he asked, 'What is that?'

'William is bound to ride north with a substantial force when his intended replacement for Morcar is done to death. When he does so, it would be fitting for him to see the flames rising from his fine new castle here in town.'

'You wish me to lead a body of men against the castle guard?'

'What is left of it, yes. William was so confident, when he so eagerly departed south, that he had cowed the north into submission that he left only a few token Normans to man his proud new castle. He was unwise enough to recruit local men to swell their numbers, some of whom were even drawn from those whose huts he burned down in order to make the land available. How strong do you think their loyalty to him might prove, if tested?'

'So your plan is that the Norman garrison will be done to death by their own locally recruited colleagues, leaving it wide open for burning?'

'Precisely. And I wish you to lead the outside party that will move in and do the deed.'

'And this is to be as William approaches from the south, assuming that he gets this far?'

'Either then, or while he is actually sweeping through the gate, in his usual arrogant manner. It must be done so as to afford him the greatest insult, and cause him the greatest grief.'

'God help those responsible, if they are ever betrayed.'

'As I said already, Selwyn, I must test your loyalty. And by this means you will also be testing my loyalty to you.'

Robert de Comines presented the scroll to Morcar with the seal attached, and grinned sadistically as Morcar admitted that he had no French.

'Allow me to translate, since I have the English,' Robert smirked. 'Basically it says that you are an untrustworthy piece of horse waste, and I am now the Earl of Northumbria.'

'I am sure that King William did not use those words,' Edwin replied with sweet sarcasm as he sought to save his brother's face, 'given that he looks like a horse and smells like the waste that drops from it.'

'You speak treason?' Robert demanded, red in the face.

'Fluently,' Edwin replied, 'but let us move into the Great Hall in order to eat. You have presumably brought your food taster with you, in order to ensure that you are not poisoned?'

'I do not intend to remain a minute longer in this town in order to be further insulted,' Robert erupted.

'By all means feel free to continue your journey north, where the insults are colder, but no less heartfelt,' Edwin countered, beginning to enjoy himself.

Robert glared at him, assured him that his treasonous words would be conveyed to King William upon his return to London, and stormed from the room, followed by the token three men-at-arms who accompanied him.

'If you live long enough to convey those words,' Edwin muttered as he heard the horses galloping away on a shouted command, 'then we are all lost.'

Robert was met on his arrival in Durham the following day by its bishop, Ethelwin, who was pale as he bowed, then held out his ring of office to be kissed. As Robert bowed his head to do so, Ethelwin had a whispered warning to impart.

'Forgive my presumption, as I hope God will forgive me for my breach of the confessional, but one of my flock confessed to me yesterday that there is a plot against your life while you are abiding here.'

'Thank you, my Lord Bishop, but your words merely confirm an opinion that I formed when entering your apology for a town, namely that this is not a healthy place to stay for longer than one night. You no doubt have a palace of some sort, where I will reside while my men commandeer such lodgings as they may find among the peasantry, whether they approve of such an arrangement or not. Lead me to your palace, and show me where you hide your whores.'

After such an insult to both the town and its bishop, there was hardly a soul to be found who did not heartily approve of what followed. As the night air was assailed by the hoot of a barn owl, it was hastily followed by other sounds that should have alerted the inebriated guards. Their last sensation was having sharp knives drawn swiftly across their jugular veins, as each of the heavily disguised mob set about their allotted task. By morning, the charred remains of the briefly appointed new Earl of Northumbria were available for morbid inspection in the burned-out ruins of the bishop's house. The news of the successful and all but silent assassination was relayed down to York, and another of Edwin's two-way messengers was dispatched on the first stage south, as far as Selby.

XXI

Will and Joan bowed as they entered Lady Richeldis's hall.

'The children?' she asked.

'We travel with my sister-in-law Elva, as you know, my lady, and she is content to sit with them until they fall asleep,' Joan replied. 'Then she will also lay her head down. My youngest is but a baby of some four months, and he was fed not an hour before we crossed the lawns to come here at your very gracious invitation.'

Richeldis smiled in appreciation of the girl's polite manner, and indicated that they should sit. A serving girl laid trenchers of bread on the table, and a kitchen hand moved swiftly forward to lay a dish of roast duck in front of them.

'You keep a fine table, my lady,' Will observed.

'Not as fine as it once was, as you shall learn in a moment. We should await the arrival of Earl Waltheof before that, since even he has not heard the whole of what I have to impart. Before he makes an appearance, tell me about yourselves.'

'I'm originally from Wessex,' Will explained, as Richeldis's eyebrows rose with sudden interest. 'A village called Sandlake, just above Pevensey, on the south coast. I was in command of the local fyrd, and I was among those who stood on the ridge they now call Senlac, to face William's army in the service of King Harold.'

'Were you there when Harold fell?' Richeldis asked.

Will nodded. 'He was shot in the eye, or so we heard. Both Selwyn — my sister's man — and I were wounded, and we staggered from the field just after King Harold died.'

'He was indeed shot in the eye,' Richeldis said quietly. 'I saw his body before they dragged it away. In fact, I was forced to go onto the field and confirm that it was him.'

A shocked silence fell as they took in the implications.

'I have not always been the Lady Richeldis de Faverches.'

'Who exactly are you?' Will asked, aghast at the thought that was forming in his mind.

'Do you perhaps remember the name "Edith Swan Neck"?'

'Of course,' Joan said, 'she was the wife of King Harold. She was fabled to have been beautiful.'

Richeldis smiled. 'Yes, they once said that of me. But that was before I was widowed.'

'You — are — were — Edith Swan Neck?' Will asked in disbelief.

'Yes, I was, and I still am, in my heart. This must remain entirely confidential, since that is part of the reason why you are here.'

'I don't understand,' Will admitted, just as a bustling movement announced the entry of Waltheof, who hurried to the table, bowed to the ladies, sat down, and poured himself some wine.

'Forgive me, my lady, but the journey from Huntingdon gets no easier.'

Richeldis nodded indulgently, and introduced Joan to the new arrival. 'This is Joan, wife of our trusty warrior here. I had just reached the point in my narrative when I revealed my true identity. I think that they are shocked — either that or they do not believe me.'

'You can believe her,' Waltheof confirmed. 'I was the one who escorted her back here as my final duty to the late King Harold, although regrettably some time after his death.'

'You were in Harold's army?' Will asked.

'Yes and no,' Waltheof replied. 'I was on my way to join it, having been alerted by one of Edwin's captains on his way south. Edwin himself was not in command, so I combined those of his men who had travelled south after the encounter with the Norsemen at Stamford Bridge into my own force, and we marched from Huntingdon. Progress was slow, because Edwin's men had been on the road for two weeks or more, and some of them were even wounded. By the time we got there, it was all over, because Harold had not waited for us.'

'He assumed that you were not coming,' Richeldis reminded him. 'We were encamped by a large lake at the very top of the hill that led down to the shore, and we could see even from there that William was breaking camp, heading for London, or so we thought. Harold took his army down to stand between him and London, and the rest you both now know.'

'Not exactly,' Will pointed out. 'You told us that you had been on the battlefield and confirmed that Harold was indeed dead. You must surely have been captured by William?'

'I was captured a little while before that,' Richeldis explained. 'After the battle, his men kept going up the hill, and overran our camp by the lake. I was quickly identified, and taken down to William, trussed like a deer. He insisted that I go onto the battlefield, and I trust in God that I will never again have to behold what I confronted there, and that such slaughter will never again stain the green fields of my native land. They had stripped dear Harold's body by then, and subjected it to many indignities which even now I cannot bear to describe, but I was able to confirm it was him by certain marks on his body that only a wife would know. But the worst was yet to come.'

'What could be worse than having to identify your own husband's body after battle?' Joan asked in a small voice.

Richeldis's face hardened. 'William's first thought had been to put me to death, but one of his men stepped forward and asked for me as some sort of battle trophy. His name was Guy de Faverches, and he was an unwashed animal covered in the blood of others, and smelling accordingly. William thought it a great jest to hand me over, and Guy violated me for the first time in a hedgerow within sight of the battlefield, and even some of his men. He continued to use my body like a limp sack for many weeks, and William made him a gift, not just of me, but of my family lands here in Walsingham. Then, when it was revealed that I was with child, William ordered him to marry me, which he promptly did, even though he was my senior by some thirty years.'

'I have seen a child being attended by a nurse,' Joan said, her eyes wide with horror. 'Is he the child of your union with this Guy de Faverches?'

Richeldis looked briefly across at Waltheof, as if seeking his permission to explain. He nodded, so she continued. 'He is my child, certainly. A son called Geoffrey, so named by the man who believed himself to be his father, a man who died from over-eating at Dover, only a few months later. It was then that Waltheof gallantly offered to return me here, where the child was born under my new name. Waltheof had by then surrendered to William, and had been granted back his lands and title. So I am twice a widow. But the child I bore was in my belly even before William made me a widow for the first time.'

'So the child is…' Will whispered, then faltered.

'Geoffrey is the son of King Harold of England, who, had he lived, might well have persuaded the Witan to appoint him as his successor. The child you see innocently tottering around the manor grounds, little older than your own daughter, is the next rightful Saxon King of England.'

'Edgar Aetheling might dispute that,' Waltheof reminded her. 'And in any case, the next King of England, after William has been put into six feet of ground, may well be another Dane. But, Will, you can now appreciate why I need a strong warrior to protect a royal heir and his mother.'

'And my shrine, Waltheof. Don't forget my shrine.'

'Is that the small house in the meadow in front of the river?' Joan asked.

'Indeed it is,' Richeldis confirmed. 'And tomorrow you must visit it with me. Please bring the children — after you have broken your fast, of course.'

The following morning, Richeldis was waiting for the family on the gentle grass slope that led down to the river. She pointed at the small house, its ornate spires catching rays of morning sunlight and reflecting them back up like arrow shafts.

'Before we go inside,' she said to the expectant group standing around her, 'I must impart the wonderful history of what you see down there.'

'It's well crafted,' Will observed. 'Your carpenter must have spent many days perfecting such symmetry.'

'It appeared overnight,' Richeldis calmly told her spellbound audience, 'and I had nothing to do with its construction.' She watched their faces carefully as she revealed the awesome secret. 'One day I was standing where we are standing now, holding baby Geoffrey in my arms and praying to God for a safe future for him. Then I had a visitor. Not from this world, but from the place in which all love and peace may first be found, before it is bestowed on unworthy people like us.'

'You mean…?' Elva asked, being the first to catch the significance of what they were being told.

'It was the Blessed Virgin Mary,' Richeldis revealed, 'with her holy child. The first time she appeared, it was to bless me. Then the second time she asked that I allow a shrine to be built here, a place in which the love and blessings of God might be made available to everyone who cares to worship here. I agreed, of course, and the next morning it was where you see it. In this time of trouble I have not revealed its origins to anyone other than Waltheof, until today. And even he was previously unaware of precisely how it came to be where it is. But you see, Will, that is the real reason why I wish you here. This shrine must be guarded for all time, and you will be the first to guard it.'

'But Waltheof brought me here to keep you and your royal child from harm,' Will reminded her.

'Which of course you can do at the same time that you add the strength of man to the blessings of God. Will you stay and keep this place secure? You have felt for some time, have you not, that you have some mission in life beyond travelling the country with a tyrant?'

'Indeed,' Will replied, 'but I had thought it to be the saving of lives from the brutality of the invader.'

'Is this not more worthy, and more likely to bring lasting peace for the entire kingdom — the entire world, perhaps?'

Will looked across at Joan, who was nodding eagerly with Thomas in her arms. Elva was holding Elston, silently transfixed by the sight of the small house glinting in the sun. Matilda sat on the damp grass, legs straight out in front of her.

'Before you decide whether or not to accept this heavy burden,' Richeldis urged them all, 'you should step inside and experience the wonderful feeling of peace it contains.'

They followed her down the slope, and she pushed open the unlocked door. Inside was a chapel of sorts, with a carved wooden figure of the Madonna and Child at the far end. Behind them the sun was streaming in through a window, casting a halo glow around the statue.

Will stood open-mouthed at the sheer beauty and serenity of it all, and sensed tears welling in his eyes. The children were gazing innocently up at the statue, and Joan and Elva had silent tears rolling down their faces.

Will turned to Richeldis. 'I will stay and guard both you and this beautiful place, of course.'

King William hurled the wine goblet across the chamber and swore as he listened to what he had just been told by a messenger.

'Summon all the members of my council who may be found within the palace precincts!' he bellowed to an attendant, who bowed and scuttled out.

One by one the men answered the summons in various stages of dress, given the relatively early hour. They all kept their distance after one look at the crimson royal countenance. William removed a mailed glove and began angrily biting his fingers before he found the words.

'The ignorant scum have killed de Comines! We ride for York as soon as the men can be assembled. Not just you and *your* men — all and every man who calls himself a soldier, and lives at my expense. It will be the largest army ever to ride north out of London, and we will pick up Earl Waltheof and his men on the way. Then we will suck up every man from every castle north of here, including those who claim to serve Earl Morcar, who shall be dead within an hour of our arrival at York, along with his brother. We will create a whirlwind of death around the towers of York, and leave not so much as a house beam standing in Durham! Widows will grieve for years over the loss of their husbands, and Yorkshire shall become the haunt of orphans! Be back within the hour, fully armed and ready to leap to horse, unless you want your heads on spikes! GO!'

The first of the longships slid up the wide estuary on the incoming tide, its sails lowered now that they were no longer required for forward movement. Sweyn Estridsen, King of Denmark, stood on the rear deck alongside helmsman Erik Johannsen and peered through the sheeting rain.

'You are sure you have the right river?' he demanded.

Erik nodded without taking his hand off the massive rudder. 'It is as described, with the hill to the right, and the marsh to the left. An hour upstream we will see the entrance to the smaller river, where we may drop our lines and await our English host.'

'I hope for your sake that you are right,' Sweyn replied, then waved his fellow adventurer Asger Jorgensen onto the raised platform.

'Where is this place?' Asger asked.

Sweyn grimaced. 'Either it is close to where we will meet with the English rat Siwardson, or Erik here will go over the side with his throat cut.'

'At long last a Dane will be back on the English throne,' Asger said.

'I may decide to accept the seat they are offering, after we have stripped the nation of anything of value,' Sweyn replied. 'Our men do not fight for my glory, Asger, any more than you do. England was ever a place for plunder — a quick raid on a wealthy house, a few women, a night of drinking, and then home rejoicing.'

'I thought you had been promised the English crown?' Asger replied, puzzled.

'That is indeed what I was promised,' Sweyn replied with a wicked smirk, 'and in due course, I may claim that. But first I'll cut the balls off the man who got here before me, that arrogant William the Bastard. Then perhaps a gentle pillage through his war chests, a night with his woman satisfying my grosser desires, and as much plate and coin as we can get in our longships. That is, if Erik has not mistaken the place where we are to meet the English traitor. If he has, then he will not live to see dry land again. If he has not, then Waltheof Siwardson will lead us to his own downfall.'

XXII

Will stepped outside their hut and gazed suspiciously at the group of ragged, sullen men who were walking up the meadow from the river, where a large boat loaded with timber was moored.

Earl Waltheof stepped from the boat and yelled up to Will. 'Behold your army. They are a sorry bunch, but I needed the real ones to fool the king when he passes through Huntingdon.'

'Why do I need an army, and what is all that wood for?' Will asked.

'Did you expect to be able to defend this place by yourself?' Waltheof replied. 'As for the wood, presumably you do not want these scruffy oafs sharing the rushes with you and your wife and children? They will require a barracks of their own.'

'My question was rather why we need an army in the first place,' Will replied sullenly.

'These are uncertain times, as King William is about to discover,' Waltheof said. 'He heads north, to lay waste to Yorkshire, but unknown to him the Danes have already landed in the Humber. That will be my excuse for not joining him on his revenge journey north, but I cannot be in two places at once, and neither can the men I command. There is a local outlaw cut loose from royal justice further west — a wild man of the Fens called "Hereward". I do not trust him, in my absence, not to move east and harry these parts.'

'And where will your journey take you?' Will asked.

Waltheof moved closer and lowered his voice. 'I go to meet with King Sweyn of Denmark to welcome him to our shores, and I will agree with him when and where he will strike at William during his northern march. Then, while William is guarding his eastern flank against Danish axes, he will feel Saxon steel at his back.'

'You plan to attack William from the rear?' Will asked, surprised by the audacity of Waltheof's plan.

'Isn't that where his backside is to be found?' Waltheof chuckled, then turned back to the men who had taken the opportunity to lie on the meadow grass.

'On your feet, and start the unloading!' he commanded, and they rose slowly and slouched back down to the water's edge.

'You expect me to create an army out of *that*?' Will asked, aghast.

Waltheof nodded. 'You told me that you commanded a fyrd that stood against William at Pevensey. I can only assume that they were originally peasants best trained to till fields, fish rivers and construct huts, and that it was you who taught them warfare. If you can do it once, you can do it again. Their armour and weapons are in the scuppers of that vessel, and as you can see they bring their accommodation with them, like snails. By the time that they have built the huts that will keep the elements from their heads, they will be fit enough for training. Lady Richeldis has graciously undertaken to feed them, since they will be additional protection for that holy house of hers down the slope.'

'And how soon must I have them ready?' Will asked.

'Yesterday, if not before,' Waltheof told him. 'At present I do not know if the rebel Hereward will join with the Danish invaders, or pillage on his own. Either way he will not offer his services to William, since he is on the run from a death sentence for his deeds in Normandy during William's absence. But like all those running from royal justice he must live outside the law, and this manor is too rich a target for him not to be tempted, even though I have let it be known that if he harms so much as a blade of grass here I will have his balls in my saddlebag.'

'And what were you saying about Yorkshire?' Will asked as he recalled the earlier conversation.

'It will become a wasteland, unless William's temper abates in the meantime, which is unlikely. He sought to replace Morcar as Earl of Northumbria with Robert de Comines, who was murdered by the resentful folk of Yorkshire as he journeyed north towards the Scottish border.'

'In York?'

'No, a place called Durham. But it's all the same to William, and according to my man at West Minster he all but had a seizure when the news was brought to him. God help York, but our business is here in Norfolk, and it is these lands we must defend — against William, or Hereward, or whoever.'

'Come inside and enjoy a mug of ale,' Will invited him. 'But say nothing of what William is planning for York. My sister Elva's man is still there, in the service of Earl Edwin.'

'Then God help him,' Waltheof muttered as he followed Will up the slope.

Three days later, Waltheof was explaining his late arrival back at the castle in Huntingdon that William had built.

'I am marching urgently north, to kick Northumbria in the backside,' William complained when Waltheof finally bent the knee in his own great hall, 'and for that I require the assistance of you and your forces. Where have you been, and why?'

'Forgive me, sire, but I think you will agree that it was time well spent. I heard a rumour that foreign ships had been espied in the Humber, which lies of course on the borders of my lands and those of the earldoms of Mercia and Northumbria. Since I knew Edwin to be detained in York, I took the liberty of venturing to Gainsborough. From there I took a boat down the Trent until we spotted the vessels in question, lying where the Trent meets the Ouse. I then sent scouts to question those who live and farm in the area, and it would seem that the invaders are Danish, and led by King Sweyn himself.'

'I was already aware of all this,' William grumbled, 'since I too have my sources of information. You will presumably also be aware that they have been there for the best part of a week, and have moved no further inland than to steal food from the nearest fields? Does that sound to you like a dangerous invasion?'

'Indeed not, sire, but you would surely not wish to leave the whole of the east exposed while you venture north? It would be better for me to remain and guard your eastern flank against attack, and block the tracks south to London.'

'Your family is Danish, is it not?' William asked suspiciously.

'Indeed, it once was,' Waltheof conceded, 'but now it is English.'

'Half of England was once Danish,' William reminded him. 'Does your knowledge of recent history extend to your recalling how they were regularly bought off?'

'By the payment of money,' Waltheof replied.

'Indeed, and might that strategy not prove successful again?'

'You intend to buy their inaction by sending an envoy to offer them money?'

'In a sense, yes,' William replied coldly. 'I wish you to travel there in person, escorting several boxes of gold coin as a suggested first payment, the second — and larger — payment to be forthcoming when they actually raise their lines and sail back east.'

'I would be delighted to carry out such a service, sire, but will you not require my men in your force when you move on York?'

William smiled unpleasantly. 'I said nothing about your main force going with you, Earl Waltheof. You will take a dozen of your most trusted men, no more, in addition to my wagon drivers. The rest of your force will continue to York, under my direct command.'

'As you instruct, sire,' Waltheof conceded, clearly not entirely content. 'Now, if you will permit me to withdraw, I have much to prepare.'

William waved languidly to indicate his permission for Waltheof to leave. He then beckoned to Ralph of Falaise and whispered in his ear. 'Your man has his instructions?'

'Indeed, sire.'

'Good. See that he does not fail.'

King Malcolm of Scotland was uncomfortable at being this far south of his border without an entire army, and somehow the twenty or so armed men that he had brought with him as a personal bodyguard seemed pitifully inadequate once he was in traditional enemy country. However, he contented himself with the thought that the young future king he had brought with him was surely guarantee enough against treachery.

Then there was the sizeable contingent from the forces of Earl Gospatric who had accompanied them south from Bamburgh, the same Gospatric who had the most to lose should the northern earls prove treacherous, given the large standing army that Malcolm kept ready and battle fit just over their border. All in all he was probably safe enough here in York, and the prospects that they were discussing were such as to make the heart quicken with anticipation.

'William reached Selby earlier today,' Edwin told the company, 'and will be here within two days, by our reckoning. When he arrives, he will be greeted by the sight of his precious castle in flames, and will no doubt hurry his main force through the south gate to extinguish them. Once he is through, the gate will be closed behind him and his men, and Gospatric's main force will be admitted through the north gate, while Morcar's men and mine come from their hiding places and encircle them. By then, if they have not already engaged the rear of his force, Waltheof will race his men in through the re-opened south gate. Once William is slain, there will be no-one to command his force, and we may take advantage of their confusion and terror. Edgar shall be anointed king by Archbishop Ealdred, and then we march south.'

It fell silent. Selwyn was in his usual place along the rear wall, within defending distance of Earl Edwin, alongside similar trusted men-at-arms. He looked carefully at the faces of the traitorous earls, which clearly betrayed their doubts.

'How will you arrange for the castle to go up in flames, when it is guarded by William's men?' Malcolm asked suspiciously.

Edwin smiled. 'That is my business — yours will be to return north. Your presence here was solely in order to witness the crowning of your future king.'

'I could have brought a stronger force,' Malcolm objected.

'And alert William to what awaits him here?' Edwin replied. 'His men will be exhausted after their long march, and may perhaps have been considerably reduced in number following Waltheof's rearguard attack on them further south. We did not need your force.'

Edwin was not to know, until it was far too late, that William's force had in fact grown considerably, and that it had not been attacked from behind. In truth, by the time that Edwin was making his confident assertions, Waltheof was securely locked in the dungeon of the recently erected castle at Lincoln.

The wagon driver in the pay of Ralph of Falaise had eagerly earned his bonus by advising Ralph, on his return with an empty wagon, that he had silently watched and listened while Waltheof and King Sweyn had gleefully loaded the boxes of gold coin onto Sweyn's longship, while cackling at William's arrogant short-sightedness. They had agreed that after they had collected the second instalment and shared it between them, Sweyn would take his fleet down the southeast coast, pillaging at every promising-looking harbour until they sailed up the Thames and sacked West Minster.

William had nodded as he received the information, then smiled sadistically as Waltheof rejoined him at Lincoln and reported that Sweyn had accepted his first instalment, and would shortly be setting sail out of the Humber estuary. Only then did Waltheof become aware of two men-at-arms closing up behind him, removing his sword and grasping him tightly while they forced him to his knees.

'And when the Dane leaves the Humber, he plans to attack London, does he not, and with your blessing?'

'Sire?'

'Don't give me any more of your devious lies, Waltheof. Your treachery is, I admit, a disappointment, particularly since I had planned for you to marry my niece. That will not now be happening, of course, and when my skilled questioners have finished with you in the dungeon, you may have nothing left to offer a wife anyway.'

'Sire, I...'

'Shut your mouth, Waltheof. I intend to hold you secure as a bargaining counter for the Danish invader to whom you may be of value as a hostage. Once I have shown the scum of the north what happens when my orders are disobeyed, I shall lose no time in returning to London, with you chained in a cattle cart, to display to Sweyn of Denmark. My first offer will be your entire body, still breathing — if a little damaged in places. My second will be your head launched from a mangonel into the front rank of his invasion force. Take him away, and if you hurt him I will not die of grief!'

It was time for Will to put his injured shoulder to the test — not in actual combat, but for long enough to demonstrate the basic manoeuvres of 'thrust', 'parry', 'slash' and 'cut'.

The resentful men he was facing were at least fit. Once they had completed the construction of the longhouse in which they lived, he had lined them up and set them running up and down the riverbank, first with nothing to encumber them, then with swords held above their heads, then with a shield in one hand and a sword in the other.

Will was watching them carefully. Two of them in particular had caught his eye, because they appeared constantly alert and seemed to command some respect from the others. At the end of one day's particularly gruelling exercises, when the men appeared at least capable of wielding swords without cutting off their own limbs, Will called the two of them over.

'Your names?' he asked.

The larger of them was the first to speak. 'Enric of Huntingdon. Blacksmith by trade. Some of our swords lack an obvious edge, and if you can set me up a forge I can soon have them sharp again.'

'And you?' Will asked of the squatter man with the matted black hair.

'Norvel, also of Huntingdon. I am a builder, and supervised the construction of the longhouse where we now live, a long way from our women.'

'How did you two come to be in this company?' Will asked.

'A bad harvest,' Norvel replied. 'We were starving, and Earl Waltheof offered bread to those who volunteered. But Enric here killed a man.'

'He violated my daughter,' Enric said.

'How come you didn't hang?' Will asked.

'Earl Waltheof is the judge in our manor court, and he offered me this option.'

'Well, Enric who has already killed in anger,' Will replied, 'you shall be my captain, in command of the men and conveying my orders. As for you, Norvel, you are excused from further combat training until you have built Enric a suitable forge. Do you each accept?'

The two men nodded, and Will dismissed them to return to the others, who by now were either lying in the rushes of their longhouse or bathing naked in the river. As his eyes drifted back up the grassy slope, he caught sight of Elva, Joan and the children on their way down to Richeldis's shrine. They seemed to go there at around this time every day, and a few moments later he caught sight of Richeldis herself, moving swiftly down towards the same place.

On a whim he followed her, and stood a few yards away from the shrine as he heard the gentle murmuring of female voices, and then Richeldis's voice raised in a solo song. His curiosity aroused, he slipped in through the open rear door, where everyone was on their knees. Only tiny Thomas was above floor level, cradled in Joan's arms, and all their eyes were on the statue of the Virgin at the rear wall.

Richeldis became aware of Will standing uncertainly in the open doorway and beckoned him in. Joan looked round almost guiltily, while Elva's eyes never left the statue.

'Do please join us, Will,' Richeldis said. 'Are you a Christian?'

'I'm not really sure,' Will admitted as he walked as silently as he could, for reasons he didn't quite understand, towards where the women were kneeling. 'We received teaching of sorts from the friars who sometimes came to our village. They told us about Christ and the Bible, but only in exchange for food and drink.'

Richeldis nodded towards Elva. 'Your sister must have listened more attentively than you did, for she prays here every day. I found her here quite by accident one afternoon, and now each day we gather here for a few prayers and a holy psalm or two. Joan has also become interested in the word of God, I believe, and most mornings we talk about the wonderful message that Christ had to impart regarding an all-powerful but merciful God.'

'I was praying for Selwyn's safe return,' Elva explained.

'And I was praying for a safer life for us and our children,' Joan added, the streaks from earlier tears still evident on her cheeks.

'God hears all our prayers, Will,' Richeldis explained, 'and He also instils goodness and strength in all those He deems worthy of his work. It was when Waltheof told me about your efforts to save Saxons from the slaughter of the Godless William that I asked him to bring you here to defend this House of Mary. You are a good man, and clearly inspired by God, but you will be severely tested in the months to come, I fear.'

'I am prepared for that,' Will insisted.

Richeldis held out her hand. 'Come and kneel here with us, and let the peace of God give you added strength.'

Will looked down at Joan's face, which was infused with such love, pride and longing that he felt all resistance and embarrassment slip away. He knelt beside her. Matilda was gazing up at the statue, transfixed, as Richeldis began to recite a prayer.

Will only heard the first few lines of it, before a peaceful feeling came over him, almost as if he were drifting into a long and much-needed sleep. He had no idea how long his mind floated before he opened his eyes and gazed up.

It was almost certainly a trick of the late afternoon light, but it seemed to him that the Virgin was smiling at him, and he became aware of tears rolling down his cheeks. Then he saw Richeldis studying his face.

'Waltheof did not choose unwisely, it would seem,' she said softly.

XXIII

Selwyn stared with horror at the sight before his eyes. He was fifty feet above the ground, on the top of the steep climb up the castle motte, awaiting the right moment. But all that was momentarily forgotten as he took in the sheer size of what was approaching. The land to the south was relatively flat, and all he could see was a snaking line of fully armed soldiers, chainmail glinting in the sun's dying rays. If he closed his ears against the busy noise in the streets below, he could already hear the trudging sound of ten thousand boots on the march, and the combined jingle of two thousand or so horse harnesses, borne towards him on the stiff but variable breeze. They had seriously underestimated what they were taking on.

Suddenly, shouts and screams came from behind him as those loyal to King William were overpowered by the local men unwisely recruited by the king after he had destroyed their former lives. The gates of the bailey creaked open, and a hand beckoned him in. He hesitated, wondering if perhaps there had been a last-minute change of plan, given the sheer size of the oncoming royal army. Then he looked towards the south gate, which remained firmly shut, and would not be opened until he had carried out his part of the overall plan.

The soldier in him kicked back into place. He slipped inside the still open castle gates and ran to the right, where a brazier was burning brightly, intended for the comfort of those who had, until minutes before, been patrolling the outer bailey. To the side was a pile of wood supplied as its fuel, and he thrust one into the flames. He was swiftly joined by half a dozen other men, all grinning and cackling with delight, some still holding glinting blades festooned with fresh blood. Together they ran to the timber walls of the inner keep and laid their blazing burdens at its base.

In the stiff wind the flames took little time to lick up the wood that had been in place for less than a year. Within five minutes, the former castle built by royal command was a blazing beacon that could be seen for miles around. Selwyn ran back down the slope and merged with the curious onlookers, most of whom were cheering loudly. He slipped between two huts on the outer fringe of the castle surrounds, and watched the dark yellow flames twisting. But something was not going to plan: they had failed to calculate for the wind.

The strengthening early evening easterly breeze was lifting small portions of the burning roof, and carrying them high until they floated lazily to the ground. Several pieces landed on the thatched roofs of huts that had been constructed close together. Once the first went up like a burning cornfield, its neighbours stood no chance. Within minutes, the cheers had turned to screams and curses as people ran for safety. Then the wind changed yet again, and it was the turn of huts to the north, and even a small church building across the river.

Selwyn stood, transfixed, until his view down the narrow alleyway between huts that were still intact was obscured by the passage of a hundred mounted men in the royal livery. He realised that the south gate must have been opened in accordance with the plan. Shortly, if things progressed as agreed, the north gate would swing open and Gospatric's forces would sweep in, while men in the service of Edwin and Morcar would surround the king's men. But everywhere Selwyn looked, people seemed more intent on putting out flames, while a captain from the royal army was supervising men as they pulled down other intact huts in the path of the blaze, hoping to form a fire-break. They were working unchallenged, and Selwyn suddenly realised that there was no sign of the rearguard attack from Waltheof's men. All those who had poured through the south gate appeared to still be in King William's service.

He weaved his way through the chaos, running towards the north gate for sight of the incoming forces of Earl Gospatric. When he got there it was still locked and barred, and he yelled to one of the men on duty on the internal platform at its top, from which the land to the north could be surveyed for approaching enemy forces.

'Is there an army on its way in?' he yelled.

'No, but there's one heading north like their backsides were on fire!' came the reply, and Selwyn finally accepted that it had all gone wrong. The retreating men must be under the command of Gospatric, Edwin and Morcar, and they were no doubt forming an escort for Edgar Aetheling and King Malcolm of Scotland. Given the non-appearance of Waltheof's army, for whatever reason, those who remained were now playing host to the largest body of armed men King William had ever brought to York. The city was on fire, and all the brave rebels had taken to their heels, leaving those left behind to face the consequences.

It was obvious to Selwyn that unless he got out of York during the current confusion, he would eventually be brought before King William, questioned, tortured, and made to disclose how his precious castle came to be in flames. Even more to the point, others would be captured and questioned ahead of him, and sooner or later his name would be mentioned. Time to leave, by whatever means presented itself.

He pushed his way through the excited throng and headed for the stables. The south gate might still be open, and he could slip away unnoticed; he still had the directions to the place where Waltheof had assured him he would find sanctuary from King William, and he would be able to rejoin Elva, Will and the children.

He was overtaken by two men carrying blazing brands. They were easily recognisable by their emblems as thugs in the service of King William, and they were laughing as they approached a line of huts that had thus far escaped the flames. Selwyn gasped as he saw each of them throw a lighted brand into the roof of a hut, then stand with drawn swords in their doorways as the flames quickly took hold in the stiff wind, and screaming townsfolk pleaded to be let out. The screams grew louder and louder, then the first of the roof supports gave way, and a shower of burning thatch landed inside the first of the huts, while the screams became those of innocent folk being burned alive in their own homes.

Without thinking, Selwyn grabbed the sword arm of the man blocking the exit to the second hut, and yelled at him to let the occupants out. He could clearly see a woman with two small children clinging to her skirts and bawling in terror, while behind her was a more elderly couple wide-eyed with fear.

'Let them out, you murderous bastard!' Selwyn yelled above the screaming, only to find himself bound from behind by a pair of massive mailed arms that gripped him as if he were a tree trunk, and hauled him out of the way. Another man stepped forward, removed Selwyn's helm, then rammed the hilt of his sword into his temple.

Selwyn came round on a hard earth floor whose thin rushes smelt of dead rats. As he gathered his senses, he realised that he was not alone. There were others like him, some still comatose, others rising groggily to their knees. They all sported the livery of Earl Edwin. After what felt like several hours, a heavy wooden door opened, and four of King William's men-at-arms strutted in with swords already drawn. They quickly scanned the twenty or so men in the chamber, and indicated with their sword tips which of them was to accompany them. Selwyn was relieved to be one of those chosen — if nothing else, the smell of fear in that cramped space was beginning to make him feel queasy.

As they hit the open air, Selwyn realised that it was fully dark, and that to judge by the smell of burned oak, and the debris lying underfoot, they were in the keep of the former castle — the one he had supervised the burning of, before the rash plans of others had come to naught. They were marched down the motte and into the streets between burned-out huts, outside of which entire families were standing with shattered, fearful looks, clutching in their hands the only possessions they had left.

Selwyn began to send a last, silent message of love in his mind to Elva and Elston as he recognised the building to which they were heading. It was Edwin's manor house, and either Edwin himself had fled the scene, or he was inside there being horribly tortured until he identified those who had been privy to the burning of the castle. By now, King William would be aware that an ambush had been planned upon his arrival, and he would no doubt lose no time in putting its ringleaders to death.

The line of men of which Selwyn was an unwilling member was ordered to form up in front of a high chair, in which sat a frozen-faced king clutching a large flagon of wine. A serving man with his arms tied in front of him was driven at sword point down the line, and as he looked into the faces of each man, he yelled back confirmation that he knew them. In

Selwyn's case, he went further and announced, 'This were one o' those what were allus wi' Edwin when 'e were plottin' the 'ole thing.'

The man next to William translated this into French, and Selwyn was accused of being one of Edwin's conspirators in the plot against the throne. He replied that he was a loyal soldier performing his duty in the service of his master. He was then asked if he was referring to the service of Edwin or the service of the king, and he wisely chose to reply that he had, until yesterday, believed it to be the same thing. William yelled out an instruction, and a burly man-at-arms stepped towards Selwyn with a knife.

Selwyn closed his eyes and anticipated the burning sensation of a blade slicing through skin as it detached an ear or a nose. But to his profound relief he felt only a tugging at his chainmail, and he opened his eyes to see Edwin's emblem being cut loose. It fell into the rushes, and the man-at-arms stomped on it with his boot, and then for good measure spat on the reviled symbol of Selwyn's former master.

Through the translation offered by the man at William's side, Selwyn gathered that he was now a soldier in the service of King William, and would be supplied with a new emblem when he had earned the right to wear it. In the meantime, he was to be under the supervision of someone more directly loyal to the crowned King of England. He would, he was informed, be required to ride out of York for duties yet to be assigned. For that purpose he was to retrieve his horse from the stables that had escaped the fire, and report for duty at daybreak the following day. For the time being, he was free to go, although if he desired food and drink, he was to steal it from local folk.

Outside, he could hardly believe his good fortune. As the sun's first rays blinded him, he waited patiently for his new tasks to be assigned to him, confident that at the first opportunity he would kick his horse into urgent life and pound southward before anyone could pursue him. Then it would be back to his beloved Elva and Elston. He half remembered the name of the place to which he would be headed, but had already discovered, with an oath, that his saddlebag had been robbed of the spare shirt that it contained, in which he had kept the scroll containing the precise directions. Hopefully the person who had found it would simply have thrown it away, but once Selwyn reached Huntingdon, if ever, he would need to ask for new directions.

'Are you one o' mine?' asked a rough voice to his right.

Selwyn screwed up his eyes to look towards the hulking shadow that loomed to his side, hoping to make out facial features. 'Probably. I was told to report for duties outside York, but beyond that I was given no more detail.'

'You one o' them idiots that was servin' Earl Edwin?' the man asked.

'Yes,' Selwyn admitted, 'but I had no idea what he was planning.'

'Yeah, they're all sayin' that, apparently. But yer'll do. Saddle up an' join the others over in the brewery yard.'

Selwyn joined the mixed party awaiting further orders. Most of them were mounted, but there was a cart containing various implements and a large quantity of wood, so those on foot would no doubt be allowed to ride inside it, rather than walk.

The man from earlier reappeared, and Selwyn was able to make out an emblem on his chainmail that he could not quite place. At least it was not that of William of Normandy, Selwyn reassured himself. Not long after they had ridden through the south gate, then picked up the pace on the track south to

Selby, he found himself riding alongside the same man, who caught him glancing at his emblem.

'Waltheof of East Anglia,' the man told him roughly. 'Another one what were stupid enough ter show King William 'is arse. The last I saw o' Waltheof, 'e were bein' taken down ter the dungeon under Lincoln Castle. I'm Wynstan, by the way.'

'Selwyn. Where exactly are we headed?'

'Howden, two days' ride, they reckon. We'll need ter stay somewhere overnight, so we won't put it ter the flames until we're leavin' it tomorrer mornin'.'

'We have orders to set more fires?' Selwyn asked nervously. 'What quarrel does King William have with the people of Howden?'

'It's in Northumbria. What other excuse does 'e need?'

'Is he planning on burning down the whole of Northumbria?' Selwyn asked, aghast.

'No idea, my friend — I just does what I'm told. And you do what I tell yer, or else.'

'Of course,' Selwyn conceded. 'It just seems to me to be a bit excessive, that's all.'

'From what we was told,' Wynstan confided, 'it's goin' ter be 'appenin' ter every place between the 'umber an' the borders o' Scotland. D'yer think we're the only ones sent out wi' a wagon full o' sticks to burn? We're meant ter burn their crops an' slaughter their animals an' all. After we've killed the folks what lives there, an' burned their 'ouses down, that is.'

Selwyn suppressed a shudder and kept his eyes on the track ahead. He hoped to make his escape early in their travels, before he was forced to witness — and perhaps even become part of — what was to follow.

Late that afternoon they approached an isolated manor house set alongside a broad stream, and Wynstan called a halt. He trotted his horse towards the entrance, where a middle-aged man stepped out from under his thatch to speak with him. Wynstan turned in his saddle and waved his hand, whereupon the entire company of twenty or so turned off the track and regrouped on the rough ground in front of the doorway. Two hours later, a white-haired lady was bringing out cooked meats and freshly baked bread, while a girl who looked to be in her late teens, with long dark brown hair and a nervous smile, offered them mead. Tasting mead again, rather than the thin wine he had grown more used to of late, Selwyn was transported back to his youth. He looked up, and a small boy of about seven years of age was staring at him as he ate.

'I'm Wilfrid,' the boy said with a slight impediment, and once again Selwyn was reminded of better days.

'I have a friend called Wilfrid,' he said to the boy, 'and I married his sister.'

'Are you one of the king's soldiers?' Wilfrid asked.

Selwyn nodded with shame.

'Have you ever killed anybody?' was the boy's next question.

The young woman Selwyn had seen earlier rushed over and scooped him up with an apologetic look. 'Please forgive 'is insolence, sir, but 'e's only six.'

'That's alright,' Selwyn assured her. 'I have a son of my own, although he's not yet two years old.'

'An' a wife an' all?' she asked, and Selwyn nodded. 'Are they ridin' wi' yer?'

Selwyn shook his head. 'No, they're … well, I'm not entirely sure *where* they are at present, but I hope to rejoin them soon.'

'God bless yer all anyway,' the girl said as she led the boy away, and Selwyn suddenly no longer felt hungry.

As soon as the loud rhythmic snoring of the men with whom he was sharing the stable floor assured him that it might be safe to do so, Selwyn untied his horse and led him by the bridle into the starlit night. After checking the leathers for tightness, he climbed onto his horse's back and walked him quietly over the grassier patches.

Once back on the main track south he gave the horse its head, and by sunrise the next day he concluded that he had perhaps put enough distance between himself and the murderous crew as part of which he had left York. He said a silent prayer for the innocent young boy who shared his brother-in-law's name, the girl who must have given birth to him while still almost a child herself, and the gentle grandparents who had been so generous with what little food and drink they had, little suspecting how their generosity would be repaid the following day — the day that was just beginning. He lay down to rest with tears in his eyes, having tied the horse to a tree at the side of the track.

He was awoken by someone kicking at the soles of his feet. He opened his eyes and squinted into the glare of full daylight. Above him stood Wynstan.

'I might've guessed yer'd desert first chance yer got. On yer feet.'

Richeldis de Faverches was not the only one for whom the shrine to Our Lady of Walsingham, as it was rapidly becoming known, had a fascination bordering upon a mania. She had been watching carefully as Elva seemed to be strangely drawn, not just to the natural peace of the shrine, but the legend that lay behind it. Richeldis had taught her all about the holy lady who'd been chosen to bear the Son of God, and how she had accepted with humility and grace the fact that he would be taken from her by the cruelty of man. Elva could relate to all that, with the chosen man in her life taken from her in the maelstrom of cruelty and wickedness that had overtaken the land of her birth.

Richeldis had also begun to spread the good word among a wider populace, and every day visitors would arrive at the shrine, bathe their feet symbolically before entering it barefoot, then bow their heads while Richeldis led them in prayer. Pilgrims, simple local folk and occasionally more elevated clergy such as monks, friars, priests, and even — on one occasion — the local bishop, would kneel humbly in front of the wooden image of the Holy Lady who had once visited this place to bestow peace upon it. On some days Elva herself led the prayers.

Word had drifted in from coastal villages such as Lynn, Overstrand, Lowestoft and Felixstowe that a great fleet of ships was working its way down the east coast, coming ashore from time to time to pillage what was available, and disembarking men with axes who would kill, rape and terrorise any villagers who were unwise enough to stand and resist. They spoke a strange tongue that was still familiar to some of the older folk, and it was believed that they were heading for London.

They also learned that there had been a massive slaughter further north, as King William took his revenge on those whose only offence had been to live in the region in which Edwin and Morcar had sought to rebel against his rule. As a final curse upon them, William had ordered that the land itself be soured with salt, so that there would not even be a harvest for the following year, or the year after that. There were also hideous rumours that in the last throes of starvation, the people of the north had begun to eat each other. It was becoming known as 'the great harrying', and the small community at Walsingham could only pray that it would not come south into the region notionally ruled by Earl Waltheof. However, they had not seen him for months, and it was rumoured that he was languishing in the dungeons of Lincoln Castle.

Aware of all these rumours, Will kept his men fully alert and organised patrols of the perimeter, just as if they were all under siege. His men tolerated the regime, if only because they were regularly fed, and would occasionally receive a gift of coin from Lady Richeldis, the source of whose wealth never became obvious. The rough peasants from Huntingdon who now constituted a credible fighting force of some twenty men were also kept firmly in line by their new captain, Enric, who most of them had feared even before they'd arrived at Walsingham.

Selwyn's first thought as he scrambled to his feet was that Wynstan had not immediately put him to the sword. Then he looked round and realised that they were alone.

'Where are the rest of the men?' Selwyn asked sleepily.

Wynstan grimaced. 'Yer not the only deserter. Killin' men in battle is one thing, but puttin' old folks, kids an' young lassies ter the sword, an' burning' their 'ouses down, that's another matter. I couldn't rightly stop 'em, 'cos that's what our orders were, but when they 'eld that lassie by 'er long 'air, an' did that to 'er in front of 'er kid, well, that were it fer me, I'm afraid. I've got a lass about the same age, yer see. Anyroad, we're both deserters now, so what d'yer think we should do next?'

'Get as far south of Northumbria as we can,' Selwyn suggested. 'How far's Huntingdon from here?'

'Mebbe two or three days. Certainly no quicker. If we keep ahead o' the king's men, we can live off the land, an' we'll mebbe be the last that ever does that, around these parts anyroad. They reckon King William's plannin' on ridin' south pretty soon, 'cos there's a lot o' them Danish types 'eadin' fer London. That's why Earl Waltheof's in trouble — it were 'im what invited 'em, or so they say.'

Two days later, just north of Lincoln, they awoke in the latest barn that they had commandeered to the sound of a massive party of men. Wynstan crept to the door and looked out.

'Ter judge by the size of 'em, an' all the bloody banners an' suchlike, it's King William marchin' south. Now we 'as ter keep be'ind 'em. Mind you, they won't be burning no crops nor killin' no animals, else they'll have nowt to eat themselves.'

Waltheof was shoved to the floor inside the Great Hall of Lincoln Castle, and William glared down at him.

'You're only half the size you were when you were locked away,' he gloated, 'and that's because the rats had most of the little food you were allowed. And you seem to find daylight something of a challenge, to judge by the way you're squinting up at me. They tell me you smell worse than a wet sheep, but I don't intend to get that close. Hopefully, the first king to smell you will be the Danish bastard, because I intend to release you long enough for you to deliver the second instalment of gold coin — closely supervised by my own men, of course. Then you'll tell him to go back to Denmark. If he gets to London before you do, you're dead, since the queen is residing at West Minster.'

'Thank you, sire,' Waltheof croaked as he grew accustomed to using his voice once again. 'I won't let you down this time. What are your orders once I get rid of King Sweyn?'

'See to your own lands,' William replied. 'I'm advised that in your absence, a local brigand has taken to helping himself wherever he and his scum take a fancy. They have been able to take advantage of your long rest here in Lincoln, but I intend to flush them out and make an example of them while you deal with the Danes.'

'It shall be done, sire,' Waltheof assured him.

'See that it is,' William growled back. 'You are the first to whom I have ever given a second chance, and in truth it is only because my niece is so ugly that forcing you to marry her will be a fitting eternal punishment.'

'Did the Blessed Virgin never have a husband?' Elva asked of Richeldis, as they sat on the grass slope looking down at the shrine.

'Yes, she did,' Richeldis told her. 'According to the Bible, he was a man called "Joseph", and he married her out of pity because of her dishonour in being unmarried while carrying a child in her womb.'

'And yet that child became Jesus?' Elva queried.

'He did indeed,' Richeldis said, 'but no-one knew at that time — apart from Mary herself, of course — that he was to become so special.' She paused. 'Do you miss your man dreadfully?'

'Of course I do, but he's been away so long now that I barely remember what it was like when he was here. I think I could live quite happily without a man by my side. I don't imagine that I will ever be the same after receiving the grace and peace of the Blessed Mary.'

'You know that there are groups of women of like mind?' Richeldis asked cautiously. 'They live in holy houses throughout the land, and they are called "nuns". Their houses are called "convents", and should you ever become single, you might wish to consider joining one of them.'

'Could I do so without being single?' Elva asked.

Richeldis shook her head. 'For as long as your man is alive, you owe it to your child to remain by his side and provide a proper home. For me it's different, being twice widowed. But I have often thought that it would be the appropriate thing to form my own holy house here in Walsingham. I would call it "The Convent of the Holy Sisters of the Blessed Virgin", and you would of course be very welcome to work with us. Just not in holy orders, that's all. For that you would need to foreswear any congress with your man, which would not be right.'

'I've foresworn it for so long that I don't think I'd miss it, to be perfectly honest with you,' Elva confessed.

Selwyn and Wynstan approached the north gate of Lincoln cautiously, having watched from a nearby hillock as the royal procession wound its way south again. There had been an earlier departure by a smaller group, and Wynstan's practised eye had spotted the pennants of his own force fluttering in the easterly breeze that seemed to be a permanent feature of the flat landscape.

They remained in Lincoln for long enough to eat and drink, and then Wynstan took himself off to the barracks and came back with an emblem for Selwyn to fix onto his chainmail, to identify him as one in the service of Earl Waltheof. By the middle of the day they were riding hard for Huntingdon. Two days later they sneaked into the town that was the seat of governance for East Anglia, and Wynstan was gleefully welcomed home by his wife, daughter and granddaughter.

The following morning he was seated outside, humming happily and deciding what to do next. When Selwyn joined him, Wynstan had concluded that he was honour-bound to find Earl Waltheof and report back for duty.

'What about you?' he asked of Selwyn.

'I had hoped to rejoin my own family, somewhere east of here, but I have no adequate directions. I only know that the place is called "Walsington", or something like that. I've never been there. Earl Waltheof gave me directions when we spoke together in York months ago, but I lost them, I'm afraid.'

Wynstan smiled. 'I'm pretty sure yer mean "Walsingham", since it's one o' the earl's favourite places. I've never been there meself, but if yer 'ead north an' east've 'ere, to a place called "Lynn", then ask again, yer'll be sure ter find it. Yer officially in the service of the earl now, so nobody's likely ter challenge yer. But mind what we 'eard in Lincoln — King William's still around these parts, so best keep yer 'ead down, in case 'e remembers yer.'

XXIV

Several weeks later, William was in a foul humour as he sat in the hall of the Abbot of St Alban's, Cambridge, awaiting the completion of the new castle he had commissioned. In better times, he could have taken out his ill humour on some local rebel, but everyone in Cambridge seemed to have been born with a bent knee, such was their instant recognition of his power. A bunch of grovelling sycophants, but at least they were giving him no trouble. Not like that evasive bastard who called himself Hereward.

He'd been pillaging local churches and monasteries, and William wished to maintain his good standing with God, so he'd set off after him with a large army. That had been three weeks ago, and every time they got close to him, the slimy lamprey would run back into the malodorous swamps that he called home, and William dared not order his heavily armoured knights in after him. The first attempt had been a morale-sapping disaster, with at least ten noble knights and their monstrous destriers sucked into the evil-smelling green slime, from which they had not resurfaced.

King Sweyn had not reached London, so William could not carry out his threat to put Waltheof to death. However, when he reached Cambridge on his return north, Waltheof was summoned and ordered to search out Hereward without delay and bring him back to Cambridge in a dung cart.

'Where will I find him?' Waltheof asked.

William grew purple in the face as he screamed back. 'It's your job to find out! If you can't put paid to one local traitor, how can you lay claim to an earldom, let alone to the hand of my ugly little niece?'

Elva was, as usual, devoting prayers to The Blessed Virgin for the safe return of the man who was rapidly becoming a distant memory. Then she pleaded for a sign as to whether or not she was ready to forgo all worldly pleasure and devote herself wholly to the worship of the holy lady who had come to feel like a mother to her.

She eased herself from her knees and made her way into the warm sunlight, marvelling yet again at the blessings that God poured down on His people. Then she heard her name being called, and turned.

A man on a horse was guiding his mount carefully across the river, and when he reached the near bank he called her name again. With a strangled cry she saw his face, and she raced down the grass towards him, heedless of her footing. Then as the man threw himself from the saddle, she saw the tears rolling down his cheeks.

'Praise be to God!' she screamed. 'Thank you, Blessed Mother! Selwyn! Oh, Selwyn — I feared you were dead!'

'Have you noticed any important change in Elva while I've been away?' Selwyn asked Will a few hours after he'd been reunited with the family. 'She seems devoted to that "shrine", as she calls it. You know — that little white house?'

'You must ask Lady Richeldis about that,' Will told him, 'since the two of them are forever huddled together in there, along with other folk who come to prostrate themselves in front of that statue. It is of the Virgin Mary, and if you remember the tales told to us in our youth by the friars, "Mary" was the mother of Christ, the son of God.'

'And Elva is devoted to her worship?'

'So it would seem. She seemed to gain great comfort from it during your lengthy absence, and she would tell us of how she was praying for your safety. Perhaps it's true, as Richeldis maintains, that this Mary once visited this place and blessed it.'

'But this is surely just peasant superstition?' Selwyn challenged him.

'You are safe, are you not?'

'Thanks to my own wits, yes. But on that subject, how safe is this place?'

Will smiled. 'We see very few here, other than those who visit the shrine. We've certainly never seen William of Normandy, or Waltheof, since he took off north.'

'And he was fortunate indeed to be allowed to return south,' Selwyn replied as he launched into a full account of the failed rebellion in York, the merciless suppression of the whole of Northumbria that had followed, and the arrest and subsequent release of Earl Waltheof.

'He's obviously still a free man,' Will told Selwyn, 'since Lady Richeldis advises me that he's to dine here in two days' time, along with some churchman or other. We are all invited.'

On the appointed day, Selwyn was playing with little Elston on the grassy slope when he became aware of the approach of four men on horseback. One he recognised immediately as Earl Waltheof. The man riding by his side was unknown to him, but to judge by his monk's garb he was the second guest they were expecting for the midday meal.

Within the hour, they were all feasting on wild turkey and washing it down with mead. Waltheof effected the introductions.

'This man is Abbot Francois of Peterborough. He is Norman by birth, but speaks perfect English, and he has both a need

267

for our services, and a means of us all being of service to King William. I will let him explain.'

The somewhat elderly abbot bowed his head in acknowledgement, and smiled benignly round the table. 'As Earl Waltheof told you, I am the Abbot of Peterborough. I replaced the previous abbot, who was the uncle of a man you may have heard of called Hereward, a Godless robber, blasphemer and murderer who lives by stealing the rightful property of others.'

'We hear of little else these days,' Will grumbled.

'Then I need hardly explain further what a thorn he has become in the side of the law-abiding Christian community around here. Also the king, who has been attempting for some time to hound him to his lair and apprehend him. Unfortunately the way into that lair is surrounded by treacherous marshland and bog, so much so that the land inside is regarded locally as an island. The Isle of Ely, they call it, and King William has thus far been unable to find a way in.'

'Francois knows such a way in,' Waltheof added eagerly.

The abbot nodded. 'How I come to know of it is a long and somewhat sordid tale involving a friar and a very young girl. I will not repeat the details in the presence of these delightful children, but it is enough to say that in exchange for preserving his soul from eternal hellfire, he shared with me his account of how he installed this girl in a hut on the island, which he would visit whenever the urge took him — and a very evil urge it was indeed, as you can imagine. Anyway, he led me to that hut in order to rescue the girl, who is now a novice in our sister house, and I have a distinct memory of which paths to take between the marshes that trap the unwary.'

'King William has tasked me with the capture of this Hereward,' Waltheof explained, 'and Abbott Francois seeks the return of some precious items stolen from his abbey.'

'King William has by far the larger army,' Will pointed out suspiciously, 'so why can he not go in after this Hereward for himself?'

'For the reason you have heard already,' Waltheof said. 'Hereward and his followers have their own secret way in and out, and William is at risk of becoming a laughing stock through his inability to capture, with a force of ten thousand, a band of men that is no larger than a hundred. He has therefore passed the task to me; either I will succeed, and retain his good offices that led to his not putting me to death, or I will fail, and either be killed in the attempt or when I report my failure to him.'

'Bringing this Hereward to heel is clearly crucial to you,' Selwyn observed, 'and it would seem that you know the secret track into his lair. So why do you need us?'

'I need you to flush him out,' Waltheof replied. 'If they are attacked from all sides, they will clearly seek to escape along this safe track. Then I will be waiting for them, with perhaps as many as a thousand men.'

'And there is only the one safe way in or out, you say?' Will asked. 'If that is so, how do you propose that this small band from Walsingham can get close enough to force them to flee to safety?'

'On the eastern side there are trees growing out of the marsh,' Abbot Francois explained. 'Trees sufficient for a silent band of men to sneak up on them, then create enough noise and confusion to cause them to flee.'

Will and Selwyn exchanged uneasy glances. Will shook his head. 'What you ask could lead only to our deaths, either in unequal combat against a hundred men, or when we are sucked down by the marsh grasses.'

'Those who earn their livelihood by harvesting the reeds from the marshes wear a special type of shoe,' Waltheof told them. 'It's a flat meshed board, and it holds a man above the marshland itself, enabling him to slide forward without sinking.'

'And it no doubt makes a great deal of noise in the process,' Will argued. 'We would also then be at a great disadvantage, fighting hand to hand while encumbered by boards on our feet.'

'The island on which they live is firm ground,' Waltheof told them. 'We know this at least from women who have plied their immoral trade in there. These women were led in and out of there blindfolded, but those blindfolds were untied once it was time for them to conduct their business, and they all speak of an area of dry land on which reed huts have been constructed. I propose that you and your men make your way in by night, suitably clad with reed-cutters' shoes, then slip them off at daybreak, when suitably hidden around their camp. Then you imitate a sizeable army and fall upon them without warning, flushing them down the safe path where we can cut them down.'

'"Imitate a sizeable army",' Will repeated sarcastically. '*You* are the one with the sizeable army, are you not? A thousand men or so, you mentioned earlier. You would need less than half of that to ambush a hundred men on the run. I still cannot for the life of me understand why you cannot undertake this task without involving my small band, whose only contribution would be to make wild noises in the trees surrounding their camp.'

Waltheof and Abbot Francois exchanged uneasy looks.

'Unfortunately, the word of God has not travelled through the western Fenlands as widely as one would have hoped,' explained Francois. 'The men of Huntingdon and Cambridge are still in thrall to old superstitions, old Gods, and folktales that were ancient even before the first Christian missionaries arrived in these parts. They still stubbornly believe the old legends handed down over blazing fires in the chill of the night, of nature spirits and hideous monsters that prowl the Fens, their dismal howling heard on the winds that blast from the halls of the dead.'

'I'll take the children out to play a game,' Joan offered with a shudder.

Once they were safely out of earshot, Will had another objection. 'If such superstitious nonsense still infects the wits of *your* men,' he asked Waltheof, 'how are mine any different?'

'Have they not, while here, come to worship the true God?' Francois asked. 'Have they lived within feet of the place which the Mother of God chose to bless, without becoming Christians?'

'My woman's certainly caught that disease,' Selwyn muttered. Both Elva and Francois stared at him in outrage.

'You call Christianity a *disease*?' Francois challenged him.

Before Selwyn could offer a retort that might be even more offensive, Will jumped in. 'Without doubt there is something in this place that offers peace of mind against blind superstition, but I hardly imagine that the simple men of Huntingdon who you first brought here, who by my estimation were formerly rough peasants themselves, have now become suitable candidates for holy orders.'

'I may be able to assist there,' Richeldis chimed in, having listened in silence thus far. 'I have long sought an opportunity to preach the word of God among the heathen, and as we have observed for ourselves, it does not take long for the peace of the Blessed Virgin to enter any heart that is exposed to it.'

'It has certainly entered mine,' Elva enthused, with a defiant sideways look at Selwyn.

'It pains and embarrasses me somewhat to have to admit this,' Francois said, 'but the early elders of my holy order soon learned that such superstitious traditions may be turned to good advantage. Instead of seeking to ridicule the ancient spirits, they came to realise that they could point men's heads toward God by persuading them that Jesus Christ and the Blessed Virgin were more powerful than woodland sprites or river monsters. The Cross of Christ has often been sold as a powerful talisman against any demon of the Old Way, even the "Black Shuck" that is said to haunt this region — a huge hound with blazing red eyes and dripping jaws.'

'You're proposing to fight devilry with even more powerful devilry?' Selwyn asked.

Francois winced. 'If you choose to put it that way, yes. I'll conduct divine service on the morrow, and instruct each man to construct himself a crude cross from the wood around the estate — one that is small enough to be hung around their necks on a piece of hempen cord — then I'll bless each cross in turn before the altar of the Virgin. With the greatest of respect to your piety and dedication, Lady Richeldis, what I propose will certainly be a lot quicker.'

'And you really believe that hanging a cross of wood around their necks will convince these hard fighting men that God is preserving them from all harm?' Selwyn asked.

'That is the essence of the Christian faith, my son,' Francois replied, 'and I'll sprinkle the one around your neck with holy water, as a double precaution.'

The following morning, Abbot Francis demonstrated his talents as a showman and piqued the curiosity of the warrior peasants by conducting a loud and dramatic Mass in front of the statue of Mary in the shrine. Will, Selwyn and their womenfolk were present. Lady Richeldis added to the mystery by donning a nun's tunic and veil and walking three times around the outside of the shrine, waving a thurible of slowly smoking incense that added to the seeming magic of the occasion.

Once the men had been drawn towards the sounds and smells of the strange ceremony, Francois emerged and invited them inside so that they might become invincible warriors. Several of those who had come from Huntingdon were no strangers to the Christian religion, having become aware of some of its manifestations in the local cathedral, but now they were intrigued to be invited to partake in what they had, as mere peasants, rarely been allowed to do.

The abbot drew a small silver cross from his robes and held it high in the air. 'With this simple cross, all the forces of darkness can be driven back to their lairs,' he told them. 'Each man who kneels and worships God shall be given the gift of everlasting life. Let each man make himself a simple cross and present it to this Holy Lady whose image is here before us, and he shall be eternally free from the evils of this world. Join with me this day and vanquish your enemies.'

'I hope they still remember how to fight,' Will whispered to Selwyn as they stood on the grass slope and watched the men forming a queue to have their newly made crosses blessed.

'I only hope I don't fall over when I try to walk on those table tops,' Selwyn replied as he saw one of the men-at-arms who had accompanied Waltheof unloading a pannier from his horse's flank, and dropping a seemingly inexhaustible supply of woven rush platforms onto the grass.

For the next few days they practised lifting their feet carefully and sliding across the grass, before moving to a rougher patch of pasture once they began to get the hang of it. Following a suggestion by Joan, Will made a game of it by organising races, with a pot of Richeldis's honey for the winners.

Soon, the entire company was ready to move off, led by Waltheof, Francois and their armed and mounted escort. Three days after their departure, as the sun set over Ely, they stood on the fringes of a tangled mass of reeds, rushes, shrubs and stunted trees, many of them willows that had seeded with high expectations, but had been lost in the perennial slime that had overpowered their roots. Waltheof look down from his saddle and wished them every success in their venture.

'My men will be ready and waiting when you flush them out,' he assured them, 'and King William will reward our enterprise.'

'I wonder how he'll reward my desertion,' Will muttered as he waved his contingent of twenty forward, with a final warning to move as silently as possible through the swamp that lay ahead of them.

For the next two hours they slurped through gaps in the foliage in pitch darkness, some of the more superstitious men holding their crosses aloft in their free hands, while grasping their shields in the other. Occasionally they would disturb a nesting wild fowl, which would flutter off noisily, causing a moment's heart-stopping fear for those who were not entirely convinced that every water spirit or marsh demon had been expelled by the elderly monk.

Finally, as the first faint streaks of a red dawn rose above the skyline to the east, they stood obscured amid a line of ash trees that had found firmer roots in the slowly rising sandbank on which could be seen several reed huts. A man sat hunched in front of a brazier that was still exhibiting a dull glow as it burned down. He seemed to be asleep.

Selwyn sidled up to Will. 'I have an idea that comes from what occurred in York. Tell the men to take off their marsh footwear, and be prepared to make as much noise as possible, without breaking cover. The sign to do that will be when men half-dressed pour out of three burning huts. Once they are out, we chase them down that track to the left, which must be their safe escape route.'

Will watched with bated breath as Selwyn emerged from the treeline, doubled up, and crept slowly up to the brazier. He gently took the knife from the belt of the sleeping look-out, and rammed it into his unarmoured gut. There was a grunt, followed by a sickening slurp, and the man pitched over sideways. With a grin of triumph, Selwyn reached down for several stick bundles and inserted them into the brazier. When they were fully alight, he ran forward and launched each of them into the roof thatch of a reed hut.

Since it hadn't rained for weeks, in less than a minute the roofs had become blazing canopies. They began to hear cries of alarm, then shouts, as the men inside the huts realised that they were in danger of being burned alive where they lay, and one by one they began to tumble out of the huts, half asleep.

'Now!' Selwyn yelled as he turned back towards the trees. His followers duly obliged with an ear-shattering racket of sword hilt on shield boss, to which they added fierce yells without emerging from their cover. The overall effect was that of a marauding army about to charge, and most of the men ran back into the huts to retrieve their weapons. Most, but not all.

Hereward himself advanced on Selwyn with a drawn sword, growling obscenities. Will realised with horror that Selwyn had left his sword propped against a tree before creeping out to set fire to the huts, and he yelled and hurled the sword in Selwyn's direction. It fell a little short of its intended recipient, and Selwyn rushed forward to pick it up. As he rose and turned, pivoting on the leg that still pained him, it gave way and he went down on one knee.

Seizing his chance, Hereward raced at him with a screaming curse. As Selwyn rose unsteadily, he provided a perfect target. The sword plunged so far, and so hard, into his chest that the sound of shattering breastbone blended with Selwyn's final death scream. He sank into the sand, blood pumping through his mail where his heart had been pierced.

Will stood transfixed by the sight, and it was Enric who yelled the command to charge. The men leapt from the undergrowth, free at last from the restriction of their strange walking platforms, and hurled themselves at the hut entrances. As each man tumbled out, he was either felled by a determined slash or stab, or was able to slip sideways behind a comrade who was being slaughtered and race down the sand path towards where Waltheof and his men would be waiting. Realising that his men had been taken unawares, Hereward yelled for them to follow him, and a handful of them were last seen racing for their lives into the ambush that lay ahead.

It was almost an hour before Waltheof rode up on his horse, and looked mournfully down at Selwyn's corpse. Will hunched over it, his tears splashing into the fatal wound.

XXV

The sad procession wound its way through the gateway to Lady Richeldis's manor, Will in the lead on his tired mount, with Selwyn's body draped over the other horse that Will was leading by the bridle.

Joan ran out of the hut yelling with joy, and she threw herself at Will as he slowly dismounted. Then her gaze drifted to the dead eyes of the man lying across the other horse, and she froze in horror. 'Oh no. Please, no!'

Will's eyes met those of Elva as she stood in the doorway of their hut. She walked slowly towards the sad group by the gate. Before Will could begin the small speech he had been rehearsing for two days, she looked up at him, tears rolling down reddened cheeks.

'I asked the Blessed Mary for a sign. I would have hoped for something other than this, but now I have my sign.'

Selwyn was buried a few feet away from the shrine two days later. Richeldis conducted the brief burial service in her own rustic style, dressed in the nun's garments she had worn before. Prior to his departure, Abbot Francois had granted his permission for the formation of a second sister house to his Peterborough Abbey, with Richeldis as its first abbess, and now she already had her first novice by her side.

Elva showed no outward sign of emotion as she watched Norvel shovel the first load of earth over Selwyn's funeral shroud, but she was whispering a prayer as she stood solemnly in the all-white habit tied loosely at the waist. Her luxuriant red hair had been shorn down to her scalp, but the results were hidden beneath a white veil. The only remnant of her former life was a lock of Selwyn's hair, woven lovingly around the cross that hung from her belt. Joan and Will had agreed to take care of Elston.

'Will we be making our home here?' Joan asked Will as they sat outside their hut a week later. They were basking in the rays of the setting sun and gazing down at the simple cross that marked Selwyn's final resting place.

'Why should we not?' Will asked sadly. 'Selwyn is buried here, and Elva will clearly be remaining. The children appear to be content.'

'You will have to learn to call Elva "Sister Grace" soon,' Joan reminded him, 'just as Lady Richeldis has become "Mother Magdelena".'

'Until then, she's still my sister Elva,' Will insisted.

It fell silent for a moment, then Joan asked quietly, 'What will you do for a living if we are to remain here?'

'The village across the river has no mill, and everyone has to go to Fakenham to have their grain ground. If I could prevail upon "Mother Magdelena" to grant me some land down by the river, I think the race is fast enough for most of the year for me to build a mill and take up my old trade.'

'Promise me you've finished with being a soldier?'

'I was *never* a soldier, until circumstances dictated the need to take up a sword. But if the need arises again, I shall not be found wanting.'

'Let's hope that it never does,' Joan murmured. 'Talking of which, what news is there of King William?'

'According to Waltheof, he's planning to return to Normandy but wishes to place men he can trust in positions of authority. Waltheof has been forgiven his past treachery, after putting paid to Hereward, and he'll shortly be marrying William's niece.'

Joan tutted loudly. 'It was *you* who drove Hereward away. You and your men, anyway. And poor dear Selwyn, of course. It cost him his life, and what reward has William given you?'

'He's let me live,' Will replied. 'I never knew William to grant mercy to anyone who showed him disloyalty. Except Waltheof, of course, but then he needed him to hold down peasants like me, who never survive William's anger. England may be at peace now, but William's wrath never will be.'

Three nights later, a shadow fell over the family's hut entrance as they sat at supper.

Will rose. 'Waltheof, what a welcome surprise! Do you come to visit Selwyn's grave?'

'No, I bring you a visitor,' Waltheof announced. He stood back as a man brushed him aside and strode in.

Will gasped and sank to his knees, and King William glowered down at him.

'A deserter caught at last! What reason did you have to scuttle from my service like a rat from a burning grain store?'

'To bring my family here, sire,' Will stuttered in French.

'And this is your family?' William demanded as he gazed round the humble all-purpose room.

'Yes, sire,' Will told him.

'You knew the penalty for desertion without just cause?' William demanded.

'Yes, sire.'

'But you deserted nevertheless?'

'Yes, sire.'

'I see your reason all around us, but I cannot condone desertion by someone of such lowly rank as yourself. Wilfrid of

Pevensey I dubbed you, but you proved that this was not an appropriate level of elevation for you. It is perhaps appropriate that you remain on your knees.'

He drew his sword, and Joan gave a strangled scream, not having understood a word of their conversation. She watched in horror as William raised his sword.

Will bowed his head, and prayed that the pain would be only momentary. Then he found himself praying to the Blessed Virgin, and wondered at his own superstition.

He waited for the sensation of a sword cutting through his neck, but felt only a light pressure on his right shoulder. He opened his eyes, and saw the smile on William's face as he transferred the flat blade of his sword to Will's left shoulder and spoke.

'You knelt as Wilfrid of Pevensey. Now rise, Sir Wilfrid of Walsingham.'

A NOTE TO THE READER

Dear Reader,

Thank you for your support for this first novel in a series that between them cover the twelfth century, a period during which England was transformed beyond recognition. I hope that it lived up to your expectations.

In 1065, England barely qualified as a nation in its own right. It was the multi-ethnic residue of every marauding race that had overrun it in the pursuit of land, precious metals or conquered populations that could be enslaved. First had come the Romans, followed by Angles, Saxons, Danes and Vikings. Its kings were drawn from these incomers, and they had names foreign to our contemporary ears such as Cnut and Harthacnut, while among the powerful barons were men called Siward, Morcar and Eadwulf, names that equally betrayed Scandinavian origins.

The 'Saxons', as our history teachers encouraged us to call them, were by no means a homogenous race enjoying self-rule under the protection of a powerful monarch. England was still seen as an offshore island to the north of mainland Europe, whose powerful warlords were themselves descended from Norsemen and who saw 'England' simply as a desirable location ripe for the picking.

The great attraction of this period of English history to an historical novelist such as myself is the fact that the plot lines are already in place, and it is only necessary to insert the fictional characters into them. Will, Joan, Selwyn and Elva are all obviously the product of my imagination, but the other main characters and events are drawn directly, and as accurately as possible, from the real events of this most turbulent but formative period of England's history.

By this date there were two 'outsiders' who considered the throne of England to be theirs to sit upon, and each of them had a mighty army to back up their claim. Harald Hardrada of Norway was a fierce warrior with bloodlust, and he was convinced that the throne of England had been promised to the offspring of his father Magnus should it fall vacant on the death of Harthacnut without heirs. When the crown slid sideways to Harthacnut's half-brother Edward the Confessor, Harald was far from amused, and began making invasion plans to prove his point.

But he was not the only one. Duke William of Normandy, with Viking blood in his veins, had been promised the throne after his death by Edward the Confessor, or so he would claim once Edward could no longer deny that. As an extra precaution William had also allegedly tricked Harold Godwinson, the likely Saxon successor, into confirming Edward's choice by means of an oath sworn on holy relics.

Two proud and powerful military leaders threatened the island from two sides at once, but they might have been beaten off by a nation united under bold and secure leaders at the head of a national army. But England had none of those things in 1066.

England during that year was best described as three provinces that co-operated under a titular leadership. Each such province was governed by a mighty earl — Edwin in Mercia, Morcar in Northumbria, and Harold Godwinson in Wessex. Between them they governed in the name of Edward, the notional King of England who spent his days with his head bowed before an altar while his warlords did as they wished, any one of whom could have unseated him with little effort.

When Edward died, the loose conglomeration of nobles that called itself the 'Witan', which was what passed for an English Parliament, met to choose his successor, and realpolitik won the day. Harold Godwinson was the late king's brother-in-law, Edward had allegedly bequeathed the throne to him on his deathbed, he was there at Westminster, and he had the largest and best prepared fyrd army.

Not that this promised military supremacy over any invader. The ramshackle defence force that was assembled in England's cause was a part-time army of 'chocolate soldiers', not unlike a Territorial Reserve Battalion, but with the important difference that members of a fyrd could only be called upon to perform military service for a given number of days a year. Particularly at harvest time, desertions were frequent and uncontrolled, and even when they were present the men of the fyrd were in the main poorly armed, if at all, and even less protected by armour. Even when the Fyrds of Mercia, Northumbria and Wessex were combined, there was a limit to the resistance that could be effected with farm implements and arms that were more like family heirlooms than state-of-the art weapons.

It was a miracle that this motley collection of conscripted farmers managed to defeat Hardrada the Viking, prior to marching south at a speed that defies belief to engage Duke William. The duke then demonstrated just how easily military tactics in the hands of seasoned soldiers bearing the latest weaponry can overcome enthusiastic but ill-disciplined peasants with billhooks and converted ploughshares.

The outcome of Hastings was never in doubt, but its long-term consequences could have taken many forms. In the century that followed, England continued to be merely one 'possession' of several warrior dynasties whose origins and primary ambitions lay in what is now France. One group of invaders had been replaced by another, but this most recent one would endure and shape an island nation.

William of Normandy may have won a decisive battle, but his original ambition to tick the box and move back home to his beloved Normandy was thwarted by a sullen and resentful populace. They did not so much care who had become their new king, and where he came from, but they were not about to sit watch their way of life transformed as they were forced at sword point to pay taxes to a man they did not know, did not respect, and had not invited over. Given William's almost ungovernable temper, and his unwillingness to pardon those who either betrayed him or simply refused to acknowledge his victory, the stage was set for bloodshed on a grand scale.

That disgraceful episode that became known to historians as 'The Harrowing of the North' was one of the most systematic, brutal and merciless acts of revenge ever inflicted by a monarch on his people. An angry King William knew no restraint, despite his professed and openly pious Christianity, and it was his way of not only venting his rage over the murder of his chosen Earl of Northumbria but also sending a message that would never be forgotten by those who were delaying his return back across the Channel.

These events are adopted as the background to the ongoing fictional fortunes of Will Riveracre and Selwyn Astenmede, brothers by marriage and social equals following the destruction of their former society in the Battle of Hastings. Waltheof was the only one of the rebel earls to survive William's wrath, but was condemned in marriage to William's niece, Judith of Lens. The failure of that marriage, and Judith's betrayal of Waltheof, feature in the next book in the series, *The Traitor's Arrow*, but conveniently for the plotline in this one Waltheof was confirmed in the Earldom of Huntingdon, from which he was required to supervise and control events in East Anglia. Which leads us to two more of the characters you have just read about, and who actually led the lives described.

Richeldis de Faverches existed, and is generally credited with having founded the now world-renowned 'Shrine of Walsingham' that draws so many pilgrims and tourists to this village a few miles inland from the Norfolk coast. As described in this novel, she was a widow with a son named Geoffrey who eventually went off to the Crusades, and reliable scholarly research also credits her with having been, in a former life, 'Edith Swan Neck', the widow of King Harold. I plead guilty to literary licence in explaining how she made this transition.

As for Hereward the Wake, most readers will vaguely remember this shady character from somewhere in their school history texts, compiled in turn from obscure, and somewhat questionable, monastic records. What is not in doubt is that this evasive brigand commanded a group of marauders whose headquarters were inside the almost impenetrable marshes of the Isle of Ely, and that he was captured more than once, only to either escape or be pardoned by King William. His eventual fate is clouded in obscurity, and there are several conflicting rumours regarding it, so I conveniently had him brought to account by Will and Selwyn.

As ever, I look forward to receiving feedback from you in the form of a review on **Amazon** or **Goodreads**. Or, of course, you can try the more personal approach on my website, and my Facebook page: **DavidFieldAuthor**.

Happy reading!

David

davidfieldauthor.com

Sapere Books is an exciting new publisher of brilliant fiction and popular history.

To find out more about our latest releases and our monthly bargain books visit our website: **saperebooks.com**

Printed in Great Britain
by Amazon